Pamela

Seeds of Doubt

To Clive
Best Wishes
Pamela Vass

Boundstone Books

First published in Great Britain in 2011 by
Boundstone Books, Little Boundstone, Littleham,
Bideford. EX39 5HW.

ISBN 978-0-9568709-0-2

Cover photo: Olgapshenichnaya/Dreamstime

Printed and bound in Great Britain
by SRP Ltd. Exeter.

www.boundstonebooks.co.uk

Author's Note

This novel is set against the background of actual events. All references to official documents are authentic and are listed in the appendix.

All organisations and characters, however, and the roles they play, are entirely fictional.

Acknowledgements

My thanks go to Laurence Shelley, Terry Sackett, Liz Shakespeare, Sarah Willans, Edward Vass, Miranda Cox, Elaine Hennessey and Shelia Bees for their invaluable scrutiny and support.

Preface

On the evening of August 15th 1952 the worst floods ever to hit the west of England destroyed the beautiful coastal village of Lynmouth in North Devon. Newspaper headlines reflected the nation's shock at the scale of this tragic natural disaster. Page after page documented the devastation left behind when a series of torrential downpours caused the East and West Lyn rivers to burst their banks. Such was the force of the water that ten-ton boulders were carried out to sea as though they were mere pebbles; roads, bridges and entire cottages were swept away.

Thirty-four men, women and children lost their lives that night.

There is no doubt that this was a disaster: but a natural one? There are those who still believe that the events of that night were not so much an Act of God as an Act of Man. This novel blends fact and fiction in a story of one woman's struggle to expose those who contrive to manipulate one of the greatest powers on earth - the weather.

Prologue

Her steps echoed along the road to the Valley of Rocks. Ahead of her, familiar formations reared up, strange headless shapes swallowed up by the sea mist.

She paused at the entrance to the cemetery, pulling her grey coat closer, throwing the hood over her hair, protection from the mist or perhaps from prying eyes. She blended so well into the damp, colourless day that her only distinguishing feature, as the vicar was later to recall, was the bunch of russet chrysanthemums she clutched in her hands.

She picked her way between the headstones, edging this way and that to peer at fading inscriptions. It wasn't the old stones that delayed her, nor even most of the newer ones, just those that took up so little space they might easily be missed. The lichen-covered headstone that finally brought her to rest was almost obscured by the roots of an overhanging beech. She knelt on the sodden earth, feeling it cast a damp embrace around her, drawing her down to her silent companions.

Shivering, she placed the flowers in front of the stone, pausing only to trace the inscription. *Sacred to the memory of Alistair and Michael Davenport, 1946 – 1952. May they rest in peace.*

Raindrops, their fall broken by the overhanging branches, sought out the nape of her neck as if anointing her. 'Forgive me,' she whispered finally. Their silence was no more than she expected, or deserved.

Chapter One

March 1982, Salisbury, England

'Rainmaking!' Nick Pearce pushed open the plate glass door and threw his dripping coat over the first available chair. 'Are you seriously saying that...?'

'Not me,' Ingrid interrupted. 'Private Dean.'

'Who's he?'

'The old boy in the photo.'

'Oh, yeah.'

Ingrid Clarke's heart sank. Her boss's off-hand response wasn't exactly encouraging. She edged round the marble bistro table to the chair opposite. 'I interviewed him yesterday for the British Legion piece. Here,' she leant down and retrieved the black and white photograph from her bag, 'there's a cutting stuck to the back all about rainmaking. And before you ask, it's nothing to do with voodoo or ancient pagan rituals. He swore he'd seen planes make it rain when he was on manoeuvres on Salisbury Plain.'

Nick slid the photograph towards him, flipped it over and scanned the text on the yellowing piece of paper. 'So according to this, planes flew overhead, the clouds got heavier and blacker and about thirty minutes later it rained.'

'Bit more to it than that, but yes.'

He shook his head. 'I'll order. What do you want?'

'Tuna roll and a coffee. Thanks.'

Ingrid took in the lunchtime crowd. Half a dozen office workers were clustered at the food bar, probably tempted in by a leaflet campaign advertising the café's grand re-opening. Although a few balloons and a free cappuccino with every meal hardly qualified. But they seemed happy enough; unlike the regulars, who looked a lot less at home with the stark black and silver art deco theme - not a trace of cosy red gingham anywhere.

A young mother struggled to the entrance with a baby asleep in a buggy and a toddler tugging at her hand. Ingrid scraped her chair back and held the door open. As the girl turned, Ingrid couldn't help noticing the heavy bags under her eyes, the lines creasing her forehead, her dull, sallow complexion. 'Sit here,' she said, moving their coats across to the next table. 'There's more room for the buggy.'

'Thanks.' The mother pulled a high chair over for the toddler, gently removed his coat, lifted him in, tied his bib, wiped his hands, found his cup and placed a banana on the tray before sinking into a chair. Ingrid felt their closeness. It was a bond she could have known, once; but it was too late now. Work filled the gap. She'd been covering stories of triumph and tragedy at the Salisbury Post for more than twenty-five years - not bad for an agency typist who came for a week. The work suited her and, according to the previous editor, she suited the work. 'You've a nose for the domestic stuff,' he'd said. And she'd been happy enough to cover the hatches, matches and dispatches and everything in-between. Until now.

She turned back to her boss, stuck in the counter queue. He'd been at the paper for five years; semi-retired from one of the nationals. In a rare moment of confidence he'd shared his frustration at being sidelined as soon as he hit fifty. His clean sweep at the Post had been brutal, but she'd survived: more than survived recently in fact. He'd started involving her at briefings and running copy past her. Not exactly a promotion but she'd definitely been invited to step up a rung.

He was different too. His clothes, routines and, lately, his mood. Ingrid watched as his eyes drilled into the assistant, intensifying every second of waiting time as she slapped two slices of tomato, some wilted lettuce, two slices of cucumber, a ring of onion and a squirt of mayonnaise onto their rolls. It was going to take more than fancy art deco fittings to up-market the market café. Nick snatched up their plates and headed back, making a point of having to negotiate the buggy and highchair.

'Oh my dear Lord, what have they done to the weather?' Dimpled elbows pushed against the door as an overweight woman backed into the café. She thrust a pile of plastic shopping bags into an empty chair and shook her umbrella out in their direction.

'For goodness sake.' Nick spun round, his face soured with irritation.

'Sorry my love, didn't see you there. Still, no harm done, it's only a bit of rain,' she said with a smile as she pushed on towards the counter, dislodging a trail of chairs in her wake.

Nick grabbed a paper serviette and began stabbing at the offending drops on his sleeve. Ingrid looked out the window, finding sanctuary in the kaleidoscope of umbrellas outside. Hopefully it would stop raining before they left.

She turned back. 'I noticed the circulation figures are up this month,' she said.

'About time.'

'Getting behind the Hospice campaign was a good move.'

'I guess so.'

She bit into the granary roll; mayonnaise oozed over her fingers. She licked it off and tried another tack. 'Are you and Liz going away this year?'

'No. She's taking Ellie to Cornwall but I don't suppose I'll get any time with her.'

'With Liz?' Ingrid asked.

'No,' he said abruptly. 'With Ellie.'

So Alice had got it right for once. The paper's young receptionist had been spreading rumours about Nick's marriage for weeks. 'I'm sorry,' she said.

The silence lengthened. Taking a deep breath, Ingrid finally summoned up the courage to get to the point. 'What do you think of Private Dean's story?'

Nick was lost in his own thoughts. 'What?'

'Private Dean. What do you think?'

'I think it's an old boy winding you up.'

'He was pretty convincing,' she said.

'Yeah?' Nick muttered, swilling his free cappuccino around an over-sized cup.

'I'd like to follow it up.'

He looked up. 'Why?'

'Why not?'

'Because our readers want to know what happened last week, not thirty years ago.'

'I still think there could be something in it.'

The toddler threw his cup overboard. Ingrid retrieved it, winning a smile.

'Where would you start?' Nick asked.

'Ministry of Agriculture might be worth a try. Remember the droughts in '75 and '76 when people were queuing at standpipes? Imagine being able to make it rain to sort that lot out.'

'But according to this,' he pointed to the faded text on the back of the photograph, 'your Private Dean was talking about the early 1950's. Any experiments couldn't have been much good if we were stuck with a drought twenty years later.'

Ingrid shrugged. 'Maybe, but think of the spread we could run if it's true. Taxpayers money being spent on making it rain, in our climate!'

Nick pushed his empty plate away. 'I suppose Danny could take a look at it, but it'd be a waste of his time.'

'No!' She didn't mean to react so violently. Danny and Mat were two young career reporters at the paper. They wouldn't be staying twenty-five years; just long enough to get noticed by a national. Of course Nick was going to pass anything vaguely controversial onto them. But not this time. This story was hers - it had to be. 'I mean, you're right; it would be a waste of his time. So why not let me see if there's anything in it first?'

He looked directly at her for the first time since they'd entered the café. His eyes were bloodshot. Was he drinking? 'Okay, as long as you bring your other stuff in on time. It could be interesting - but I won't hold my breath.'

'Thanks.' Ingrid grabbed her coat.

'Just a minute.' Nick delved into each jacket pocket before retrieving a crumpled piece of paper. 'Fancy this next time?' He smoothed the flyer out on the table. A pub round the corner was advertising lunchtime jazz sessions. She enjoyed jazz; that wasn't the problem...

'I don't know...'

'Think about it.'

'Okay. But just now I've a story to follow up.'

Nick took his cue and held out her coat. As Ingrid slipped it on he rested his hands on her shoulders, just for a moment.

They stepped out into the drizzle. Ahead of them lay the Salisbury streets, bedded in history and bustling with lunchtime shoppers intent on snapping up a few essentials before the pre-season, post-season, out-of-season sale came to an end. Behind them, in the vast square, formal facades presided over the tented encampment that market day always brought, full of billowing awnings, overflowing stalls, eager crowds - and noise.

They turned away towards the quieter, more dignified streets that converged on the Cathedral Green. Buildings of substance and solidity rose up on either side. One of them - a double fronted, stone-faced converted bank - housed the offices of the Salisbury Post.

'Let me know about the jazz,' Nick said, holding the heavy oak door open for Ingrid.

'Is it still foul out there?' Alice was perched on the edge of the enquiries desk, swinging her impossibly long legs back and forth. Everything about Alice was sleek, even the straightened blonde hair that fell around her face. Definitely an Afghan hound in a former life, Ingrid thought.

'It's still raining if that's what you mean,' Ingrid said, shaking out her coat.

'Thought so. Anyway, I'm off. Oh, you've got a visitor Mr Pearce.' Alice nodded in the direction of a stylishly dressed, impeccably made-up, middle-aged woman standing at the window, her auburn hair lit by the afternoon sun.

'Hello, Liz,' Nick said. 'Been waiting long?'

She emitted a sharp laugh. 'Only about twenty years!'

He turned to Ingrid. 'Do you mind holding the fort for a bit?'

'I guess not.'

'We'll talk in my office,' he said, shepherding his wife out of embarrassment's way.

Nick followed her into the wood panelled room and waved her towards one of the two upright leather-seated chairs on the visitor's side of the enormous companion desk. It was perfect for editorial meetings - smoke filled, coffee laden affairs when Mat and Danny covered its vast expanse with copy for the next edition. For a couple of hours each week Mat, Danny, Nick, even the office itself, colluded in a delusion of self-importance. Under the overhead strip light - the only alteration Nick had made since its previous incarnation as the bank manager's office - they argued over which story should lead as though the Post's headline could make or break the government.

'Can't this wait?' he said. 'I'm busy.'

'So I see,' Liz replied, looking over her shoulder in Ingrid's direction. 'And the answer is no, it can't.' Shunning the chair, she walked to the window.

'What's so urgent?' he said to her back.

'Walking out on our conversation this morning. That's what.'

'Conversation! Is that what you call it?'

She turned round. 'Well it would be if you tried listening once in a while instead of telling me what I think before I've had a chance to open my mouth.'

'Telling *you* what *you* think...! Take a look in the mirror, Liz.'

'Oh that's right; turn it around - like you always do.'

He gave an exaggerated sigh. 'Change the record.' He looked at his watch. 'I've got work waiting.'

She screwed a tissue up in her fist. 'It's not working.'

'What isn't?'

'This: us. Trying to hold it together... for Ellie's sake.'

'Who says it isn't?'

'My solicitor has advised...'

'Your solicitor!' Nick pushed himself out of his chair and began to pace in front of the fitted oak shelving that ran the length of one wall. 'So when exactly did he put in an appearance?'

'She says that...'

He shook his head. 'I might have known. So much for your "let's give each other some space, time to see how we feel about things". You had it all stitched up from the beginning didn't you?'

'No! I...' She dabbed her cheeks. 'She says I have every right to ask you to leave, at least while I'm Ellie's main carer and until she's eighteen next year.'

Nick stopped pacing and fixed his eyes on his soon-to-be ex-wife. 'Leave? It's my house for Christ's sake.'

'It's our house, and for the moment I need it for Ellie. She's in a bad way with all this.'

'Oh, so the fact that our daughter is having a rough time is all my fault now is it?'

'Please don't use Ellie to score points.'

He leant over the desk and thrust his finger in her direction. 'You know I'd do anything for her. Anything.'

Liz perched on the edge of one of the upright chairs, smoothing her skirt as she sat. 'So prove it. Move out, just for a bit. She needs a break from it all. Her diabetes is barely under control with all the stress. She's struggling to manage her injections.'

Nick looked at his wife. Had she planned this strategy before she walked through the door? Don't talk about the relationship, the rights and wrongs of who's doing what to whom, just keep it simple - Ellie needs you to move out. And she had the nerve to tell him not to use Ellie to score points.

'So will you?' She was looking straight at him. 'For Ellie's sake.'

'Do I have a choice?'

'Thank you.' She hesitated at the door. 'Will you be okay?'

'Just perfect.'

The paper's offices were open plan, but beyond the long oak counter that dominated the reception area, glass partitions gave the illusion of privacy. They were a small team. Reception was Alice's domain. Beyond her were two desks occupied by Danny and Mat. Next to them was the casuals' desk, shared by the free-lancers who contributed anything from the farming news to cinema reviews. Ingrid's desk, behind the last partition, was the only one with a window that opened. She was forever being told to close it, that the air conditioning wouldn't work, but who wanted to be shut in?

Nick, as editor, was insulated from the ebb and flow of the general public in his office off the main area. The short corridor and closed door provided some insulation, but the raised voices still filtered through. Ingrid cast around for something else to focus on. Private Dean's photo stared up at her from the desk. 'So how reliable a witness are you?' she murmured. Nick could be right; the line between fact and folklore became impossibly blurred when filtered through elderly country folk. 'Let's see if there's anything in your story shall we?'

Ingrid twisted and turned her way along the spines of the paper's reference section until she arrived at *Understanding Weather*. She flicked through the index. *Weather fronts; depressions; cloud formation...* That could be useful. She scanned the pages. Suddenly the word 'clouds' was about as useful as 'feelings' or 'flowers': wonderful as poetic imagery but hopelessly unspecific. The skies were actually filled with blanket stratus, fluffy cumulus, strained altostratus, towering cumulonimbus, scatty cirrus and more. 'Oh so it's called cirrocumulus.'

'What is?' Nick demanded, as he watched his wife disappear through reception.

'When you get that high cloud rippling across, the one they call a "mackerel sky".'

'Oh... I'll be in my office if anyone needs me.' He strode back down the corridor, and slammed his door.

Ingrid returned to the book. 'Enough of clouds. How about rain?' *Air contains moisture. When warm air rises it cools. Some of the moisture condenses into droplets that form clouds. Millions of these droplets need to merge before they are heavy enough to fall as raindrops or hailstones.* Hardly riveting stuff. Basically air needed to rise and cool to form clouds, then the droplets clustered around a nucleus, usually dust, salt or sand, and fell as rain.

Alice returned in time to pick up a call from the print room. 'Are the hatches, matches and dispatches ready, Mrs C?' she called across the room. Ingrid looked at her watch. Private Dean would have to wait.

Two hours later, her page was done. Every message, every photograph told a story - and she had a gut feeling Private Dean's was going to surprise them all.

There was a tap on the partition. Nick walked round and sat on the edge of her desk. 'Sorry about that,' he said.

Ingrid put out a hand to steady her overflowing in-tray. 'No apology necessary.'

'What were you doing earlier?'

'Dealing with hatches, matches...'

'No,' he interrupted, 'you said something about clouds.'

'Oh, I thought I'd check out Private Dean's story with a bit of cloud study.'

'And?'

'I had a crash course on rain but I couldn't find anything on artificial rainmaking.'

'In that case you might be interested in this.' Nick pushed a piece of paper towards her. 'I rang a source at the Met Office. It's not something he's too well up on, but it seems cloud seeding is a well known procedure.'

'Cloud seeding?'

'Spraying clouds to produce rain.' He pointed to the fax. 'That's the definition Guy came up with.'

She read. *Cloud seeding - the process of dusting clouds with particles to trigger the formation of raindrops. Experiments have chiefly taken place in the USA and USSR, largely on the margins of farming areas where rainfall is needed for crop growth.* 'So it *was* the Ministry of Agriculture.'

'Looks like it.'

'How would they do it?'

'Specialised planes I guess. Maybe crop sprayers.'

Ingrid glanced up at her boss; he was being unusually helpful. 'Thanks for getting this.'

'Contacts are there to be used.'

'Thanks anyway,' Ingrid said, smiling.

Chapter Two

'Mrs C,' Alice bounded across the room. 'Your husband's here.'

Ingrid glanced at the clock. Five exactly. Predictable as always.

'On her way,' Alice chirruped in the general direction of the well-built, grey haired gentleman slumped in the one and only easy chair the paper provided for visitors. Climbing the short flight of steps had left him breathless and flushed.

At the entrance, Ingrid found herself pulled back beneath the umbrella Jack held ready.

'I'm fine, Jack, it's not far to the car.'

'Nonsense.' He escorted her to the door, the rain drenching his back. He folded the umbrella with practised precision, placed it in the boot, removed his damp coat and hat and settled himself into the driver's seat. She watched as his hands ritually checked the gear stick, brake, mirror, before pausing to select radio four. Several minutes later Ingrid was finally on her way home.

'*A small group of islands that most people have never heard of are at the centre of an international storm this evening. The Falklands are a bleak, windswept British outpost off the coast of Argentina, a country that has long disputed sovereignty. Today...*'

There was an urgency to the newsreader's voice. 'What's this about?' Ingrid asked.

'Looks as though there's something serious brewing with Argentina over the Falklands.'

'Why are we hanging on to somewhere so far away?'

'They're strategically important. And I shouldn't be surprised to hear there's oil in those waters.'

'Might have known it was all about money. It's what all these disputes come down to.'

'Not necessarily.'

'Course it is.'

'Think what you like but it could get serious. Mrs Thatcher isn't going to take this sitting down.'

'Well I hope someone has the sense to try diplomacy before she gets carried away with war-mongering.'

Jack turned the car into the driveway of their 1950's detached dormer bungalow, one of eight making up a classic cul-de-sac. Jack's choice. But the view across the meadows at the back more than made up for its shortcomings. Weeping willows traced the course of the stream across the swathe of green, leading the eye to the towering centrepiece, the Cathedral spire. Ingrid loved her early morning walk to work through the mists that hovered above the water, casting the city adrift like a mystical island. And the walk home was the perfect antidote to the urgency of the pressroom - unless it was raining, when Jack was always there.

He parked beside the new caravan. Ingrid's choice. Whenever she stepped into it she felt... at home. Crazy thing to say but there it was. Maybe it was the freedom of being able to roam wherever and whenever she wanted that appealed. But they hadn't been out in it yet. 'Best to wait for the fine weather,' Jack had said the last time she suggested it.

Ingrid grabbed her case from the car and made a dash for the front door before Jack could repeat the charade with the umbrella. Thirty minutes later, with a hastily prepared salad consumed, Jack rolled up his napkin and placed it in a silver ring, a christening gift from his grandmother. He'd presented an identical one to Ingrid at their wedding breakfast. She'd almost burst into tears. No one had ever treasured her the way Jack did.

'Coffee?' she asked, 'then I'd like to show you something.' She cleared the dishes, retrieved the photo of Private Dean and took it through to the sitting room. 'Look on the back.'

Jack, as always, was in his leather recliner to the left of the fireplace. He studied the article. 'What's your interest in this?'

'It's such a crazy idea - weather being manufactured.'

'I don't know about manufactured. Influenced maybe.'

'Whatever. It's still something we think of as in the lap of the Gods. Like that insurance get-out for disasters.' She sat down opposite him. 'We're obsessed by the weather. It's all you hear: "turned cold this week," or "I'll be glad to see the end of this rain." But we don't really think about it.'

'A lot of people study it.'

'Maybe you do, but you're a pilot. Most of us just want to know whether to take the brolly or not.' She stood up. 'But what do you think? Could there be any truth in it? Can rain be produced artificially?'

'Depends what you mean by artificially.'

Ingrid sighed. What happened to words in the space between them? Words were her life, her work, yet here... Some days it felt as though all the pieces of her life had been thrown up in the air and fallen back in the wrong place. One day she would have to put them together all over again.

Jack pulled himself out of his chair, eyes focused on the bookshelves he'd built into the symmetrical alcoves on either side of the fire. He began to search the titles, all aligned to avoid any unnecessary twisting and turning, finally selecting a comfortable read to take him up to the evening news.

'Well that's it.' Jack turned off the TV. 'If Galtieri doesn't back down soon this is going to get nasty.'

'Uh huh.' Ingrid was immersed in the latest P.D. James.

'You should take more interest. This is going to affect us all.'

She looked up. 'I don't see how.'

'The stock market won't like it; our investments could be hit.'

'There's still time to try diplomacy, surely.' There was no response. Her husband was already on his way to the bedroom, switching the sitting room light off behind him.

The radio alarm clicked into action '...*a warm front will move across from the west bringing some rain, but not before evening. Most of the south should remain dry with clear sunny spells...*'

Ingrid stretched. Something was different. She opened her eyes and saw the sun playing on the bedroom wall. What a wonderful sight, a rare, wonderful sight. January had been unbelievably dreary. First non-stop rain, then bitter cold as the rain turned to snow, leaving everyone shivering their way through the rest of the month. The cold eased, but the sun was lost as part of the bargain: grey, mizzly days filled February. But today the sun was shining and she felt like embracing the day.

She swung her feet out of bed and wandered through to the bathroom. On the way back, the full-length mirror caught her reflection. 'Hmm, not bad,' she murmured. Jack stirred. She dressed quickly, anxious to be off before he could insist on driving her to work.

'I'll be late tonight so don't worry about picking me up,' she said.

'Why's that?' he asked.

'Just some research - not sure how long it'll take. Then I'll probably go for a swim.'

'Can you get me copies of the emigration lists to Canada?'

'Not today. This is about that photograph. Bye.' She gave him a quick kiss, ran down the stairs, scooped up her case from the hall table and was opening the back door when he called.

'Well ring me when you're ready to come home. You don't want to be walking back alone at that time.'

'I don't mind, I like the air.'

'Not when it's dark. Call me.'

'Okay, I'll call,' she shouted back.

Ingrid pounded down the path, grateful for release. Sometimes it was suffocating being indoors.

Jack pushed himself out of bed and went to the window. He needed to remind her not to leave it too late but when he finally found the key she was gone. Oh well, at least he could take it easy getting dressed. And when he was ready to face the day - what then? All that time stretching ahead with precious little to fill it. The day was never so long at work.

He made for the shower. On the return trip he managed to open the window to hail the postman.

'Morning, Mike, any news?'

'Morning, Mr. Clarke. Yes, a girl. 7lb 2ozs, arrived at three minutes past one this morning. Mother and baby doing fine thanks.'

'Unlike father. You look terrible.'

'You try doing a full round on top of an eighteen-hour labour and forceps delivery. I'm not going through that again I can tell you.'

'Surely you can take some time off.'

'Sue and I decided it would be better when she comes home. So I can help out.'

'Well, congratulations.'

Jack shut the window, adjusted his dressing gown and tackled the stairs as quickly as he dared to collect the letter, keen for confirmation of the celebration he had arranged for their twenty-fifth wedding anniversary. When Patricia, his first wife, died he thought he'd lost all chance of ever celebrating a twenty-fifth. They'd made it to twenty, just. He'd spent it sitting by her bedside, intent on remembering the good times. He never, ever, wanted to feel so helpless again.

But then Ingrid appeared out of nowhere, bowled him over, literally, up on the Downs. He could still feel his surprise and pleasure at being singled out by someone so much younger. His proposal to this attractive, timid, but undeniably besotted girl had seemed the most natural thing in the world. He was relieved when she suggested a small civil ceremony. Most first-time brides wanted the works but they were kindred spirits - neither wanted any fuss. Once the hitch with her birth certificate was resolved there was nothing to stop them marrying straight away. It was so simple, sincere and, ah... shocking. For Ingrid anyway. He could still see her face when reached the airfield and she saw his Cessna waiting. He'd enjoyed springing surprises even then.

He held on to the bottom stair post as he bent to pick up the letter. It was a confirmation, but not the one he was expecting.

It was such a lovely morning Ingrid was tempted to join the elderly couple sitting in the Cathedral Close. She swung her bag down from her shoulder and perched on the end of the bench.

'Hello dear, taking a break are you? We're just the same; know all the benches right down to the day centre now.'

Ingrid smiled, picked up her bag and walked off a little too vigorously. She slowed down across the green, regretting the short cut. She should have realised the grass would be sodden after all the rain. But it was still a beautiful day. Danny took the time to share a joke with her, Alice was almost bearable and it was a treat to hang up a dry coat for once.

'Morning, Alice. Is Mr. Pearce in?'

'No. Head office all day,' she said, putting the finishing touches to her face from the multi-coloured palette wedged in her hand.

'Oh yes, I'd forgotten.' Probably just as well he was out of circulation - it gave time for the gossip to die down. Ingrid hurried towards the sanctuary of her desk, returned Private Dean to his rightful place, and made a start on her in-tray.

A few hours later she was settled in Salisbury's reference library at a table overlooking the canal. Young mothers with pushchairs were jockeying for position with experienced old timers' intent on claiming the two feet of bench the birds hadn't christened with their droppings. With only himself to consider, a retired general (he had to be ex-military with that bearing) definitely had the advantage. He'd taken up his position and feigned complete absorption in *The Telegraph* before the nearest mother had even marshalled her troops.

Ingrid was tempted to wait to discover who the young girl on the bridge was waiting for - but time was short. She forced her attention back to a tome on Wiltshire airfields. There were forty of them. How on earth was she going to find the one engaged in some obscure research on weather, possibly organised by the department of agriculture?

A familiar name caught her eye: Old Sarum. Jack kept his Cessna there. *Old Sarum, one of the oldest airfields in the country, played a critical role during the sea-borne invasion of Europe, and continued to be active after the war.* And, in Private Dean's time, there was a school of Land/Air Warfare based there. She jotted it down as a likely candidate. Eliminating those put on care and maintenance eventually left her with fifteen still active in the 1950's.

Ingrid checked her watch. Almost five-thirty. She should be going. There was dinner to prepare; Jack would be waiting... She half closed the book, paused, pulled her sleeve down over her watch and turned the page.

In June 1948, Overton Heath was transferred to the Ministry of Agriculture and Food. It was a possibility. She skipped the pages on Boscombe Down, Upavon, Netheravon, Porton Down, and Ramsbury... Ramsbury. Something caught her eye. *In 1947 some of the airfield's domestic sites were taken over by Wiltshire Agricultural Committee - as a hostel for the land army.*

Ingrid smiled as memories flooded back of early mornings in the fields dressed in her regulation green jersey, brown breeches and wide-brimmed brown hat. She closed her eyes, saw herself sneaking out of the farm and running through the woods to the river. It was so alive as it leapt over the boulders, splashing against itself in its hurry to reach the sea; plopping down into a pool worn out by the advance guard, whirling round and round while it waited for the rest to catch up. She would stand there, summoning up the courage to plunge into one of the dark pools, fed by water straight off the moor. It was freezing, even on the hottest summer's day.

She'd felt so free, but wary too, ready to flee at the slightest sign of anyone watching. Things always changed when someone was watching. She changed. Even the river changed...

The thundering of the rain on the corrugated roof was threatening to drown out the seven piece band. Louder and louder... the band racking up the volume to compete; great gusts of wind thudding against the walls of the hall and thirty or more children inside oblivious to it all, their staccato shouts simply adding to the din.

Much more of this and Moira would be screaming herself. She had to get out, if only for a minute. But it wasn't any quieter outside. With each step the roaring grew worse, drowning out the music, the shouting, even the murderous percussion on the tin roof. Her eyes were useless in the pitch black, but there was no escaping the noise; not of the rain or even the wind, but what? The gentle stream hidden in the valley never sounded like this. But if it was so well hidden why was water coursing across the gardens, surging round her ankles, sweeping up everything in its path?

'No!' She was pushing against the flow, finally breaking free, bursting through the doors of the hall, screaming. 'It's flooding; the river's flooding!'

Parents and children spilling out into the rain; scurrying up the slippery valley sides, scrambling over rocks towards the lights of the village, desperate to escape the terrifying force breaking through the night behind them. But suddenly the lights weren't there anymore. Blinded, they were losing their bearings, running back towards the torrent. 'Up, up. Keep climbing up.' Useless words thrown back at her by the storm. Only touch was any good, guiding the terrified children until, numbed by exhaustion, they slumped on the fern covered hillside for the final count.

But two were missing. Moments later she was plunging back towards the hall, forcing her way through the water surging across the dance floor, calling 'Alistair, Michael,' again and again. No answer. Where were they? The relief of finding them... turning to agony as they were torn from her grip, swallowed up by the flood. In the dark and confusion stumbling after them, out of the collapsing building into the rising water, tugging at her legs, refusing to release her, pulling her down, stealing her breath...

Ingrid was gasping, the sound intruding into the furthest corners of this unnaturally silent room. She fumbled in her bag for her inhaler, painfully conscious of the sideways glances her asthma attacks always attracted.

Jack cursed as his head hit a rafter. Ingrid was right. They should have put a Velux up here when the other windows were done. He paused to steady himself, shifting a couple of boxes of old sheet music further under the eaves. He hadn't the heart to get rid of them. Listening to Patricia play the baby grand was his most vivid memory of her. They'd even invested in a duet stool so that he could turn the music without blocking out the light. 'Jack, you're looming,' she'd say.

Patricia was the reason he was up here. Well her easel anyway. It had seemed such a good idea when she couldn't get about so much. He swung the torch around the cramped loft, illuminating more than seventy years of memories. He stumbled against boxes full of paperwork from his self-employed days. They could probably go. How long did the tax people insist you kept records for? He'd forgotten.

The easel would probably be leaning against a wall at the back somewhere. He lifted the torch, revealing two long, slim pieces of polished wood. His stilts! How old had he been? Six, seven at most, when he'd pestered his father to make them for him. Being tall, or not being small, was a matter of life and death for, oh, weeks. Why on earth had it been so important?

His army kit bag was wedged between the stilts. That could go. Leaning over his father's fishing rods and a pile of old drawing room curtains (much too big for here) he lifted it out. Pushing a couple of redundant stools aside, he edged towards the back. Funny how small things could be so painfully significant. A mouldy bottle cork (twenty-first birthday), rough carved stick (scout camp - 1923, or perhaps 4), broken penknife (ashamed to say, stolen from his brother). He couldn't help exploring a box of childhood books. Why on earth were they hidden away up here? They were beautifully illustrated; might even be some first editions amongst them. They should definitely go down.

He tried to pull the box towards him. But it resisted. Perhaps the other boxes were pinning it at the back. He wedged his shoulder against the pile. If he could shift it a few inches it should be enough to release the...

For a minute he thought a loose board had pivoted and hit him in the chest. He slumped on to a rolled up carpet, upsetting the contents of another box over his legs as he fell. For a few minutes he struggled to force each breath into his rigid chest.

The torch had fallen on its side, illuminating cobwebs in the rafters. He followed the efforts of a spider retrieving a newly caught fly. Rich pickings up there, he thought. Funny how everything happening six feet above his head was crystal clear but all else was cotton wool.

Slowly his chest relaxed, his breathing eased. So that's what it felt like. Next time he saw his cardiologist an apology was in order. He'd been so convinced they were making a mountain out of a molehill. He bent to pick up the torch. 'Aaahhh...' The pain was still there. Keep calm, be still, relax, his mind urged. But the stuff on his legs was uncomfortable. He shone the beam along his body to get a better look and managed a wry grin. He was shivering uncontrollably, from the shock probably, and resting against his left leg was a fluffy hot water bottle cover.

He nudged a small, square piece of cloth towards his hand. It was a needlework sampler of some sort. He drew it closer to the light.

Psalm 124
If it had not been the LORD who was on our side,
now may Israel say;
If it had not been the LORD who was on our side,
when men rose up against us;
Then they had swallowed us up quick, when their wrath
was kindled against us;
Then the waters had overwhelmed us, the stream had gone
over our soul;
Then the proud waters had gone over our soul.
Blessed be the LORD, who hath not given us as a prey
to their teeth.
Our soul is escaped as a bird out of the snare of the
fowlers: the snare is broken, and we are escaped.

It was a long time since he'd studied the Psalms; the language was strangely comforting. He worked his hand towards the books wedged under his knee, edging his leg further over... 'Aaahhh.' He fell back against the carpet. Once he could shrug off as a warning, but twice - twice meant it wasn't over. He closed his eyes and tried to relax. Slowly the grip eased and the darkness resolved into boxes, curtains and stilts again.

He'd have to wait for Ingrid. She could just about see the ladder from the hall, if she looked up. At least he had the torch. He eased the spine of the nearest book into the torchlight. *Practical Cookery*. He'd pass on that one. And *The Nation's Archives* wasn't exactly what he was hoping for.

There was one more volume just within reach. He grasped the frayed edge and edged it towards him. It hadn't suffered too much from its fall but the tooled leather cover was grubby. He rubbed his thumb across the contours, removing a powdery layer. What a shame, it had been dropped in mud. The edges of the pages were discoloured too. Stop... breathe... rest... he reminded himself. No consequences so far but he wasn't going to risk moving yet. He unfastened the catch and turned to the title page. Only it wasn't a book.

Reading a diary felt an intrusion, but it was a long time ago, and he desperately needed something to take his mind off the prospect of ending his days sprawled across a moth-eaten carpet. He scanned the first few entries.

Keepsake Diary
January 1952

Tuesday 1st
Spent New Year's Eve in a lay-by just outside South Molton. One minute Frank was stopping for a pee, the next he was out like a light. I was stuck on that cold leather seat all night. Happy New Year.
Saturday 5th
According to Mr. Harris in the post office, 1951 was the wettest year on record. Can you believe that? I can. Going to Julie and Hugh's tomorrow.
Sunday 6th
Not many at chapel this morning.
I was so embarrassed. Julie said it's the last time Frank will cross her doorstep, but I'm invited whenever I want, day or night. He won't let me.

Tuesday 8th

Last night was magic! Frank was down south so we went dancing, Julie and me, in her sitting room! The programme was 'Come Dancing', from a Manchester ballroom. They gave a dancing lesson too. We laughed so much, but got it right in the end. I was late back.

Wednesday 9th

A bad day. That's all I'm going to say.

Thursday 10th

I had a puncture again. Mr. Atkins at the garage was so kind. It was awkward when he called Mrs Atkins to do something about my other bruises. Anyway bike plus face now sorted.

Friday 11th

Julie told me about a film called 'The Man in the White Suit'. The suit's made from an everlasting material and always stays clean. Now that's what I call an invention! She asked me to go and stay with them at the Manor again. She doesn't understand.

Sunday 13th

The sermon was Isaiah 41:10 'Fear thou not for I am with thee; be not dismayed for I am thy God, I will strengthen thee; yea I will help thee.' When?

Monday 14th

Frank isn't going away this week. Says he's collecting local orders. Don't believe a word of it. They've given him the sack haven't they? He's out drowning his sorrows (if only). I'm going to Julie's.

Tuesday 15th

Another letter from my father. Not sure how much longer I can fob him off.

Thursday 17th

One is presently sitting in the palm conservatory at the Manor. Philip has brought me a cup of tea on a silver tray and left a bell in case I should require any further assistance. My am I Lady Muck! Not really. Just babysitting Michael and Alistair. Julie and Hugh have gone to...

For a second Jack feared his sight was failing, but it was the torch of course. He shone it across the eaves. It barely picked out the rafters let alone the spider's web. He wasn't comfortable with the thought of disappearing into the darkness.

He flexed his legs. No obvious repercussions. Very, very gingerly he placed his hands on the floor and eased his body further up. Nothing. He risked lifting himself onto a low stool - slightly breathless but no more than usual. He eyed a box to his left. Placing his hands on either side he pulled himself up, pivoted round and sat on the edge. Oh, the relief of being vertical. He would never, ever take being able to get up for granted again.

He'd have to learn to live with this. But no sense in worrying Ingrid. If he could just get downstairs she needn't know. Boxes lined the route to the hatch. Shuffling from one to the next he made it to the opening. Foot-by-foot and hand-by-hand he inched down each rung until he reached the landing. A slightly raised heartbeat but that was all. A few minutes later he was at the bottom of the stairs. It was over, for now at least.

The official letter he'd discarded earlier was lying by the phone. He checked the number and dialled. 'Cardiology please.' He waited while they put him through. 'It's Mr. Clarke. I'd like to confirm my appointment with Mr. Bridges.'

Ingrid was silent as they sat down to dinner. Jack had been offhand on the phone and, after all his fussing, had told her to get the bus home. And still expected her to cook.

'What research are you doing?' he asked.

'Something for work.'

'Oh yes?'

She took a mouthful of wine.

'Anything interesting?' he persisted.

'Following up that photograph.'

'About rainmaking?'

'Yes.'

'Anything in it?'

'I don't know.' She looked across at Jack. Was he really interested? 'I need to find out more about cloud seeding.'

'Where did you hear that term?'

'Nick rang a contact at the Met Office.'

'Oh? You didn't say.'

'Didn't I?'

Ingrid piled up the plates and took them through to the kitchen. She loaded them into the dishwasher and sat down on a stool. She was tired; too tired for games.

'Would you like some coffee?' She called as he settled himself into his chair in the sitting room.

'Yes, I would. Thank you.' His voice softened. 'We'll go into town on Saturday, Ingrid. It's time you had something a bit brighter now that spring is coming. Replace all those winter greys.'

Chapter Three

'The Prime Minister is expecting a response from President Reagan by 3pm today. If he fails in his attempt to persuade President Galtieri to abort his planned invasion of the Falkland Islands then it leaves Mrs Thatcher with very few options. Our reporter is outside Downing Street. Dominique. What are the latest developments?' Jack's cereal spoon hovered above his bowl.

Dominique took his cue. 'The situation is looking pretty grim. You may recall that last week, armed Argentinean military personnel landed on South Georgia.'

'What's Mrs Thatcher's reaction likely to be?'

'We can't be certain. An unconfirmed source has stated that the Ministry of Defence has advised against a military response, but will Mrs Thatcher take their advice?'

'Thank you Dominique. And now the weather with Michael Fish.'

Jack turned the radio off. 'She's made of stronger stuff, thank goodness.'

'What's the point of having military advisers if you don't listen to them? I can't believe one woman can take us to war against all advice,' Ingrid said.

'That's all it is; advice. Mrs Thatcher is in the driving seat; she has to be.'

'Well she's driving in the wrong direction. She's talking about going to war! Don't we even have a say?'

'You elected her to govern. That's what she's doing.'

'I didn't elect her. What gives her the right to ignore the wishes of over half the population?' Ingrid cleared the dishes.

'I'm off to work.' She deflected Jack's peck on the cheek as she turned to go. Why did he always have to argue?

Alice ushered an elderly lady out of reception and appeared round Ingrid's partition. 'I'm off to lunch, Mrs C. There's no one in at the minute.'

'Okay Alice. Is Mr. Pearce in his office?'

'No. Hasn't been in this morning.'

'Not at all?'

'No.'

'Do you know why?' It was unusual for Nick to be absent without saying anything.

'Nope. See you later.'

Ingrid took some work out to the enquiries desk; it was easier than having to listen for the door all the time. But personal callers were few and far between at the end of the week. It was a good twenty minutes before she heard anyone. It was Nick. He looked dreadful.

'Are you okay?' she asked.

'I've been at the hospital. With Ellie.' He slumped into a chair, his head in his hands.

'What's wrong?' Ingrid asked.

'Don't know yet. They're doing some tests.' His hands covered his ears, as if trying to block out the voices he'd been enduring all night. 'She may have kidney failure.'

'Nick, I'm so sorry.'

He swallowed repeatedly, then lost the battle and began to sob. Stranded in unfamiliar territory, Ingrid rested her hand on his arm; he gripped it with his own.

'I'm sorry. It's been a difficult night,' he said.

'Can I get you anything? Goes without saying I'll cover for you. You'd better get home.'

'No, I can't. I mean... I'd prefer to be here. Thank you for... well, thank you.' He squeezed her hand and walked unsteadily to his office.

Alice returned in time to deal with a flood of calls about a fire on the industrial estate.

'Have we got anyone out there?' Ingrid asked.

'Mat's on his way.'

'Okay. I'll field anything you can't deal with. Mr. Pearce is in his office but don't disturb him unless it's absolutely necessary.'

'Oh?'

Alice could interrogate with a single word. Ingrid left her to fester.

She'd been back at her desk for less than half an hour when Nick appeared. 'Am I disturbing you?' He looked marginally better.

'No, course not. Heard anything?'

'She's responding well. Might just be an infection.'

'That's a relief.'

'Yes.' He paused. 'Thank you... for asking.' He pinched the bridge of his nose between his thumb and forefinger. 'Did you find out anything interesting on Friday?' he said eventually.

'Friday?'

'At the library.'

'Oh, no. It was a waste of time really. One of the airfields had been taken over by the Ministry of Agriculture but that's all,' she said.

Nick leant on her desk. 'I've been thinking. If there's any truth in this the implications are staggering. Imagine Africa without drought. People would be desperate to get their hands on the technology. It could be worth a fortune.'

'Strange to think of the weather as a commodity.'

'Might explain why you're having trouble getting information.'

'Well, I haven't tried very hard,' she replied.

His phone echoed down the corridor. 'Better get that.'

Ingrid unearthed her file. It was unlikely to win her journalist of the year but she was beginning to see what gave Danny and Mat such a buzz. This wasn't about regurgitating the same stories each week. This time she could be creating the news.

Nick was soon back with a fax in his hand. 'It was Guy.'

'Guy?'

'My contact at the Met Office - the expert on this sort of thing. I told you about him. Anyway, he's sent us another fax.'

Us. She hadn't thought of the two of them as an 'us'.

The fax was brief but very much to the point. *About your call. Does this help? Cloud seeding is commonly achieved by releasing minute particles of silver iodide or dry-ice crystals from an aeroplane into a cloud. The particles provide surfaces onto which water vapours can freeze. More water freezes on top of this and so on until a droplet weighs enough to fall as rain or snow. Some experts believe the difference in rainfall between seeded and non-seeded clouds to be as much as ten percent but data is unreliable. 'Project Popeye', however, is quoted as a demonstrable example of its effectiveness.*

'What's Project Popeye?'

Nick shook his head. 'Haven't a clue.'

'Come away from the window. You know you don't play outside on a Sunday.' Her father's voice rang in her ears as she pressed her seven-year-old nose harder against the windowpane. They were all out there, jumping and running and falling over the scratchy hay bales; building a magic castle right outside, so close she could almost touch it.

Then into camps for the real game to begin... chasing each other through the maze of tunnels... shrieking with laughter. 'I want to go.' She wanted to go so badly. Surely one more voice amongst the many wouldn't have made so much difference? But there was never any route of appeal to her father.

Miserable Sunday faded, for now. Although it would be replayed through many more dark nights. Ingrid turned restlessly in her bed, unable to prevent the next scene pulling her back.

'Be sure to keep the house in sight. And be back well before dark.'

'Yes dad.'

'Put your winter coat on or you'll catch your death.'

'But they're going.'

'You'd be better off playing without that rough crowd. Make sure they don't get you into trouble.'

'Bye.'

'Be careful.'

Her legs carried her along the track. She wouldn't look back: she looked back. As always her father was there, watching her, fearful of unseen dangers. It trapped her breath. She tried so hard to do everything right, to take his fear away but she never could. A single magpie flew across the path. Quick, wave, take away the sorrow. She ran on, bursting into the woods, breaking free of her father's gaze.

In the woods everything was different. The sounds, the smells, the sensations soothed her, like nothing else could. Nurtured her like a seed buried deep within leaf mould waiting for the right conditions to burst into life. The danger wasn't there at all. It was somewhere behind her, at home, suffocating her...

'Ingrid. Wake up. Wake up. Here, take this.' Jack finally got her to grasp the inhaler. 'Now breathe. That's it. That's better. Slow deep breaths.'

The bedroom slowly came into focus.

'You were thrashing around again,' he said. 'You need to get some help.'

'No. It was just a bad dream. I'm fine now.'

'You don't look it. It's time you went back to the specialist.'

'I'll see.'

'You'd better take today off, build your strength up.'

Ingrid threw the covers back and balanced on the side of the bed. 'I can't do that.'

'There's no point exhausting yourself at work.'

'I enjoy my work. You know that.'

'You say that, but there are so many things we could be doing here. And we certainly don't need your money.'

Ingrid wandered through to the bathroom. She hadn't the energy to try, yet again, to get him to see things through her eyes. To Jack love and possession were indistinguishable.

The jazz wasn't quite as far in the background as Nick had suggested, the smoke was irritating and the food predictable but

Ingrid felt surprisingly relaxed. Unlike Nick.

'How's Ellie?' she asked.

He pushed the remains of a cottage pie around his plate. 'The last results weren't so good, but it'll be okay. She's always been so fit.'

'What did the consultant say?'

'Not much. Ellie needs more tests, but there's a delay.'

'Why?'

'Understaffed, no emergency cover, doing twenty hours a day already. The father of the girl in the next bed is going private.'

'Is that an option you can...?'

'Don't you think I would if I could,' Nick snapped. He paused. 'Sorry, I shouldn't lay all this on you.'

'Not a problem. You'd do the same for me.'

'You know I would. At least I hope you do,' he said, with unexpected emphasis. 'Speaking of which...' his face broke into a smile, 'Got something for you. Project Popeye - I know what it is, or was.'

'What?'

'Strictly speaking it's US military code for in clouds or areas of reduced visibility.'

'US military! I don't understand.'

'Neither did I at first. Turns out we were barking up the wrong tree with agriculture. For anything to do with cloud seeding we've got to go to the experts.'

'To the what?' A well-oiled group at the bar had joined forces with the jazz trio. Much more volume and she'd be reduced to lip-reading.

Nick moved closer. 'The experts - the Ministry of Defence. From 1966 onwards the American military were cloud seeding along the Ho Chi Minh trail in Vietnam.'

'Why?'

'To extend the monsoon season and bog down the Viet Cong supply chains.'

'How would a few extra inches of mud make a difference?'

Nick shrugged. 'Maybe they'd have to rely on coolies to get

supplies - people can get seriously sick in those conditions.'

'So cloud seeding was being used... as a weapon of war?' Her words hung in the air, brutally exposed in a momentary silence between numbers. She looked down.

'Sounds like it.'

She leant closer. 'Did it work?'

'Well according to this,' he took a scrap of paper from his pocket, 'they were still doing it in 1972.'

'So they were cloud seeding for six years. It must have worked. What do you think? Could we have been doing it even earlier?'

'Odds-on chance we were.' Nick left a dramatic pause. 'Ask me when the process was discovered.'

'You know?'

Nick beamed. 'Try Schnectady, New York. Guy dug out this great story. Forget high tech. research budgets, this discovery was made by a man breathing into a chest freezer at the General Electric Company's research laboratory.'

'What happened?'

Nick pushed their empty plates aside and scanned his hastily scrawled notes. 'Some high shot Nobel prize winner discovered he could produce millions of ice crystals by dropping dry ice into a cloud of water droplets below freezing point. Then they discovered silver iodide did the job even better.'

'I get it. So the silver iodide was there to stimulate ice crystals to form.'

Nick smiled at Ingrid. 'I'm impressed.'

'Not just a pretty face you know.'

'Never doubted it, but it is... very pretty.'

Ingrid looked down, conscious of the blush creeping up her neck. 'So... when was this amazing man-freezer moment?'

'1946.'

'46! So they could easily have been experimenting with it over here in the '50's.'

'Yep. Guy is pretty keyed up about weather experimentation. He said something about having a contact at the MoD he could rope in.'

'I knew it! Weather experimentation on our doorstep - that's got to be worth the front page.'

'There's a way to go yet. But get some copy together and I'll take a look at it.'

'I'll interview Private Dean again. There may be stuff I've missed.'

'Worth a try. And I'll get Danny to follow up on the MoD angle.'

'Danny? Why?'

'Investigations are his baby.'

'Not this one.' She lowered her voice. 'This is mine. I did the interview. I picked up on it. I have to see it through.'

'Sure, you've an instinct for a story, but you haven't got the experience to run with this.'

'Then it's time I got it. I've been in the business long enough.'

'Precisely.'

'What's that supposed to mean?'

'You know exactly what I mean; this is a young person's game.'

'There's no reason you can't give me this job. I got the lead, there's no deadline and we're talking thirty years ago. What does Danny know about the fifties?'

He studied the dregs in his glass. 'Well,' he sighed, 'it goes against all my instincts but...'

She squeezed his hand. 'Thanks, you won't regret it.'

'You might need to remind me of that.' He smiled, 'but okay. Alice can take over the village correspondents and charity events while you get yourself up to London. Guy suggested taking a look at the declassified records at the Public Record Office.'

Mike Hoskins tapped his pen in time with the chimes of Big Ben. It was the most productive thing he'd done all day, apart from rifling ancient MoD files as a favour for a mate. Three years ago, this desk job in records had seemed like the better bet, but now...? His whole body, all six foot four of it with a physique to match, ached for a challenge.

It had been a different story when he and Guy were in Northern Ireland, handling covert missions, volunteering for additional terms - until Guy had developed a conscience and opted out. The lucky bastard had had a choice and actually volunteered to put himself out to grass at the Met office! A bit different to his own choice. When he'd decided to put a stop to all the shit those louts on the Shankill Road threw at them day in day out, he'd been offered a court martial or a desk job buried somewhere they wouldn't hear from him again.

The phone rang. 'Yeah?'

'Thanks for the information.'

'Guy. How did it go down?'

'Great. It's whetted their appetite, and mine.'

'Can't see why. Now if you were talking about the Falklands - boy, could I get my hands on some stuff that would blow the government out of the water.'

Lay off, Mike. Just how many dishonourable discharges are you planning on collecting?'

'Do you want me to nose around here or not?'

'You know I do.'

'What's in it for you?'

'Not sure yet.'

'Okay, let's try an easier one. What's in it for me?'

'Revenge maybe.'

'I'll settle for boredom relief. What do you want?'

'Anything on weather modification. Not in or by the US - over here. Anything the MoD was involved with directly.'

'When?'

'Anytime, but particularly the early fifties.'

'Okay so that'll be Air Ministry. This could get interesting.'

'Be careful.'

'Piss off.'

Jack was in his seat in reception at five exactly. He ushered Ingrid out to the car. 'I thought we could eat out tonight,' he said, as soon as he'd got his breath back.

'What's the occasion?'

'Nothing in particular. I've booked the George for 6.30pm.'

Ingrid looked at him. They hadn't been out for months. Why tonight?

Ninety minutes later, an Italian waiter was pulling out her chair, placing a crisp white serviette across her lap and filling a glass with her favourite Frascati. Two meals out in one day felt very decadent. Not that she'd said anything to Jack about lunch.

In a welcome pause between courses, he placed an envelope on the white linen cloth beside her.

'What's this?'

'Open it.'

She ran her finger along the crease and drew out two sheets of headed paper. They were from the local travel agent.

'I'm taking you up to London, for our wedding anniversary.' Jack said.

Ingrid read the printed itinerary. *Two days dinner, bed and breakfast at the Piccadilly Hotel, a show of your choice on the Tuesday evening and afternoon tea at the Ritz on Wednesday.* 'Jack, this is such a surprise. Why didn't you say anything?'

'That would have spoiled it.'

'But you should have asked if I could get time off.'

'Have you taken any this year?'

'Well no, but...'

'There you are then.'

Nick wasn't impressed. 'One minute you're begging me to give you an investigation, the next you're asking for three days off - with hardly any notice.'

'Yes,' said Ingrid.

'Does that strike you as reasonable?'

He was right. It was completely unreasonable. 'I'm sorry. I didn't know anything about it until last night; only Jack's already booked a hotel, for our wedding anniversary.'

'Have I made a mistake, Ingrid? I mean, you're either

investigating this story or you're not. When did you last see Mat or Danny take lunch, let alone three days off when they're onto something? I knew I should have given this to them.'

'We're going to London. I could go to the Public Records Office while I'm there - and you won't have to pay expenses.'

'I don't know...'

'I can put a day to it. Maybe more.'

He paused. 'Okay. But don't do this to me again, Ingrid.'

'Thanks, Nick. I'll make it up to you.'

'I'll see that you do.'

Ingrid stood. 'I could do with a date to search on.'

Nick lifted a manila folder out of his drawer and pushed it across to Ingrid.

'What's this?'

'Take a look.'

Ingrid opened it. 'My God! How did you get your hands on this?' She was holding a dozen or more sheets of faxed minutes and reports stamped *SECRET*. The first was headed *Tactical use of Rainmaking*. She read. *A paper on rain and snow making by artificial means written by Mr I.P.Krick, the President of the American Institute of Aerological Research, was received in this office at the beginning of this month. It was passed to the War Office...* Ingrid looked up. 'The War office!' The War Office was studying a paper on rainmaking. 'So the British Government was involved.'

'Might not be able to go that far, but they were definitely interested.'

Ingrid read on. *It was passed to the War Office for study and a subsequent meeting was held in the War Office to hear Mr. I.P.Krick's personal views on the subject and to make some evaluation as to the tactical use to which this science could be put.* 'Who was this Krick?'

'Some guy making a packet out of rainmaking contracts; snow for skiers, rain to fill State reservoirs, that kind of thing. He got paid if it rained - without having to prove it had anything to do with his seeding. That's the sort of job I could do with.'

'But he was hardly sending a paper to the War Office to make sure the skiing at Aviemore was up to scratch that winter.'

'Take a look at the letter from Searl, Krick's rep.'

She read. '*I became aware that the U.S. Air Force was investigating methods of rainfall increase and a possible application when linked to the strategic use of the atom bomb.* The atom bomb! How does rainmaking link to the bomb?'

'That's what I'm paying you to find out.'

'This was written on December 16th, 1953. It's the right time but... all it says here is, *to make some evaluation as to the tactical use to which this science could be put.* That's not evidence we were actually doing it.' Ingrid started to work her way through the other papers.

'Here,' Nick said, 'give me some of those.'

It was strange, working together. They'd worked side-by-side for five years but never actually collaborated. She smiled at the memory of the frosty reception she'd given him. An abrasive brummie with a short temper wasn't the person specification she'd had in mind when the old editor retired. The paper needed shaking up - it was losing out to the free sheets - but there were the old ways and Nick's ways. He didn't suffer fools gladly. Two of her colleagues were made redundant within months; but she'd survived. A bit of continuity maybe? Or a talent for keeping her head down. No wonder it had taken so long to get on friendly terms. And now? How would she describe their relationship now?

'What have you got?' he asked.

She focused on the paper in her hand. 'A memo from Air Vice Marshall Sinclair. He's a G.C., C.B., C.B.E, D.S.O. Seem like pretty impressive credentials wouldn't you say?'

'Not bad.'

'So probably a reliable witness.'

'What are you getting at?'

'Take a look at this.' Ingrid held out a brief memo headed *Loose Minute ops 7643* and stamped *SECRET*. Nick reached across to take it from her, brushing her arm for a second. It was an accidental intimacy, but the sensation lingered.

Nick scanned the memo. *'Reference your loose minute dated 12th November. I had heard about the tactical use of rainmaking while I was Commandant at OLD SARUM...* Old Sarum. That lands the story right in our patch.'

'When was he Commandant there?'

Nick read to the end of the memo. 'Doesn't say.'

'I need a date.'

'Come on.' Nick grabbed her hand.

'What are you doing?'

'You want answers. You shall have answers.' Out in the corridor he put his arm behind Ingrid's back and ushered her past a startled Alice who was directing a young girl to a newly opened boutique in the High Street. Blushing, although she wasn't exactly sure why, Ingrid was almost relieved to be thrust into the darkness of the archive. 'Don't move.' A strip-light fizzed into action. 'Sit,' Nick said, pointing to a wooden chair wedged between the grey metal bookshelves and a couple of open crates. 'Okay. We've got a history of the RAF on Salisbury Plain here somewhere.' He began to scan the shelves.

'You could humour me by using the index. I hardly saw the light of day for nine months, two weeks and three days - give or take a few hours - putting that damn thing together.'

'Aahhh. Sorry about that. But Alice is unreliable and...'

'Just use it!'

He reached for the green filing box and flicked through the cards. 'Great system.' He smiled at her, selected a card and turned to a shelf just above his head, removing a large black bound volume. 'There's a whole section on biographies in here... there you go... Air Vice Marshall Sir Laurence Sinclair. He certainly got around; Mediterranean, Aden, Iraq...'

'Let me look.' She pulled at his arm.

'...before returning to take up his post as Commandant of the School of Land/Air Warfare at...' he paused for effect, 'Old Sarum.'

'When?'

Nick closed the book. '1952.'

'No month?'

Nick turned, bringing his face closer to hers. 'You're a very hard woman to satisfy, Ingrid Clarke.'

Impulsively, she squeezed his arm. 'Oh, I wouldn't say that.'

'Why don't we find a pub and celebrate,' he said, taking hold of her hand.

'I... I'd love to... but...' But what? But I don't want to upset Jack? But this could get complicated? She took a breath. 'But I have to get back.'

Nick released her hand and replaced the book. 'Another time,' he said, switching off the light and guiding her back into the corridor.

'Yes, I'd like that. Thanks for your help this afternoon.'

'Lift home?'

'I'll be fine on the bus thanks.'

'In this weather?'

He was right. She'd been so absorbed she'd been oblivious to the rain bucketing down outside... And that wasn't all she'd missed.

Chapter Four

Jack was in full flow on the train up to London. 'I told you this was going to be significant. The Task Force is leaving Portsmouth today.'

'So that's it, is it? She can single-handedly commit us to war. What about Parliament - have they had any say in this?'

'And it looks as though HMS Endurance won't be scrapped after all. It's about time they saw sense.'

Ingrid tried again. 'I can't believe she's doing this.'

He looked up. 'Well what would you do? Let Galtieri walk all over the Falklands?'

'Why does it have to be so black and white? What about economic sanctions? The US must have some clout.'

Jack sighed and immersed himself in his paper.

'You can't just...' Ingrid stopped. What was the point? He didn't want an argument, or even a debate; just an audience. 'Surely they'll try diplomacy.' Silence. His paper was already dropping towards the table revealing half closed eyes. Jack fell asleep at the drop of a hat these days, and his face was becoming so lined and sallow. Age was catching up with him. Was that why he was always trying to take over her life?

He'd been so full of energy, on top of everything. Every moment of his precious spare time he'd spent with her, at home or whisking her off in his Cessna. But they hadn't been up in the plane for months. He hadn't done much, except potter about in the garden and set the agenda for their home life. How could she have let it happen all over again?

Ingrid snatched her book, pressed the spine against the table and stared at the page. This trip was a mistake. She should have said she couldn't get the time off. It wasn't fair, letting Nick down like that - especially now, with his worries about Ellie.

She stared at the countryside flashing past. They'd left the fields behind and were skirting Salisbury Plain. Rain was lashing against the carriage window, the wheels drumming out the mantra, rain on the Plain, rain on the Plain. But what kind of rain? What exactly did Private Dean see? She looked at the book on Wiltshire airfields. It was filled with detail on the decoy airfields built during the war, K sites for day decoys and Q sites for night. Then there were Starfish, specially ignited fires, QL's, special lighting effects and SCI's - whatever they were - obscuring targets with smoke. By the end of 1941 the Luftwaffe had made more attacks on the dummies than they had on genuine airfields. Quite a success story.

Ingrid paused. She'd missed something. Jack would know. But Jack was slumped in his seat, mouth half open, a trickle of saliva making its way down his chin. Maybe she'd try Nick. He should still be at work. She could call from the hotel, see if he'd heard from Guy.

The countryside metamorphosed into city streets, unkempt backyards, and creeping highways; great sweeps of land without a genuine sod of earth to be seen. London was so claustrophobic, it numbed her senses. How could people exist there, shut in by walls of concrete and glass?

The train pulled into Paddington. 'Jack, we're here.' Ingrid shook his arm. Even without the few minutes he needed to collect himself, they would have been last out of the carriage. He placed their bags on a trolley and guided Ingrid through the barrier and out to the taxi rank. It was an alien world - people and traffic alternating between bursts of activity and restless waiting. But the hotel was comfortable, the meal exceptional, and instant oblivion in the down-covered, king-size bed a welcome reprieve from Jack's determination to make this "an occasion". He must have spent weeks putting it together. She should have looked more disappointed at breakfast.

'Are you sure you don't mind me leaving you on your own?' Jack asked.

'Of course not,' she smiled. 'You haven't been to the Imperial War Museum for ages. You'll enjoy it. Besides, I'm looking forward to a wander down Oxford Street and you'd hate that.' Oxford Street? Why not come right out with it - tell him she had work to do?

'Well don't wear yourself out. I've booked dinner after the theatre tonight.'

'After?' Ingrid groaned inwardly. It would be gone midnight before she got to bed.

'Much better than rushing it beforehand. It will be just perfect, you'll see.' Jack lifted her hand and squeezed it affectionately.

Less than an hour later Ingrid fell into the Public Records Office. At least the bedlam was kept at bay inside these walls. She slipped into the nearest seat to get her bearings. Nick was right about one thing - she was flying blind. She hadn't a clue where to start.

'Yes?' the clerk called.

Ingrid stepped forward to the enquiries desk. 'Can you tell me how I access Ministry of Defence files please?'

'What date?'

'The nineteen fifties.'

'The MoD didn't come into existence until 1964. It was the Air Ministry before then and most of those papers have a thirty-year release on them so you may not be lucky.'

'What does that mean?'

'The public aren't allowed access to classified material and it usually isn't de-classified for thirty years. Anything after April 1952 will be unavailable. Anything before then you'll find indexed in the cabinets over there.'

Ingrid cursed. She turned to the polished cabinets. A plethora of labels greeted her. War Office, Ministry of Supply, Air Ministry, Air Historical Branch, Ministry of Aviation, the Department of Scientific and Industrial Research and God knows what else. She returned to the enquiries queue. Five minutes later the assistant handed her a request slip for RAF logbooks, 1951-52.

The first set of logbooks delivered to her desk was in surprisingly good condition. Ingrid skimmed through page after page of technical jargon, hunting down references to manoeuvres on Salisbury Plain. She scribbled down dates, places and brief details, just in case.

A break for coffee and an extended lunch helped with the tedium of it all but by mid-afternoon she'd completed March 1952 back to 1950 without a single mention of rainmaking. She was either looking in the wrong place or the experiments hadn't started until later in 1952. They could have been seeding the entire country in April or May for all she knew. She threw down her pencil and strode out to the lobby. What the hell was she doing here? Jack was bound to be back at the hotel, probably waiting with her afternoon tea tray, complete with a single red rose.

But she'd made a commitment to Nick.

Back at her desk, Ingrid scanned the seemingly endless pages until an entry in the logbook of flight commander John Hart brought her up short. *August 3rd 1949. Time of take-off, 1700. Aircraft type, Wellington. Registration letter, 'D'. Pilot's name, Flight Lt Otley. Duty was special duty. Remarks - Seeding dry ice into cumulus cloud to produce rain. This was successful. Time of flight 50 minutes.*

'Yes!' Ingrid exclaimed, breaking the dignified hush pervading the room. The student opposite blushed for her. Surprisingly, Ingrid didn't care. She had proof: they were cloud seeding. How many times had she watched newsreaders turn to the forecaster and jokingly ask them what they'd done to the weather? But someone, somewhere could actually be deciding whether it would be sunshine or showers in the morning. Had they gone on experimenting? Was someone out there controlling the weather?

Ingrid fixed her eyes on the young man playing the grand piano in the corner of the dining room. Whatever had possessed her to spend so much time at the record office? And to phone Nick as soon as she'd got back... Jack was no fool. Why didn't she just explain? What was there to hide? She was only doing her job.

'Penny for them?' Jack said. She allowed him to scoop up her hand across the table. 'You know you mean everything to me Ingrid don't you.' He paused. 'Only sometimes, well, things change. But we're still the same people, underneath.'

'Mostly, I suppose.'

'Anyway something happens and you realise what's important.'

'What are you talking about?'

'Nothing for you to worry about but I did want to give you this. Just a reminder of how much you mean to me.' He opened a small box, took out an eternity ring and slid it onto her finger.

Ingrid felt her chest tighten. Jack never talked emotions. It wasn't in his repertoire. She didn't know how to respond. 'Thank you,' she gasped. 'It's beautiful.'

'You need some air. We'll go.'

'Thanks. Just the strain of a day in London.'

'The fumes along Oxford Street are always bad,' he said.

She hesitated. 'Yes, they are.'

Ingrid leant against Jack in the taxi. He lifted his arm and tucked it around her, no longer firm and possessive but somehow tender, a gentle, comforting touch. She relaxed into his embrace, breathing easy. It wasn't the ring. It was beautiful of course, but still a thing. No, it was the care he had put into these few days, into those few words, that was the real gift.

'Jack.'

'Yes?'

'Thank you; for everything.'

He squeezed her hand. 'No more than you deserve.'

Chapter Five

'So how was your break, Mrs C.? Did you get wined and dined then?' Alice said.

Ingrid was trapped by the kettle. 'It was lovely thanks.' Surprisingly their last day together in London had been... what? She'd got so used to describing their relationship as comfortable that she was stuck for an answer. Afternoon tea at the Ritz had certainly done the trick. Rose coloured chairs, marble tables and the most flattering light in London falling from the frosted glass ceiling had peeled back the years.

'Mr Pearce wants to see you before you start.'

'Thanks Alice.'

Ingrid knocked on Nick's door. 'Come in.' He looked up over his glasses.

'You wanted to see me?'

'Yes. How did you get on?' he asked.

'We had a lovely time thank you.'

'Oh,' he hesitated. 'I meant at the Record Office.'

Ingrid cursed. 'Of course.'

'You said you'd found evidence they were seeding in '49.'

'Yes. Only it was up north. We still don't know what was happening here.'

'Don't we?' He was starting to look smug.

'What?' She moved round to perch on his side of the desk.

'After you rang I contacted Guy. He'd already passed on stuff from '53 so I persuaded him to get his contact to look at the rest of '52.'

'And?'

'Both their jobs are on the line if this ever gets out but he found a reference to a programme of cloud seeding experiments being conducted by a team of international scientists. Guess when.'

'1952?'

'Yep, in August.'

'August! What were they doing?'

He leant towards her. 'Don't get too excited. Apparently a team of observers watched from the ground as a pilot threw salt from a glider into the clouds, so it can't have been the same planes Private Dean spotted.'

'Where?'

'Guy didn't say. But it gets better. The BBC was interested in doing a programme on the advantages of controlled rainfall. They interviewed the scientists, followed the experiments, everything. This was the middle of August right? The film was due to go out a few days later but it was suddenly pulled.'

'Why?'

'Does August 15th 1952 mean anything to you?'

Ingrid froze. 'No. Why?'

'Call it coincidence, but this film on rainmaking was abandoned the day after the worst floods in living memory destroyed a small town on the North Devon coast.' He looked down at the fax on his desk. 'It was...'

'Lynmouth,' she whispered.

'You know about it?' There was no response. 'Who do you think pulled that programme and why? Ingrid? Are you okay?' He was standing now, a hand on each arm, supporting her.

'I've got to do something.' She pushed herself away. 'Back in a minute.'

Ingrid felt her way along the corridor to her desk. She had to get there before her mind closed in on her. She needed air. Why wouldn't the window open? Where was her bag, her inhaler? Left in Nick's office. She couldn't go back, not yet. She had to get a grip on reality first, this reality, now reality, before she could face anyone.

45

The iron band tightened around her chest; she had to think, to clear the images. But with each gasp they became stronger, filling her head with the pictures, the sounds...

...the roaring growing worse second by second, drowning the music, the children's shouts, everything. And the overwhelming darkness, smothering her, making her gasp as she called again and again 'Alistair; Michael.' The touch of a hand, depending on her for life, safe in her grasp for a few precious seconds - then torn from her by the water, tugging at her legs, pulling her away into the blackness...

'I couldn't hold them. I couldn't...'

'Mrs Clarke. Ingrid. Can you hear me?' The medic placed a cushion under her head and adjusted the oxygen mask. 'Just breathe steadily. That's it. Now let's see if we can sit you up a little.'

Nick knelt behind Ingrid and eased her up until she was leaning against his shoulder. 'Will she be okay?' he asked.

'I don't think we need to take her in. Can someone get her home?'

'Yes,' Nick said.

'Just leave that a bit longer, Mrs Clarke.' The medic gently stopped Ingrid from pulling the mask away.

'I'm sorry, Nick,' she gasped, 'I'll get on soon.'

'You'll do nothing of the sort. I'm taking you home.'

'There's no need... Really... You've got enough to worry about. I haven't asked you how Ellie is... I'm sorry.'

'Just be quiet and do as you're told.'

She leant back, vaguely aware of his hand over hers.

'Nothing to worry about sir. It's just the shock and the oxygen. She'll be herself again soon.' He removed the mask and packed the equipment away. 'We'll leave you to it.'

'Thanks.'

'I'm so sorry.' Ingrid struggled to sit.

'Will you stop apologising and stay still. I don't want you scaring me like that again.'

She closed her eyes, relaxing into the support of his arms; all embracing, protection from the nightmare.

'Ingrid. Ingrid. Oh my God. What happened?' Jack burst through the door, flushed and breathless.

Nick helped Ingrid to a chair, relinquishing her to her husband. 'Your wife had a bad asthma attack. We called the ambulance but they were happy for her to go home. I'll get the car.'

'No need for that. Mine's outside.'

'Oh, Jack, don't fuss. I wish everyone would stop fussing.' Ingrid pushed him away and reached for her coat.

Nick held it out, gently resting his hands on her shoulders. 'Take care of yourself.'

'I'll be fine. I'll see you tomorrow,' Ingrid responded.

'We'll see about that,' Jack interrupted. 'Now, hold on to my arm.'

'I'll start with all of the south and the west up as far as the Midlands. You'll notice a distinct improvement in the weather over the next few days. A clearer, drier spell is moving in from the west and should stay with us until the end of the weekend.'

They had kept her at home for a week, the doctor and Jack. *It's time something was done about these attacks. They're getting more frequent. Working full time can't be helping, she should be resting more.* That was the pot calling the kettle black. Jack was the one who needed to rest every five minutes, not her. Work had nothing to do with it. But then her opinion didn't seem to count for much.

The phone rang. 'I'll get it,' she called in the general direction of the sitting room. 'Hello?'

'How are you?'

'Nick, it's good to hear your voice. I'm fine, thanks. How about you?'

'Looking forward to having you back, but not a second before you feel up to it. Danny's on standby.'

'And that's meant to reassure me! Don't you dare make me redundant. I'm plotting my escape as we speak. I'll be back on Monday.'

'You're a long way from being redundant. And apart from being good to see you, I've got some stuff here you'll want to see.'

'What?'

'Sorry. Under orders not to talk about anything specific.'

'Who from?'

'Jack, of course, when I rang the other night.'

'Oh? He didn't say.'

'That was predictable. Everyone's out on Monday so we'll have the place to ourselves. Plenty of time to catch up. See you then.'

'Who was that?' Jack was standing in the doorway.

'Nick. I told him I'd be back on Monday.'

'That's ridiculous. Surely you can see how much better you've been at home. Retire on grounds of ill health; get your pension made up. Couldn't be a better time.'

'I don't want to retire. I enjoy my work. I don't want to be stuck at home with...'

'With me?' She might as well have struck him across the face.

'I was going to say with nothing to do.'

'You haven't touched my family tree for ages.'

'I mean something outside home.'

'It's your decision, but you know how I feel about it and surely that counts for something.' Jack stared at the television. *Mr Alexander Haig, the American Secretary of State, left for Buenos Aires today to continue his attempt at mediation with the Junta.* 'I don't know why he's bothering. We need to meet force with force. Weather allowing, the task force will be within the exclusion zone in ten days, then we'll see an end to it,' he said.

'And do you know what the task force will be meeting?' Ingrid retaliated. 'It was in the paper yesterday.' She picked it up from the coffee table and scanned the paragraphs. 'Here. The Argentinean force consists of a British carrier, an American cruiser, two British and six American destroyers, corvettes from France, submarines from Germany and the US, and as for the bombs, perhaps the task force would like to deliver some more while they are down there. Save on carriage charges.'

'Don't be ridiculous.'

'It's knowing young British men will be killed and maimed with British exports that's ridiculous. No not ridiculous, criminal. How can they sleep at night?'

'Who?' he asked.

'The government officials who sell this stuff.' She could hear her voice becoming shrill. 'What do they do? Ask for a sworn undertaking that Her Majesty's weapons won't be used to slaughter anyone other than acceptable enemies? I'm going to bed.'

Ingrid slammed the door and ran up the stairs, each breath becoming more and more laboured. How could they find something and lose it again so quickly? Had she been kidding herself in London?

'I'm sorry, Jack didn't tell me you'd called. I'd have come to the phone if I'd known.'

Nick pulled out her chair. 'Sit down.'

'It's okay. You don't need to treat me like glass. It was only an asthma attack. It's Jack who's got it all out of proportion. You should be devoting yourself to Ellie anyway. How is she?'

He hesitated. 'Not good. There are complications.' He turned to look out the window. 'I'm thinking of moving her.'

'To private care?'

'Maybe. It won't be easy.' His voice faltered.

Suddenly she was beside him. 'I wish there was something I could do to help.' She rested a hand on his back. It was one of those gestures you do without thinking, like rubbing a child's knee when they fall over... wasn't it? Nick's response was immediate. He bent his head towards her. Probably just to say something about Ellie, something confidential, but she couldn't think, being so close. She eased away. 'You said you had something for me, about the cloud seeding.'

Nick was suddenly serious. 'I've had a bit of a re-think. After the way things ended up maybe you should go back to covering domestic stuff.'

'No! It's only because it came out of the blue, the mention of Lynmouth. It jogged a few memories, that's all.' A few memories! Only one word that had changed everything, absolutely everything. Now she had to know.

'Anything I should know about?' Nick said.

'No. Not yet anyway. What have you got?'

Nick fetched a manila folder from his office. 'Listen, Ingrid, we're treading on thin ice with this. Unauthorised access to classified material is a criminal offence.'

'I'm sure it's not the first time you've done it.'

'No, but it is yours.'

'Give me the folder, Nick.'

'Okay, but I'm worried that Guy's MoD contact has crossed some fundamental boundaries to get hold of this.'

Ingrid opened the folder. Inside were several sheets of official Air Ministry paper. She took out the top sheet. *'Minutes - November 1953. Item 1 - discussion on the rationale for increasing rain and snow by artificial means. Possible uses: A: to increase rainfall over a given target area in order to bog down enemy movement in that area.*
So we were at it. And well before the Americans in Vietnam.'

'Yes. But read the next bit.'

'B: to explode an atomic weapon in a seeded storm system or cloud. This would produce a far wider area of radioactive contamination than in a normal atomic explosion.

'They... we... were researching cloud seeding to increase radioactive fallout!' The paper dropped from Ingrid's hands. 'They don't want to control the weather to relieve famine, or even to make life difficult for the enemy, but to kill as many civilians as possible!'

'Take my advice - keep this to yourself. These papers won't be de-classified until next year; we've got to tread carefully. According to Guy the MoD denies having had anything to do with cloud seeding.'

'What, in 1953?'

'Ever.'

'But they're lying. This proves it.'

'Not quite. They used "would". Nothing to say they had.'

'But the logbooks detail the flights. How can they deny that?'

'I don't know how, but they are. They want it kept under wraps. Which is why we have to be careful.'

'Could Guy find out any more at the Met Office?'

'Already tried.'

'And?'

'According to his boss the official line is they tried some cloud seeding experiments in '55 but they weren't particularly successful and no experiments in weather modification have been tried for years,' he said.

'Weather modification. So that's what they call it. And did he believe it, the official line?'

'Not a word of it. He's doing some more digging.' He leant closer. 'But we need to keep our distance Ingrid. Getting prosecuted won't be much fun.'

'But they can't prosecute,' she said, 'not without exposing what's been going on. And aren't you just a bit curious that our weather can be modified to order? Don't you want to know what they've been up to, and if they're still doing it?'

'That depends.'

'On what?'

'On whether we can discuss it over dinner tonight.'

Ingrid froze. She couldn't... could she? She gazed through the plate glass windows fronting onto the road, at the people rushing by like satellites spinning back and forth around the one or two stationary figures queuing for the bus. For a moment one of them reminded her of Jack.

'I... I don't know. It's difficult.' She jumped as the front door opened and a young lad strode in to reception.

'Is this where I sell my Escort?'

'It's where you can advertise it.' Ingrid placed a form on the counter.

Five minutes later, when the heavy oak door closed behind him, it was easier to pretend nothing had been said. Ingrid picked up the folder. 'Listen to this. *Seeding carried out from the ground is capable of creating rain up to three hundred miles away.* Three hundred miles. So there's every chance those experiments in

August 1952 caused the Lynmouth floods.'

Nick moved away. 'Theoretically, yes. But it depends on wind direction and speed. And I don't see how a couple of one-off experiments could produce enough rain to devastate an entire village.'

'What if it was more than a one-off? What if there were several, enough to waterlog Exmoor? Then one more downpour like August 15th could have been the final straw,' she persisted.

'I don't see how.'

'Nine inches of rain fell in a day. It was enough, believe me.'

'How come you're suddenly an expert on Lynmouth?'

'Suddenly!' Ingrid stopped. She was meant to be investigating a lead, not obsessed by an event she wasn't supposed to remember, somewhere she hadn't even been, that killed thirty-four people she'd never even heard of. She took a deep breath. 'Sorry. Was I getting a bit carried away?'

'Yes, but over the weather. What a waste.' He threw his sandwich wrapper in the bin, walked to his office and closed the door.

Chapter Six

Ingrid stopped Alice on her way back to reception. 'Mr Pearce has been closeted with those men for a long time. What's it about?'

'No idea. They were talking about his daughter when I took their coffee in, something about private care.' A movement behind Ingrid distracted Alice. 'The "What's On" page is all sorted, Mrs C.'

Nick escorted his visitors to the entrance.

'Morning, Nick.'

He glanced briefly at Ingrid. 'Morning.' On his return he paused. 'Come in for a minute.'

Ingrid followed him into his office. 'Was it good news?'

'Good news?'

'I know she shouldn't gossip but Alice overheard your visitors talking about private care for Ellie. Have they managed to organise something?'

'Yes.'

'You don't look very happy about it.'

'My daughter will be cared for. You know how important that is to me, don't you?'

'Yes, of course. You must be so relieved.' He didn't look relieved, or even pleased. She laid a concerned hand on his arm 'Is there a problem, Nick; finances or something?'

He shrugged her hand away and walked to the window. 'No. Everything has been taken care of. Just a few details to tie up, then we can get back to normal.'

Ingrid addressed his back. 'Have you heard any more from Guy? Only it's a week since he came through with the Air Ministry notes and I wondered...'

Nick spun round. 'There won't be anything else. I've pulled the investigation. This is a small provincial paper. I can't afford to have you tied up on something and nothing. Destroy your notes and anything else you've got on rainmaking. I've asked Alice to leave a folder on your desk of local stories that need covering today. I want the copy in twenty-four hours.'

It was a long time since he'd pulled rank on her. 'I'm sorry. I hope you don't think I've been abusing my position. I...' She was in unfamiliar territory.

Nick shuffled the papers on his desk with intense concentration.

Then the penny dropped. He'd made a move and she'd rejected him. He was nursing his bruised pride. But his attitude still rankled. 'I'm sorry I've been taking up so much of your time. I'll leave you to it.'

Ingrid marched into the corridor. His comments were so unjustified. She'd put in hours of unpaid overtime without a word of thanks. But this had nothing to do with work, did it? Just one small moment of indecision and she was out in the cold.

She leant against the wall. 'Damn!' Was her hesitation so unreasonable? After all she was married. Was - past tense. Ingrid tried the idea on for size. Jack had been driving her mad for ages, so maybe it was time to... to what? Work at it? The thought paralysed her. But when she thought about Nick, her body was suddenly alive.

This was ridiculous: whatever was going on could wait - until after work anyway. She needed another focus, right now. She settled herself at her desk and picked up a folder balanced on her in-tray. A headline caught her attention. *Plain Talking*. The local museum was staging an exhibition on Salisbury Plain. Ingrid grabbed her coat. 'I'll be at the museum if anyone wants me Alice.'

'Okay, Mrs C.'

The museum was housed in The King's House, a fascinating building made up of a cluster of wings of varying ages; all unique, but each somehow lost without the company of the others. Inside the air was laden with centuries of living, and the worn slate floors reminded her of the fleeting nature of her own footsteps. Ingrid showed her press pass at the desk and walked through to the exhibition of photographs and personal anecdotes.

There was a whole section dedicated to the residents of the village of Imber.

'Seven miles from any town
There stands Imber on the down.'

Such a sad place. The homely cluster of thatched cottages surrounding the church and manor were all empty. The War Department had evicted everyone, in December of all months. Sitting room walls were peppered with bullets, lovingly tended gardens trampled and overgrown. So depressing. But then without the pilots trained on the Plain, the manoeuvres practised on the Plain and defence strategies developed on the Plain, what would life have been like? Why did each generation have to make such horrendous decisions?

She pressed the mental rewind button. Defence strategies. She took out her pad. They were designing decoy airfields. What else? Something she'd read on the train. Smoke. That was it. The use of smoke propelled from the ground to screen installations. The Americans had been working on smoke generators to create artificial fog before they moved on to seeding clouds. The Air Ministry minutes had talked about cloud seeding from the ground. Maybe planes were only part of the picture. What if they were seeding from the ground as well?

Ingrid made a few notes on the rest of the exhibition and headed back to the Post.

'Any messages, Alice?'

'The print room called about the "What's On" section so I sent it down. They were pestering about the wedding anniversary ads too so I sorted them. Hope that's okay.'

'Brilliant, you'll be doing me out of a job next.'

'Oh no, Mrs C. I'm not applying. That wouldn't be right.'

'What?'

'How are you doing, Ingrid?' Danny burst through the door.

'Could be better,' she said.

'Not you as well. What's got into the boss?'

'He's got... personal problems. To do with his daughter.' Not exactly the truth but near enough. 'Did he talk to you about something I've picked up?'

'The rainmaking investigation? Kind of.'

'What does that mean?'

'Well one minute he was dead keen for me to take it on. The next he's asking for all the stuff back and swearing me to secrecy.'

'When did he change his mind?'

'This morning. He was going to give the council fraud story to Mat and get me to take over the rainmaking.'

'He had no right to do that.'

'No skin off my nose. I've almost nailed this guy for taking back-handers anyway.'

'Mrs C. Phone call for you,' Alice called.

'Put it through to my desk please.' It was bound to be Jack checking up on her.

'Mrs Clarke?'

'Yes.'

'This is personnel. We're updating your pension record and wondered if you could answer a couple of queries?'

'Of course.'

'We have your first contribution in June 1956. Is that right?'

'As far as I can remember.'

'So taking it to the end of next month, that gives you twenty-six years of contributions. Now, we need to consider whether your pension will be made up. Is ill-health likely to be a factor?'

'No. Nothing serious anyway.'

'I think that's all for now. Thank you, Mrs Clarke.'

In all her time at the paper it was her first conversation with personnel. Hopefully it would be her last. Being quizzed about pensions made her feel redundant.

'With a cold front coming in from the North it's going to feel unseasonably chilly throughout the week. There may even be a chance of snow on the hills to the north and east. And now for the headlines. On the Falklands...'

Jack listened intently. 'Galtieri won't last long now.'

'Do you want coffee?' Ingrid called from the kitchen.

'The task force will be there in three days; once our Harriers get stuck into them it will all be over bar the shouting.' She handed him a cup. 'Thank you.'

'You were flying during the war weren't you, Jack?'

'Spitfires, out of Boscombe Down. They were built in Salisbury you know.'

'No, I didn't know,' she said. 'I was still at school. Besides, I wasn't even here.'

'You weren't?'

She changed the subject. 'Did they use smoke, to disguise the bases?'

'Of course. Common practice.'

'How?'

'Using planes, or from the ground.'

'But how could they get it high enough, doing it from the ground?'

'Oh that's easy. Rockets,' he said.

'Rockets? As in fireworks?'

'I don't know why you're so surprised. Same mix of charcoal, saltpetre and sulphur public displays use every bonfire night.'

'Only these smoke pyrotechnics were anything but public.' Ingrid muttered.

'WAECO were big in smoke generators,' Jack was getting into his stride.

'WAECO?'

'Wessex Aircraft Engineering Company. They made the campfire simulator, a cluster of pyrotechnics and sawdust that crackled and smelt like a fire. Attracted enemy jungle patrols like bees to a honey pot.'

'What about after the war?'

'Diversified into rockets for marine use; and they made the Olympic torch of course, for the games at Wembley – '47 was it? Sometime just after the war anyway. But that was about it, oh and Fumite.'

'What did you say?' Ingrid caught the tail end of Jack's comments.

'Fumite - developed at Porton Down. Brought many a thing to its knees from jungle guerrillas to the death watch beetle.'

Porton Down, the UK Government's chemical research establishment. Like the fireworks it was so obvious once you knew.

It was a cold day and the atmosphere inside the Post's offices was no warmer.

'Morning, Nick. Can I have five minutes sometime this morning?' Ingrid said.

He looked at his diary. 'I could do eleven.'

It wasn't exactly the open-armed greeting she'd been hoping for. 'Thanks. By the way, I'm sure he knew what he was talking about.'

'Who?'

'Private Dean. Jack came up with something last night...'

His forehead creased even further. 'I told you. That investigation is over. Don't waste any more time on it, especially mine. Now if you don't mind...'

Dismissed, Ingrid returned to her desk. Was he angry with her, or with himself? At eleven she knocked on his door and waited.

'Come in.'

'Coffee?'

'No. We'll get on.' He pulled out a chair on the opposite side of the desk.

Thirty minutes later she was back in her office with hardly a glance having passed between them. There was a sound behind her. Bracing herself for her usual miscommunication with Alice, she threw a greeting over her shoulder. 'I'll be right there.'

'Good morning.' The voice was deep, dark and definitely did not belong to Alice. Ingrid turned. 'I apologise if I startled you.' The man standing in front of her was a stranger.

'I thought you were our receptionist. Can I help?'

'I understand you cover the front desk over lunch.'

'That's right, for Alice.'

'Well I've taken over from her and I'd like to go for an early lunch so if you wouldn't mind...'

'I don't understand. Where's Alice?'

'She's moved on.'

'Bit sudden isn't it?'

'I couldn't say. I'll be back at one.' His soft leather shoes hardly made a sound on the tiled floor. Quite unexpectedly, she was missing Alice already. Why hadn't Nick said anything? She walked along to his office.

'I'm sorry to disturb you, Nick but Alice...' The room was empty. He'd gone to lunch without a word to her. There was no need for him to give her the cold shoulder quite so emphatically. She hadn't actually said no. And it was his fault for springing it on her like that. She sat at his desk. His aggressive about turn on Private Dean didn't make sense either.

Ingrid looked at the fax machine, took up a plain sheet of paper and began to write. A few minutes later the fax was on its way. If Nick was going to be uncooperative she'd have to deal direct.

'It's not going to be pleasant for the ground troops when they land. Temperatures are dropping and they've got biting winds, rain and snow to contend with. And goodness knows what it's like at sea. The Argentineans are blocking all forecasts.' Jack was reading the paper after dinner.

Ingrid put her book down. 'Can I have a look?' She scanned the article ...*But this apparently petty response... is in recognition of the vital part weather could play in any battle or blockade of the Falklands. As the fleet approaches the climax of its 8,000 mile journey, weather is going to be a very important factor in the war...*

'Listen to this Jack. The Met Office told *The Times* yesterday that the weather around the Falklands was relatively calm for this time of year. That's confirmed by a reporter on *Invincible*; he describes the sea as curiously leaden and calm. But according to a reporter on *HMS Hermes*, not a million miles away from the *Invincible*, they were battling through mountainous seas. So who's bending the truth about the weather now?'

'You're becoming obsessed, Ingrid. Find something else to occupy you.'

'Something else to occupy me! You were interested enough to start with.'

'I'm too tired for this. I'm going to bed.' Jack steadied himself on the back of the chair, bent to kiss the top of her head and shuffled out the door.

Ingrid leant back and shut her eyes. 'You're tired!' she muttered to herself. 'You should try it from where I'm sitting.'

'Morning, Mrs Clarke.' Their new enquiries clerk - Ingrid still hadn't thought to ask his name - delivered his greeting with only a passing glance. With Alice gone and Nick barely communicating, it was getting more and more difficult to haul herself in each day. A call from a teacher wanting to arrange work experience for three students brightened things up for a while. She wanted to come next Wednesday, but only if the peripatetic trombone player cancelled. If not, it would be a week on Thursday, transport allowing and only if five thirty would be okay. Otherwise she would have to call again. Ingrid decided it would be quicker to agree to the overtime.

A few grey hours later, she left for an early lunch, hesitating outside Nick's door before fetching her umbrella from the kitchen. Not that it was much use on the dash to the café. The wind blew it inside out within yards.

She sat at a table just inside the window. He might come.

'Excuse me, can I join you?'

By the time Ingrid had taken in the stranger's soaked overcoat, pulled close around his face, the man had already settled himself at her table. She grabbed the menu, angry that she couldn't tell him she did mind, very much; that his seat was being kept for someone.

'You don't know me, Mrs Clarke, but we've communicated.'

Ingrid looked up. 'Excuse me?'

'I'm Guy.'

'Guy? I didn't realise... why didn't you call? I'm sure Nick would have wanted to be here. He may still join us but he hasn't said. Did you call?'

'Of course not - not now.'

'I don't understand,' she said.

'Nick didn't say anything?'

'About what?'

'Let's move,' he said, already on his feet and moving to a table at the back. Ingrid fumbled for her bag and umbrella and joined him, conceding the seat with a view of the door.

'What should Nick have told me?' she asked.

'Why he's done an about-turn on this.'

'On what?'

'Our mutual interest in the weather.'

The way he was looking over her shoulder was unnerving. She was beginning to regret sending the fax. 'Um... if you'll excuse me I really should order something.'

The wait at the counter gave her a chance to think. She knew nothing about this man, other than that he was mid-forty-ish, around six foot tall and an acquaintance of Nick's. It was crazy to get involved - but if he knew something...

'Mr... I'm sorry, I don't know your surname.'

'Guy will do just fine.'

'Guy, I've been really grateful for the information you've sent Nick and...'

'How serious are you?' he interrupted.

'What do you mean?'

'Is this just a story or is there more to it for you?'

'I suppose, well, I'm fascinated.' Ingrid wasn't sure why she was holding back.

'Fascinated!' Guy pushed his hands through his hair in

frustration. 'God help us. According to Nick you were obsessed. He's obviously had second thoughts; I need to know where you stand.'

'Why?'

'They know I've been passing stuff to you.'

'Who? How?'

He shrugged. 'Who knows, but yesterday my name came up for redundancy.'

'Cutbacks happen...'

'Not at the Met Office, not now. And my phone's been tapped.'

'That's crazy,' Ingrid blurted out. 'I mean... I'm sorry. If I'd thought it could land you in trouble... Nick said something about treading on thin ice but I thought he was over-reacting. Oh my God. The fax. Could anyone have seen my fax?'

'No. I was alone when it came through. But this isn't down to you. I could have said no. But I didn't. Do you know why?' He didn't wait for an answer. 'Civilian casualties; what does that mean to you? To anyone? Just words I bet. You have to see them. Kids in Belfast; full of attitude one minute, bits of them spattered across the pavement the next. Mothers screaming hate into the divide, hurling anything within reach at the bastards threatening to blow their brains out.' He paused.

'I got out - swapped warmongering for the weather. Okay, people still die in hurricanes and floods, there are some tragedies we can't prevent, but at least I wasn't responsible. Nothing any of us could do about natural disasters. But if I did my job properly and got the warnings out in time I could save lives. That's what I thought - until I started picking up bits of information that said otherwise.

'It's not true anymore is it? Do you really think there's any such thing as a natural disaster? They're turning the weather into a weapon - knowing they'll never be held accountable. Now those kids won't see the lunatics about to destroy them.' His face contorted with rage.

Ingrid hadn't given a thought to the person behind the name. To question why he was being so helpful.

Guy thrust his hands through his hair. 'Ever heard of ENMOD?'

'I don't think so.'

'It's the convention on the prohibition of military or any other hostile use of any environmental modification techniques. Adopted by the United Nations in 1978.'

'That's only four years ago!'

'Precisely. ENMOD banned military forces from using any weather modification techniques for combat purposes - hardly something they'd do if nothing was going on is it?'

It was too much to take in. 'Did you find out if Porton Down's involved?' Ingrid asked.

He reached into his coat pocket and handed her some photocopied sheets. 'You're sharp. This was written by a Lt Col. Kent in 1960. Look under physics.'

She read the uneven words, typed twenty-two years earlier. *'Development of new sampling instruments for assessing particulate clouds ...Laboratory and field studies of nucleation by silver iodide, in connection with the artificial production of rain.'*

'The artificial production of rain.' It was there again.

'There's more.' He flicked through the pages until he came to meteorology.

'Which part?' Ingrid asked.

'It's all relevant background stuff, like the development of instruments to measure airflow and, he read, *'...co-operation with physics in design and development of apparatus for use in rainmaking trials.'*

'So our local top secret chemical research establishment was definitely involved in cloud seeding.' There was a satisfaction in getting it right but... She shivered. 'Do you know when?'

'Before 1960, but other than that, no.'

'What planes did they use?'

'Hunters probably. Flights for chemical, biological, smoke, pesticide and meteorological trials were provided by B Flight, based at Boscombe Down.'

It was definite. They were cloud seeding over Salisbury Plain, quite probably in August 1952. And she already knew that the effects could have been felt up to three hundred miles away. If she could prove the Government were to blame it would change everything. Everything.

She scanned the café. Why hadn't Nick come? She needed to talk to him. 'I need proof. Any way we can get it?' she asked.

'Not a good idea.'

'I've got to have it,' she insisted.

'This isn't some walk in the park. You've got to understand what you're risking.' He paused. 'Why are you so keen to find out?'

'I have my reasons.'

'Which are...?'

'Personal.'

He was staring at her now. 'Nick has opted out of this. So should you.'

'I don't know what you mean.'

'I think you do. Why else did you send the fax, not Nick?' He pushed his chair back. 'I've got to go but listen; you've rattled a few cages. I should know. Please, Mrs Clarke, go back to your quiet respectable life while you still can and leave this alone.'

'I can't.'

He hesitated. 'Think about it. Take a few days, a week, whatever, but think carefully. Then if you still want to go on call me on this number. Only use another name.'

'Is all the cloak and dagger really necessary?'

'I've got to go. Give me a name.'

'Moira. Moira Williams.'

'Okay, Moira. Don't take this the wrong way but, for your sake, I hope I don't hear from you.'

Ingrid hurried back, her feet touching the pavement but her mind anywhere but on the Salisbury streets. What was going on? She was a reporter on a local rag, living an ordinary life in an anonymous suburb. Where did clandestine meetings over lunch with a stranger who'd persuaded her to use an alias fit in? And what on earth had possessed her to use Moira? She needed to get a grip.

'Nick.' For once his door was open. 'Can I have a word?'

'I'm busy.'

'You never used to be.'

He rested his pen on the desk. 'What is it?'

'What's going on? You've hardly spoken to me since... since the other day. Alice has been replaced by Mr Personality out there...'

'James. His name is Tony James. Things change, Ingrid,' he paused, 'however much we might not want them to.' He looked at her. 'We should have left things as they were.'

'Do you mean that?'

'We all do things we regret.'

What the hell was going on? This Nick, slumped in his chair, despondent, uncommunicative, was a stranger. 'I'm sorry you didn't make it, for lunch.'

'Perhaps...' he paused and resumed his examination of his desk. 'Perhaps it would be best if we staggered our lunch hours. Just until Tony is familiar with the set-up. It's not fair to leave him holding the fort.'

Mr James was capable of holding just about anything. They both knew that wasn't the point. The silence lengthened. Ingrid glanced at Nick; he looked shattered.

'Nick...'

'I'm sorry, Ingrid.' The discussion was over.

'So am I,' she said.

'This is for you.' Nick pushed an envelope across the desk. He wasn't even going to risk an accidental touch of their hands.

Well, she could do formal too. 'Thank you. I'll be at my desk should you need me.' She paused. 'I saw Guy at lunchtime. I'll give him your regards next time shall I?'

'You what!' Nick met her eyes.

'Mr Pearce. Could I have a word about my shifts this week?' Ingrid jumped. Tony James was standing in the doorway behind her. There really should be a law against soft-soled shoes.

Chapter Seven

Mike Hoskins balanced his enormous frame more or less comfortably on a bar stool alongside a pack of Fleet Street drinkers. Their competitive talking should ensure that nothing he said would be heard by anyone other than Guy.

'So what's the panic?' Hoskins asked.

'You need to watch your back. We're attracting attention.'

'How do you make that out?'

'They've tapped my phone and someone has been snooping around the flat.'

'Come off it.'

Guy stared at him.

'Okay, okay,' Hoskins said. 'But how do you know it's got anything to do with this?' He nodded at a file in Guy's open briefcase.

Guy pushed his hands through his hair. 'They've got to Nick Pearce. Miraculously his sick daughter is suddenly receiving the best private care on offer - and surprise, surprise he's stopped returning my calls.'

'Why should anyone give a damn about a paper in the sticks poking into stuff that's ancient history?'

'I don't know, but we intend to find out.'

'We?'

'There's a group - they track this kind of thing.'

'What kind of thing?'

'Illicit weather modification. And there's Moira.'

'Who the hell's Moira?'

'Moira Williams, the woman.'

'Last thing I knew she was Ingrid somebody.'

'Just being cautious.'

'If you're that worried chuck it in.'

'They're not going to shut me up. Have you been reading any of this?' Guy nodded at the file.

'Some.'

'The MoD denies any link with weather modification - but that's bullshit. I've got the evidence. So why the cover up?'

'You tell me.'

'There's too much at stake isn't there? If we could prove they've been interfering with weather patterns across the country creating catastrophic events... I'm getting my hands on stuff from the US about a stream of court cases. 1950 - New York got some Harvard University Meteorologist to fill the city's reservoirs. The area was swamped and the City landed with claims to the tune of two million dollars.'

'Who from?'

'Local farmers, for damage to their crops. Two million dollars is a whole load of claim in 1950.'

'So it's all about money?'

'Maybe, maybe not. It depends.'

'On what?'

'On whether it's history.'

'Get to the point, Guy, I haven't got all day.'

'Project Popeye, ENMOD, and a whole load more stuff. All about the use of weather modification for combat purposes.'

'So?'

'If we prove the Government are lying, people are going to start asking questions. What exactly are they so keen on keeping under wraps? Are they still experimenting with weather modification? Maybe they're not experimenting any more; maybe they're using it - as a weapon, in violation of the NATO treaty.'

'How? Where?'

'I don't know, not yet, but think about it; if you hadn't been retired from action where would you be now?'

'On my way to the Falklands.'

'Precisely. We already know the weather down there is diabolical - maybe it's another Project Popeye.'

'Who's going to give a toss about that? The Argies started it; the public will support anything that means we win.'

'Anything? How about exploding nuclear devices in seeded cloud systems to increase radioactive fallout? According to Mitterand and Reagan, Thatcher has got a submarine armed with missiles at Ascension Island on standby for a nuclear attack on Cordoba.'

'That's bollocks!'

'Is it? And what about the so-called "natural" disasters going on year in year out? Funny how they happen in areas where the super-powers have some kind of vested interest. There's stuff going on that would scare the shit out of you. They're shooting enormous bursts of energy into the ionosphere...'

Hoskins drained his glass and pushed the stool away. 'You're crazy.'

'Crazy! So you don't care that they're experimenting with global weather patterns, us even, without having a clue what reactions they might set off? Christ, you can change the behaviour of an entire population experimenting with electromagnetic waves that way.'

'Stick to the day job, Guy.'

'Read Nicholai Tesla's work, it's all there. They're manipulating electromagnetic waves to affect the brain. They're working on it now. I know they are.'

'Yeah, sure.'

'Remember the Iran raid to rescue the hostages? It failed, so we're told, because the helicopters got lost - the pilots got confused and crashed into each other. Crack teams flying the latest equipment. Lost? Confused? Does that make sense to you? Of course it doesn't. That raid was sabotaged.'

'Where do you get all this stuff from?'

'It's all there - open your eyes.'

'So you're going to take these guys on single-handed. Is that the master plan?'

'I'm not that crazy. But this,' Guy nodded towards the file, 'this might be the one provable mistake that flushes them out. They know that. Why else would they give a fuck about some harmless amateurs? We've a right to know what's down to their interference. I'm damned if I'll be shut up.'

Hoskins shrugged. 'Not your decision. If they want to stop you they will.'

'I'll take that chance.'

'Your funeral. But if all this stuff is happening, there's one hell of a deal to be made.'

'What?'

'It must have cost a packet to buy Pearce off. You could name your price. Better than any civil service pension.'

'Forget it.'

'Like I said, it's your funeral. So what are you going to do?'

'I can prove they were cloud seeding over Exmoor.'

'Oh yeah. How?'

Guy looked around at the crowd at the bar. 'Not here.'

'Hey, who's taken all the risks with this stuff? I deserve to be in on the pay off.'

He hesitated. 'Okay, I'll let you know when I'm going.'

'Where?'

'Lynmouth.'

A few hours later a memo appeared on the broad expanse of a leather-topped desk in one of the newly appointed offices at MI5's headquarters.

Re Project Cloudburst

1. For Ingrid - try Moira, Moira Williams
2. My guess is - no, he won't be bought at any price

Two hours later Mike Hoskins took a tea break, and walked to the public telephone box to make what he hoped would be a highly profitable call to SkySearch UK.

Steven Carmichael pushed through the revolving door into the lobby of the Piccadilly Hotel; paused, then chose a seat with a clear view of the lift. Seconds later he was on his feet again, adjusting the leather wing chair until he could also see the entrance. He pulled at his collar, adjusted his tie and finally settled down to wait.

The elderly gentleman sitting opposite woke with a start and began anxiously scanning the lobby. 'Excuse me,' he said, 'but have you seen a lady arrive in the last few minutes. Probably wearing a blue trouser suit.'

Steven smiled. 'No, I don't think so.'

'Gets to you after a while, doesn't it; waiting,' the man said.

Steven selected a couple of newspapers from the rack by the door and offered one to his companion.

'No, thank you.' He picked up his hat and after a couple of abortive attempts, managed to push himself out of his chair. 'I think I'll make myself comfortable upstairs. Good afternoon.'

'There you are.' Richard Powell strode across the lobby and threw himself into the empty chair. He was a short, powerhouse of a man, accustomed to imposing himself on situations and people. It made for a troubled partnership, but Carmichael had long ago recognised that he lacked the business nous to make a go of SkySearch alone. His Met Office background and Powell's Air Ministry experience had been a perfect combination for launching their own weather modification company. With Krick's success in America it definitely felt like a case of right place: right time.

'Okay, mission accomplished. We draft the contract and they'll sign.'

'What the hell do you mean, "mission accomplished"?'

'Exactly what I say. They buy it, all of it. All Elliott needs to do is finish the experimental work and draft the exact specification for the...'

'Where are they?'

'Who?'

'You know who. Your MoD contacts.'

'On their way back to Whitehall,' Powell said.

'So you just decided to ignore the fact that Elliott and I are a part of this deal?'

'I told Elliott he didn't need to come and they were happy with the written stuff you supplied - didn't have any questions I couldn't answer.'

'You did what! You've no right to decide who is or is not involved with this project. How dare you go ahead and finalise everything without me?'

'I don't see your problem. Negotiations have always been my baby.'

'And this project is Elliott's and mine.'

'Keep your voice down for God's sake.'

'This is the biggest thing SkySearch has ever handled and you're treating it like a used car deal.'

'Get off your high horse, Steven. It's sorted. Your retirement plans are safe as long as Elliott comes up with the goods. I think it's time to celebrate.' Powell headed off in the direction of the bar.

'Take it easy, dad.' Alex Carmichael nodded at the Ford barely a couple of feet in front. 'Whatever Powell said, get it out of your system some other way; I've got plans for the rest of my life.'

'Get it out of my system! I've just been treated like an office junior by my so-called partner and you tell me to get it out of my system!'

'So what exactly did he do?' Alex asked.

'Met with the clients, negotiated the finer details and as near as dammit signed the whole bloody deal - the biggest deal this company has ever handled - while I was making small talk with some old boy in the lobby.'

'Isn't that what he's there for - negotiations?'

'What's that got to do with it? He left me sitting there thinking they hadn't even shown!'

'Watch out!' Alex's feet hit the carpet as the car clipped the curb. Maybe getting his father to talk wasn't such a good idea. But he was less guarded when he got emotional. 'What's the deal?'

Steven looked across to his son. 'That's not the point.'

'But you just said...'

'Leave it will you.' Steven negotiated a junction. 'I'm sorry, I didn't mean to shout.'

'Why can't you tell me?'

'Just a minor matter of the Official Secrets Act. How did you get on at your interview?'

It was a blatant change of topic. Alex conceded defeat - for now. 'Good. They offered me the job.'

'Great. What will you be doing?'

Alex smiled. Did he come clean or follow his father's example? At Earthshield's offices he'd been quizzed about what he could bring to the organisation. On the face of it there wasn't a lot. Fresh out of university with no work or campaign experience, no evidence of involvement in any environmental projects or in-depth knowledge about any endangered species, it wasn't looking good.

Then he'd mentioned weather modification. God knows why; probably the same kind of unconscious indoctrination that condemns budding artists to slave as house doctors following the family tradition instead of their passion. But it did the trick. Suddenly Madeline Cox, Earthshield's founder, had fixed him with her eyes - so like his mother's. They were looking for a new angle, she'd explained, something with an interesting edge, explosive even, to pitch to their funders and he, Alex Carmichael, had just walked into their offices with the perfect solution.

Madeline Cox had leant across the desk and fired a string of questions at him. 'We want to know what this government are involved in. Have they sanctioned any weather modification experiments? Do they go wrong? Are any so-called "natural" disasters the result of experimentation? What is it costing the taxpayer? Can weather modification be used as a weapon of war? Is that something you can tell us Alex?'

If he'd paused a fraction longer the job would have slipped through his fingers. 'Yes,' he'd said.

'Welcome aboard.' Madeline had offered her hand and smiled, a transformation that caught him by surprise; the sudden warmth in her eyes so familiar...

'Alex... I said what will you be doing?' Steven asked, glancing sideways at him.

Alex paused. 'Just some environmental stuff, nothing earth shattering.'

Steven smiled. 'Your mother would have approved.'

The sprawling SkySearch UK complex was an unmissable landmark on the main Salisbury road, particularly with the recent addition of approximately eighty, three hundred foot high towers and a brand new, barbed-wire topped, perimeter fence. Inside, the interconnecting mid-1960's single-storey blocks had been practically rebuilt when SkySearch's main client insisted on stricter security controls. All the windows were now sealed and obscured and strictly controlled codes were required to move between sections within the building. It was a world away from the early days. Steven Carmichael still felt uncomfortable approaching the main gate.

'Morning.'

The uniformed guard nodded and held out his hand for Steven's pass. It was scrutinised, compared with his face and returned. Same pass, same face, same routine for years now. How did people live with such distrust day in day out? He waited as another guard, a new face, walked around the car, opened the boot and bent down to check underneath. That wasn't part of the usual routine - Steven felt strangely uneasy. The guard returned to the booth and released the barrier; he would already be telephoning the main entrance to report.

Steven parked in his allocated space, avoiding a self-conscious glance at the cameras covering this side of the building. There were more at the entrance, watching as he keyed in his unique access code. He stepped forward and paused, waiting for the doors to close behind him as a signal for those in front to open. The reception area was one of the few large open spaces in the building, but any sense of freedom was dispelled by the security guard waiting to frisk him. Today, according to his name badge, it was G.R. Farthing's turn. Steven wondered whether it was George or Gary or Greg. He returned his keys and wallet to his pockets and walked across to the semi-circular reception desk.

'The meeting was definitely called for two?' He asked their receptionist.

'Yes sir. Mr Powell confirmed the time by phone and fax,' Glenda replied, her voice finely tuned for mediation. Steven knew he and Powell presented her with a challenge. He might be the brains behind the operation but he definitely wasn't suited to the hard-nosed world of business dealing. Unlike Richard Powell.

'Well please tell him I'm in the board room and expect him to join me in the next five minutes.'

'I'll certainly tell him you're there,' Glenda replied diplomatically.

Steven Carmichael checked his watch again and removed a report from his briefcase. It had been compiled by Elliott Grigg, head of research and development for exactly seven more days. Which reminded him, he had to confirm numbers for Elliott's retirement do with the caterer. It was going to be a wrench losing him. Next to himself and Powell, Elliott was the longest serving member of the company and responsible for the breakthrough that was going to net them an unprecedented profit at the end of this financial year.

'Morning, Steven,' Richard Powell was through the door and into his chair at the head of the table in one fluid movement. 'We'll get down to business shall we?'

'If I knew what that business was,' Steven responded. 'The only information I received...'

Richard Powell held up his hand. 'That will be all, Glenda.' The receptionist had followed in his wake. 'No calls.'

The sound of the heavy door sealing was Steven's cue.

'What's the meaning of this? I get less than two hours notice of a, quote, "critical" meeting with no agenda, no details whatsoever. It's the farce at the hotel all over again. What the hell do you think you're playing at?'

'It depends what you mean by playing. I've got thirty-four fatalities that could destroy our entire business. How do you want to play that?'

Whatever response Steven had been expecting, this wasn't it. 'What on earth are you talking about?'

'The lucrative contract that we're about to sign with Her Majesty's Government will end up in the bin if we don't do something right now. And they'll be looking for someone to take the rap for the mess they've got themselves into. We're probably already in the frame.'

'You'd better explain because I'm damned if I know what you're talking about.'

'How are your retirement plans coming along, Steven?'

'Stick to the point.'

'This is very much to the point.'

'You know very well what my plans are. A place abroad and then to travel, maybe get a boat and do it under my own steam.'

'I've got my eye on a bit of cruising too, but first class of course, private decks, cabin service...'

'Get on with it.'

'Take a look.' Powell spun a document across the table towards him.

'What's this?'

'The transcript of a call I had yesterday afternoon with a low life at the MoD.'

The colour drained from Steven's face as he scanned the sheet. 'How reliable is this?'

'Difficult to say but if even half of it is true the only boat we'll be enjoying is a pedallo in the park.'

'But cloud seeding couldn't cause all this.'

'That's not the point. Think of the fall-out. Once they start asking questions in Parliament nobody's going to touch weather modification with a barge-pole. Where does that leave us?'

Steven struggled to take it in. 'Who is this Hoskins? How do we know there's any truth in this? Why has it come up now?'

'Thirty year rule. I bet they've been sniffing around the recently de-classified stuff at the record office.'

'They...?'

'A couple of amateurs and a Met Office employee called Guy somebody or other who seems intent on sabotaging any kind of weather modification experimentation. Four if you count this Hoskins at the MoD.'

'But won't the government do their own housekeeping? They'll hardly want anyone exposing their involvement in cloud seeding if there's the slightest chance it's true.'

'They are, to a point. They've bought off one of the amateurs and they've got a handle on the other one. But this Guy is a loose cannon. Leave him any longer and they'll be cancelling any contracts, present or future.' Powell looked at Steven, 'and they'll be looking to pass on liability.'

'But we only ever contract to provide technical input; liability is definitely theirs, not ours.'

Powell weighed his words. 'There were two reasons we got the contract with the MoD in the fifties. First, it meant they could get away with saying, "No, Her Majesty's Government is not conducting any experiments in weather modification". But that wasn't enough to get them to sign. The bureaucrats were scared shitless any experiments would land them with massive compensation claims. So I agreed to help them out.'

'How exactly?'

'The contract transferred liability to us.'

'What! You signed away our immunity? Without consulting me?'

'I couldn't spell out every clause. Besides you'd swanned off to America to cosy up to Krick. What was I meant to do? Global Chemicals had pulled out; it was looking like there would be nothing for you to come back to.'

'But I would never have agreed to such a...'

'It wasn't that big a deal,' Powell interrupted. 'Still isn't. There was case after case in America, none successful. No one ever proved cloud-seeding was to blame. So I patted the Government on the head, told them everything would be all right and they've kept writing the cheques ever since.'

'But this Guy can prove cloud seeding experiments caused the tragedy at Lynmouth. And you're telling me we're liable!'

'So we deal,' Powell said.

'Deal?'

'With Hoskins.'

'No. This company has never done anything disreputable and it's not going to start now.'

'Wake up, Steven! If we don't do something right now you won't have a company. You can forget all about retirement, travel, boats. You'll be lucky to come out of this with a tin roof over your head.'

'I need to think.'

'We don't have time. Hoskins is in the loop already. He'll know when, where and how this Guy is going to get his proof. He just needs the go-ahead to stop him: it's as simple as that.'

'If we buy them off, how do we know they won't be back for more? Besides, we don't even know if cloud seeding was to blame.'

'No, but we're not going take that chance.'

Steven Carmichael cursed as he struggled to close the garden door before the rain soaked the maple wood flooring of his sitting room. He paced back and forth, replaying the conversation with Powell. Damn the man. How could he calmly discuss damage limitation as though it were a run-of-the-mill negotiation! How could he let the company be blackmailed like this when they obviously weren't to blame? Damn him! If their stock hadn't slumped he'd have been travelling the world already. Healthy trading figures at the end of the year were his only hope. He'd spent thirty years building SkySearch. 'And now that bastard is going to screw it all up,' he exploded.

'Talking to yourself again dad; first sign of madness.' Alex Carmichael swung himself over the back of the leather sofa, drawing up his legs until all six foot two of him was more or less comfortable.

'Could be the only way I get an intelligent conversation.'

'No chance. So what's Powell going to screw up this time?'

Steven sat down in his favourite steel and leather chair; one of his few impulse buys. He'd fallen in love with its low, clean, functional lines. It suited the uncluttered feel of the house - uncluttered, that is, until his son had arrived post finals. It was great to have him around but he wasn't accustomed to sharing his space. Hopefully Alex's new job would expand to full-time sooner rather than later.

'Thirty years I've spent building SkySearch and just when I want to cash in it's all falling apart.'

'What's happened?'

'A group of interfering amateurs are hell-bent on bankrupting me. Thanks to Powell the company may be liable for massive compensation on some experiments they claim caused a disaster.'

'What experiments?'

'Some cloud seeding years ago. Ancient history compared with the stuff we're doing now.'

'Do they have a case? Can cloud seeding make that much of a difference?'

'An increase of ten, fifteen percent maybe. When we first set up there was a guy called Krick making a packet in America predicting increases of up to fifty percent...'

'Fifty percent! So what figures was he massaging?'

Steven raised his eyebrows; that was an unusually perceptive question. 'He got those figures from one experiment over mountains in the west. Seeding is more effective at altitude. All our experiments showed a much lower success rate but if a potential customer quoted Krick's figures I'm ashamed to say we didn't contradict them.'

'Or Powell didn't.'

'Yes. Richard clinched any deal he came within sniffing distance of - one way or another.'

'So how's he screwed up with this one?'

'He got some lucrative government work, but it turns out the bastard signed a contract where we took on liability.'

'How did he get that past you?'

Steven shrugged. 'I took the easy option.'

'What happens now?'

'I don't know... but we're not the only ones with a vested interest in sorting it.'

'Government?'

Steven nodded.

'What does sorting it involve?' Alex asked.

'Money; lots of it.'

'Theirs or yours?'

'Both.' Steven began to pace.

'Do these amateurs have a case?'

'Not a chance in hell. The seeding wasn't anywhere near enough to cause the devastation they're talking about.'

'If you're going to have to shell out anyway why not line a lawyer's pockets and call their bluff?'

Steven stopped in front of his son. 'In a word? Publicity. Just one seed of doubt and contracts disappear overnight. And the one we're negotiating now... Anyway, we can't take that chance. And they know it.' He sat down next to Alex. 'Thanks for the listening ear, but I've been over this a hundred times. It comes down to one simple choice. Let Powell buy off some over-enthusiastic amateurs or wave good-bye to retirement of any kind, let alone the one I'd planned.'

'Can the business survive? Are there any other buyers out there or have you got all your eggs in one basket with the MoD?'

'Why the interest?' Steven asked, suddenly alert.

'Can't I be interested in what my old man does?'

'Maybe, but I'm not convinced.'

Alex hesitated. 'There was something...'

'I knew it. Spill.'

'I've had a lot of expenses, with the graduation and...'

'No more handouts, Alex. You've got to get a grip.'

'I know; that's not what I'm asking for.'

'So what do you want?'

'A job.'

'I thought you had one. Don't say you've blown that already, you've hardly been there five minutes.'

'No, but it's only part-time and I'm up to my overdraft limit. I was wondering if there was anything going with you?'

'At SkySearch?'

'Why not? Maybe it's time for Carmichael and Son. I'm a dab hand at filing, office stuff, anything routine.'

Steven smiled. 'It's got a ring to it! Seriously though, it's not that simple. The security checks take weeks.'

'Even with a reference from the boss?'

Steven smiled. 'I could certainly do with some moral support.'

Chapter Eight

'Morning. Terrible news about the Belgrano isn't it?' Ingrid said.

'I'm not aware of the details.' Tony James picked up his tea and left the kitchen. She wasn't getting far with anyone this morning. Even Jack hadn't risen to her condemnation of Mrs Thatcher. In fact he'd gone back to bed without saying good-bye.

By mid-afternoon she'd finished a piece on the archaeological dig taking place just south of Old Sarum. The team only had a few more weeks before the bulldozers moved in to cover yet more of Salisbury's green belt with concrete. Protests over an out-of-town shopping centre had been successful but holding the high moral ground over affordable housing was more difficult.

Ingrid was sure of one thing. She searched her bag for the piece of paper Guy had given her, lifted the phone... and paused. Maybe she was being naïve. She put the receiver down. 'If anyone needs me, Mr James I'll be back in five minutes, ten at most.' She still couldn't call him Tony.

The sun and the onset of the season had brought the tourists out. The Cathedral surrounds were packed with families craning their necks to appreciate the spire against an unusually blue backdrop. She was greeted by a Japanese party, stopped for directions by a backpacker and just beaten to the phone box by a BT engineer.

'Excuse me; are you likely to be long?'

'No. Ready in two minutes.'

Surprisingly he was true to his word. Exactly two minutes later she was wedged in the box balancing her purse in one hand and Guy's number in the other.

'Guy?'

'Yes?'

'This is... Moira, Moira Williams.'

'Okay. Listen; I know how we can get it.'

'Get what?'

'Proof.'

'How?'

'Not on the phone.'

'I can be in the café at lunchtime tomorrow.'

'No. Somewhere different. Do you know the canal, behind the library?'

'Yes.'

'Be there at twelve. Bring some bread.'

'Why?'

'For the swans.'

The afternoon dragged on as Ingrid attacked her in-tray. Underneath a pile of returns she noticed the envelope Nick had given her - correction, that he'd pushed across the desk. They'd hardly talked since. His door was always shut, they took different lunch hours and the charismatic Mr James acted as messenger if necessary. Speak of the devil.

'I'm locking up now, Mrs Clarke. Will you be long?' he asked from the doorway.

'I'll be leaving at five, when Jack arrives.'

'It's gone that already.'

'It can't be. What do you make it?'

'Five twenty.'

'Are you sure?'

'Quite sure.'

'Have there been any messages for me?'

'No. None.'

Ingrid put the unopened envelope back in her tray. Jack was never late, at least, not without letting her know.

'Jack. Jack.' The house was empty. She scanned the kitchen worktops. Nothing. Habit took over. She filled the kettle and took the teapot down from the shelf. It was ironic really, being thrown by this break with routine, the one thing she spent a good part of every day complaining about. She had to sit. Get her breath back. Think. He must have said something this morning, only she was too angry about the Belgrano to listen. Yes that must be it. Either way he'd want feeding when he got back.

She'd just begun preparing dinner when the phone rang.

'Mrs Clarke?'

'Yes.'

'This is Salisbury Hospital. Could you get here?'

'Is it my husband?'

'Yes. He was taken ill this afternoon and brought in by ambulance.'

'What's wrong?'

'The doctor will fill you in, Mrs Clarke. If you ask at the enquiries desk they'll tell you where to find him.'

'Thank you.' She lowered herself onto the stairs. He would need things. Would he be staying in? She should have asked. Toothbrush, flannel, pyjamas, what else? She had to get there. In a minute. When she could breathe.

He lay so still. A lattice of wires draped across his chest connected him to a bank of machines. Ingrid couldn't take her eyes off the screens, afraid the peaks and troughs would resolve into a single, lifeless line if she wasn't there to witness their regular leaps. What should she do? He would be so uncomfortable. Bed was where he lay on his right side, legs curled up against her, his hands tucked under his chin. He never lay on his back.

'Mrs Clarke?' The voice came from behind. 'We've been expecting you.' The nurse pulled a chair over. 'Here.'

Ingrid responded to the gentle pressure on her arm and sat. She should ask something, but no words came. She should be reacting - crying, demanding to know what had happened... anything.

'Here, take this.' Young willing hands were folding her own around a hot mug. 'The tea will help. It's always a bit of a shock.' The words floated almost near enough to grasp. She drank.

'Thank you,' she said. 'What happened?'

'Your husband was crossing the street when he collapsed. He was admitted a couple of hours ago.'

'What's wrong?'

'I'll leave you to talk to Mr Bridges about that, your husband's consultant.'

'Consultant? What in?'

'Mr Bridges is a cardiologist. Your husband was lucky he's on this week. It's always comforting to be seen by someone who knows your case. I'll leave you for the moment. Call if you need anything.'

'Knows his case? I don't understand.'

'The doctor will fill you in.'

'Can he hear me?' Ingrid asked.

'Difficult to say. Best to assume he can. A familiar voice is sometimes all it takes.' The nurse adjusted the drip, re-checked the monitors and left Ingrid alone, more alone than she would have thought possible in such a noisy place. She took his hand. It felt heavy in hers. 'Jack. Jack. I'm here.' She looked for a response, reassurance that he was there, hearing her, sensing she cared. Despite everything, she did care.

'Why didn't you say? I know I've been preoccupied but I would have listened.'

But would she? She'd given him so much grief, but he'd never said a word. Just absorbed all her complaints. Ingrid felt sick. It all made sense now. She saw him slumped in the train seat. He'd been ill. Not awkward, not ignoring her. Just ill.

She rested her hand on his cheek, grateful to find it still warm.

'Mrs Clarke. We need to make your husband comfortable. Would you like to stretch your legs? The canteen isn't open for another hour but you can get a drink from the machine in the foyer,' the nurse said.

'What's the time?'

'Six thirty. The next shift will be coming on soon.'

'When can I see the doctor?'

'Mr Bridges will be round between ten and eleven.'

'Thank you.'

It had been a long night. They'd eventually left her alone when they realised she wasn't going anywhere. But she felt wretched. How could she have drifted so far, become so blind to him? He was a good man. All he'd ever wanted was her happiness and she'd thrown it back in his face.

Back at Jack's bedside, the consultant was cautious. 'It was a severe attack, Mrs Clarke.'

'How severe?'

'He'll stay in intensive care until we can assess his recovery. I should be able to tell you more tomorrow.'

'Thank you.' She moved to the nurse's station. 'Is there a phone?'

It was strange to hear Nick sounding so warm and concerned. 'At the hospital? What's happened? Are you all right?' he asked.

'I'm fine. It's Jack; he's had a heart attack.'

'When?'

'Yesterday, on his way to collect me. I've been with him all night.'

'Oh, Ingrid. You must be feeling terrible.' She couldn't handle this. Nick filled the silence. 'You need some rest. I'm coming to take you home.'

'No, no. Thank you.'

'He must understand you can't be there day and night.'

'He hasn't come round yet. I want to stay here, be with him when he wakes up. I'll need to take some time off,' she said.

85

'Sure. No-one's expecting you here anyway. You've annual leave left and you're still entitled to compassionate leave. Take as much time as you need; all of it if necessary.'

'All of it?'

'Until the end of the month.'

'Oh I won't need that much.'

'Take it, Ingrid.'

'Thanks for being so understanding. I'd better get back.'

A week later she was still waiting. 'There's a picture of the QE2 on the front of the Times, Jack, and the UN have entered peace negotiations. Mrs Thatcher will have to take notice of them now.' She missed his usual retort.

'There's nothing much else to report. I don't know what's happening at work. But it's not the same there now anyway. Perhaps I ought to leave. You'd like that wouldn't you? We could go travelling, when you feel up to it. You've always wanted to see your ancestral home haven't you? Let's do it.' She studied his face. Occasionally his eyes moved, as though he was dreaming. His lids flickered once or twice. But it never meant anything. They said he was reasonably fit for his age, that he had every chance of recovering, but there was never any answer to when.

She walked over to the window, to her familiar spire. Strange how she'd started dredging comfort from the sameness of everything outside. As comfort leached away inside this anaemic cocoon, small things in the normal world gained almost painful significance. She'd gone into the cathedral on her way home one night, conditioned to turn to God in times of trouble. But he wasn't interested. Perhaps she was beyond the pale. Shouldn't that make her even more of a catch? Where was the satisfaction in saving a petty offender when he could take on someone like her?

Someone like her.

Ingrid turned back to the bed. It wasn't God's forgiveness she needed was it? It was Jack's. Forgiveness for deceiving him, for living a lie. 'Is that what this is all about, Jack? My take-it-or-leave-it chance to set the record straight?' She pulled her chair closer and took his heavy hand in hers. 'I...,' She tried again. 'You know how...'

It was no good; the right words wouldn't come. But if she waited for the right words she'd never speak... and he probably couldn't hear anyway.

'The lie was never for you, Jack. You must believe that. It just happened, fell out... out of a time when normal life stops and you are somebody and nobody; where going back isn't relevant or even an option; when it's suddenly easy to give up such a shadow of a life.

'I'm not sure I know how to do this, Jack, how to fit the pieces back together.' She paused. 'It was years ago, at the end of the war... I was only 18... a few of us heard about the Land Girls. We decided it would be more fun stacking hay bales with all those muscular farm workers than dodging bombs around London. Two of us, Julie and me, ended up on a farm just above Lynmouth, at the end of March 1945. The recruitment department certainly knew how to work up a rumour. No bronzed rippling torsos. Just an old biddy that could barely lift a pail and a hard bed in a draughty farmhouse.

'But being close to the land was wonderful. I felt so... so free I suppose. The country has always been my escape, ever since I was little. You know all about that, Jack, about my childhood, about my father's fears. How I couldn't be the child he wanted. You know how children have imaginary friends? Well I was his imaginary daughter. He was convinced he could see me clearly but I wasn't there at all. The real me only appeared in the woods; my friendly, whispering woods where the tight knot in my stomach started to let go.

'I suppose that's what drew me to Exmoor. That's right, Jack, no munitions factory, no spinster days in a London insurance office. Lies, all lies.' She dropped his hand. It wasn't right to take advantage; he would have snatched it away if he could. She began to concertina the edge of the sheet into tiny, neat folds. 'The war was my passport to freedom, Jack. Is that an awful thing to say? Well it's true. I ran, as far as I could until I was just a blur.'

Ingrid walked to the window. She had to block out the image of his trusting eyes or she would never be able to inflict the rest on him. 'The first time I sat by the West Lyn river I knew I'd found the real me. I bet you can see me there, Jack, watching the dippers dance on the boulders, the wrens nipping in and out along the banks. Spring was the best time. The slopes were covered with all kinds of flowers - primroses, violets, wood anemones. It was so beautiful. So peaceful. You wouldn't think I was talking about wartime, would you? So different from your war.

'It wasn't all idyllic; the work was gruesome. Julie found it hard but she was good with the horses; so confident, not frightened like me. We enjoyed the dances in the town hall, took to bebop like ducks to water and showed the local boys a thing or two. It was such fun. After a few weeks of flirting the inevitable happened. Julie was the first to pair up, with the owner of an estate on the edge of Exmoor, old money and all that. Hugh Davenport his name was. He was well out of my league, but Julie loved the whole country tweed scene.

'He was dazzled by this sophisticated creation from London. It was galling. She could look stunning in dungarees.' Ingrid could see her now, mucking out in wellies and overalls and still managing to keep her hair in place. 'They married; Julie joined the County set and never looked back. After the war she chaired just about every committee in town...'

The sound of an ambulance startled her. Someone else's life was about to be turned upside down. She hadn't given a thought to normal things for over a week. Milk was piling up in the fridge, about all that was. She must do some shopping. But it seemed pointless. Everything she'd done before. Work, people. People... Guy! She'd forgotten their meeting.

The phones were down in the lobby. She waited for one to come free. 'Is that Guy? It's...'

'I know.'

'Sorry I didn't make it.'

'So you changed your mind. Probably just as well.'

'I didn't. My husband was rushed into hospital. He... he's very ill.'

'And that changes things?'

'It might. I don't know.'

'Not following in the footsteps of our mutual friend then?'

'What do you mean?'

Guy laughed 'He's sold out.'

'Sold out?'

'Our Nick is now Editor in Chief of the Wessex group.'

'That's great. I'm happy for him.'

'Oh please.'

'I don't understand.'

'I know. That's why you shouldn't be anywhere near this. Think about it. When did Nick's luck start to change, or rather his daughter's?'

'If you mean when he managed to get her private care, a couple of weeks ago.'

'About when he pulled the plug on your investigation.'

'Yes, but it had nothing to do with that. It was personal.'

'Really?'

'Yes. But I don't want to discuss it.'

'Listen to me. You're way out of your depth. We all are. But if you still want to get the... wait... I'll be in touch.' The line went dead.

'Sorry, Jack. I had to call someone. Still, it spared you a blow-by-blow account of Lynton parish council. I was probably boring you senseless. See what happens when you're not here to keep me in line?' She studied his face, reading far too much into the random flicker of his eyelids. 'Are you here, Jack? I want you to know but I don't want to lose you. It's someone else's story now. The real me is the one you've shared a life with all these years. But I know you. You'll want all the detail, to get to grips with why. Well I can't tell it all, you don't need to hear it, but I do have to tell you what happened that night in Lynmouth.

'Julie and Hugh had organised a dance for the local children. Hugh wasn't there on the night, I don't know why. He was always being called away for something or other so Julie roped me in to help. I didn't take much persuading; by then I was back to escaping from the house at every opportunity. But that's another story.

'She had a good band lined up, and a noisy one - that's why we were in the hall up the valley - so we doubled the usual amount to cater for a healthy turnout. Mind you, the weather was so awful I began to wonder if we'd over-catered.

Do you think many will turn out in this weather? The rain is set in by the looks of it.'

'It'll take more than a downpour to keep the youngsters away.' Julie said. 'Did I tell you it's okay to do sausages? Managed to get the parish council to cough up enough to get a cooker installed. There's a boiler too so you've hot water on tap for the washing up.'

'You know how to spoil a girl, Julie.'

'How did you get a pass for tonight?'

'He's on the road canvassing new business. Won't be back 'til late.'

'You're looking peaky. How are things?'

'Same as ever.'

'You know the Lodge is yours whenever you need it.'

'Thanks, Julie, really; I appreciate it. But I'd need to run a lot further to be free of him.'

'Just remember the offer's there. Come back to the Manor after for a drink. And bring your diary.'

'Yes, but...'

'Must dash. I've finally persuaded everyone to form an association. People are starting to drift back. We must advertise ourselves; tell all those folk stuck in the cities how lovely it is here. When it stops raining!'

'Julie was on a roll. She'd got everyone mobilised and a bright new leaflet promising visitors rest and restoration in 'Little Switzerland' was winging its way around the country by the spring. I admit I was jealous. I couldn't remember the last time I'd achieved anything.

'It was a diabolical night, Jack; you've never seen anything like it. The rain started in earnest about mid-day and got heavier and heavier. But Julie was right; the kids didn't notice, even though you could hardly hear the band over the rain hammering on the roof. That was one of Julie's rare failures. She'd been on at the Parish Council for years about getting the corrugated sheets replaced with a proper roof. But they insisted that it was good for a few years yet.'

'How's it going out front, Julie?' I called.
　'Pretty good. Might have to finish early though.'
　'Won't be a popular move.'
　'Maybe not, but I've had a message there may be flooding. If you get a chance, check out the back will you?'
　'Thanks a bundle. I'll get soaked out there!'

'I needed some washing up liquid from the store, so I put my coat on and headed out. Oh, Jack, as soon as I was a few feet from the hall I knew something was wrong. The river was deafening. It had broken its banks and was surging across the terraces just below. Huge branches were being washed downstream. I rushed back inside, grabbed Julie and screamed at her that we had to get the children out.

'Suddenly everything got worse. The electricity works sat right on the river and the buildings flooded, taking the generator out. The whole village was plunged into darkness. It was impossible to tell where everyone was. The girls were screaming. Some started to run. You can't imagine how awful it was, Jack. I thought we'd lost control, but somehow we managed to calm the children down and get them filing up the hill. I suppose it took fifteen minutes, maybe more, until they were all safe.' Ingrid paused, painfully aware of the still figure in the bed. She so wanted to feel his arms around her.

'But they weren't all safe.' Her voice was shaking. 'Somehow Julie lost track of her boys, of Alistair and Michael. I was nearest so I went back. It was tricky. All I had was the torch from the fuse cupboard. But I waded through the entrance, calling them.

Someone had left the takings on a table. I picked the bag up and put it in my pocket. Seems petty doesn't it? But at the time we didn't know it was so serious, and there was no sense losing a month's funds for nothing.

'There was so much noise, from the river and the drumming of the rain on the roof; like nothing I'd ever known, pounding at my head. I waded through the hall, feeling my way along the pillars at the side. It was so dark, that kind of absolute darkness that makes you lose your bearings.

'Then I realised - the noise was me, screaming for it to stop. You know how I am, Jack. Never been able to stand being closed in. Well this was ten times worse than anything before or since. I had to get out - but I couldn't, not without the boys. God forgive me but I started shouting at them to stop being so stupid and to come out right now. I threatened two frightened children with every punishment I could think of to make them come to me. As if they could. The water was already up to my waist - it would have been well over their shoulders.

'And then I felt a hand. Either Michael or Alistair was leaning down from the stage gripping my arm. I slid my hand up to grasp his. I don't know which of us was shaking more but for that moment we had each other. Then... then there was a surge. It knocked me off my feet and when I surfaced, I was on my own. One minute his hand was in mine, the next, nothing.

'I called and called and called... but they were gone. I couldn't hold on to them, Jack. And my angry words will be the last thing they heard.' Ingrid was sobbing, her tears dropping onto Jack's hand, resting gently over hers.

'The whole building was collapsing by then; there was nothing I could do. You have to believe me Jack. I forced my way out after them; only the water was getting deeper, it was dragging my legs out from under me. In the darkness I lost all sense of direction. I couldn't tell if I was struggling to safety or further into the path of the river. Someone was calling, but then it all went black.'

The torrent of words ceased, leaving Ingrid's gasping breaths the only sound breaking the silence of the sterile room.

Chapter Nine

Ingrid joined the crush on the station platform waiting for the carriage doors to open. Once inside, she swung her coat onto the overhead rack and settled into a seat well away from questioning eyes. As the train drew out, she strained to hear the guard's voice over the intercom. *'I would like to welcome all passengers joining at Salisbury for this inter-city service between London Waterloo and Penzance stopping at Dorchester, Axminster, Honiton, Exeter, Torquay, Plymouth and all stations to Penzance.'*

'He's got my seat mum. You said I could sit by the window,' the pouting girl in the next seat complained.

'Come and sit round this side then you can both have a window seat.'

'No, I want that seat,' she persisted.

'It's no different from this one. Just sit down.' Her mother was losing patience.

'I want to see coming not going.'

Ingrid smiled. It sounded like a great philosophy. And what difference, she wondered, would it have made if she could have seen coming not going? Probably not a lot then, but how about now? She'd dearly love to see what was in front of her now. How different from the last time she'd travelled this route with Jack. He'd insisted on booking first class. She closed her eyes and conjured up the indulgence of wide seats and waiter service; but the vision disintegrated into a bleached room filled with pulsating monitors.

'Please don't wake today, Jack,' she whispered, 'not today.'

Two hours later the train pulled into Exeter St David's. Ingrid joined the flow into the combined booking hall and exit where industrial sized fan heaters failed to make any impact on the reclaimed passageway. Queuing for chocolate used up five minutes, flicking through a surplus of women's magazines another ten, then Ingrid turned back towards the platform - and stopped. Whether the idea had been there before she saw the flowers she couldn't say, but it was irresistible now. She selected a bunch of vibrant russet chrysanthemums, placed the exact money in the woman's gloved hand and hurried to catch the Barnstaple train.

Even without her own memories, this journey would have erased the last thirty years. The carriages alone were vintage stock and once they were free of urban Exeter the rolling fields, thatched cottages and stone bridges of mid-Devon shrugged off the present like an ill-fitting coat. Apart from a handful of fellow travellers she was alone with the buzzards, the rabbits, the herons and probably a lot more that her town-hardened eyes failed to spot. The river Taw was a constant companion, running first this side then that, meandering its way to the coast. She could have been seventeen again, or between lives even. Was history about to repeat itself?

The weather had closed in by the time she reached the multi-arched stone bridge leading to Barnstaple clock tower and the bus station. She slipped into the queue for the bus to Lynton and Lynmouth, wedged between a walker and a group of shoppers. Half an hour later the bus was within touching distance of the bracken covered slopes of Exmoor, an expanse that concealed the prettiest of valleys; hidden worlds where you could disappear at will.

At Lynton Ingrid's fellow travellers dispersed, leaving hers the only steps echoing along the road to the Valley of Rocks. Ahead of her, familiar formations reared up, strange headless shapes swallowed up by the sea mist. She paused at the entrance to the cemetery, pulling her grey coat closer, throwing her hood over her hair, protection from the mist or perhaps from prying eyes. She blended so well into the damp, colourless day that her only distinguishing feature, as the vicar was later to recall, was the bunch of russet chrysanthemums she clutched in her hands.

She picked her way between the headstones, edging this way and that to peer at fading inscriptions. It wasn't the old stones that delayed her, nor even most of the newer ones, but those that took up so little space they might easily be missed. The lichen-covered headstone that finally brought her to rest was almost obscured by the roots of an overhanging beech. She knelt on the sodden earth, feeling it cast a damp embrace around her, drawing her down to her silent companions. Shivering, she placed the flowers in front of the stone, pausing only to trace the inscription. *Sacred to the memory of Alistair and Michael Davenport, 1946 - 1952. May they rest in peace.*

Raindrops, their fall broken by the overhanging branches, sought out the nape of her neck as if anointing her. 'Forgive me,' she whispered finally. Their silence was no more than she expected, or deserved.

Leaning heavily on her arms she stood, pulled her coat tighter about her and turned towards the narrow path that led through a gash in the rocks to the seaward side of the cliffs. From here the path wound its precipitous way back to Lynton. Sometimes Wales was so clear she felt she could reach out and touch the mountains but today... today Ingrid was marooned on a misty island, seagull calls echoing eerily around her.

The path rejoined the main street through Lynton just short of the entrance to the cliff railway. It was a beautiful way to descend to Lynmouth five hundred feet below but it was always manned, and today Ingrid preferred anonymity.

She dropped down by the side of the Valley of Rocks hotel on a path that criss-crossed the railway track as it wound its way down. Her muscles complained at the unaccustomed exercise but it was nothing compared to the pain she felt on reaching the bottom.

The pictures she'd pored over and the personal testimonies she'd read with tears streaming down her face cast a sepia filter over her surroundings. The Pavilion was immediately behind her; a place of music and laughter where tourists and residents had been enjoying a concert party on the night of August 15th 1952. Until the lights failed. Feeling their way outside, the audience were confronted by rising floodwater. Most turned up Mars Hill, finding respite in the Rising Sun Hotel or further up in Lynton but others, linking arms and ready for adventure, strode on through the surging water, some to their deaths.

Ingrid shivered and walked quickly on around the corner, past the site of the Beach Hotel where, later that night, guests were forced higher and higher as a wall of water roared down Lynmouth Street. Desperately grasping the offered ropes, they climbed to safety as the hotel crumbled beneath them, the whole surreal scene lit by the eerie glow of car headlights as, one by one, the water shorted their electrics.

Ingrid looked for Lynmouth Street. It had been a pretty lane encased by tall buildings backed on one side by steep cliffs and on the other by the brawling stream that pushed and shoved its way along its narrow winding course to the sea. But a new road had displaced the river, and balconies that for years had overhung the water, now had pedestrians and cars streaming beneath them. She crossed to the river's edge. It was tamed, submissive, barely touching the sides of its broad, over-sized channel. No longer a threat.

The new road carried Ingrid up to an equally foreign bridge where the two rivers now joined. This was all wrong, so wrong. The West Lyn had always flowed under the bridge at the foot of Lynmouth Hill to join the East Lyn for the run out to sea. But the West Lyn had chosen its own course that night, demolishing the chapel, the fruit shop, the garage and more. After climbing from floor to floor, residents of the Lyndale Hotel found themselves trapped, caught between the torrents of the two rivers. But they were lucky. Despite being pummelled by ten-ton boulders, uprooted trees and crushed cars, much of the hotel was still standing as morning arrived and the waters began to subside. Ingrid looked across to where familiar buildings had clustered at the heart of Lynmouth, and saw only an empty expanse, marked with white lines and occupied by a handful of cars.

So much had changed, so much gone. The reality was overwhelming. Her breathing faltered as picture after picture flooded her brain, washing away the last thirty years. So much devastation, the awful loss of life, six from one family alone. And the bodies, from a baby of three months to an eighty year old woman, all needing to be identified as a much loved grandmother, brother or child. Gulls wheeled overhead, their shrieks echoing the cries that had once filled this dark, raging valley, cries she had run from then. But what about now? Rash words had destroyed her life and could do as much again now. But if that was the price of retribution then... 'Do I really have a choice?'

'Can we help?'

Startled, Ingrid turned to find a Pekinese dog at eye level, its nametag glinting in the streak of sun fighting through the gloom. Oscar's mistress gushed. 'I didn't mean to startle you. Only you were talking out loud.'

Relieved to discover an unfamiliar face, she relaxed. 'I'm sorry, I didn't realise. No, I'm fine thank you.' The elderly couple and Oscar continued along by the river, a little more briskly than seemed right. Probably walking off their over-indulgence at lunch before dinner. She smiled. Julie would be pleased the holidaymakers were here so early in the season.

'I don't see how we can possibly justify the cost of wet weather insurance. I suggest we move on to the next item.' Despite thirty years of chairing just about every committee in Lynton and Lynmouth, Julie Davenport despaired of ever getting to the end of the 1982 Twin Towns Literary Festival planning meeting. But Bill Pope, retired bank manager and constant thorn in Julie's side, refused to be sidelined.

'1979 is how. Heaven's opened half an hour before the start. Made a £300 loss! Some fundraiser!'

'What does everyone think?' Julie asked.

'We could try some more quotes.' Mark Forrester, the vicar, was well practised in the art of mediation.

'Everyone in favour of Mark's suggestion?'

Hands rippled upwards in a fine example of mass procrastination - with two exceptions.

'Is that a vote against, Gill?'

Mrs Bryce-Jones bristled. She resented interlopers making free and easy with her Christian name.

'It is, Mrs Davenport. The thought Mr Pope has given to this issue is to be commended and I propose we ask him to take out an appropriate policy. Time is getting short.'

Julie couldn't argue. They were well into May; the festival was no more than six weeks away and they still had to award the refreshment franchise, finalise the stalls in the book tent and confirm a guest for Saturday afternoon.

'For goodness sake, woman, the majority have voted for the vicar's suggestion, now can we get to the end of this,' said Frank Williams, waving the agenda in front of Mrs Bryce-Jones's face.

'Sorry, Gill but he's right,' Julie said.

'That must be a first,' Frank jibed.

'I beg your pardon.'

'Mrs Julie Davenport agreeing with me.'

Frank Williams was the only person who could unite the committee at a stroke. Even Mrs Bryce-Jones and Bill Pope mentally lined up behind Julie. She picked up her agenda. 'I suggest we move on to item six, the refreshment franchise.'

Fifty minutes later Julie finally declared the meeting closed. Experienced as she was, Frank Williams was causing her major headaches. But then he was good at that, as his fourth (or was it his fifth?) wife knew all too well.

'Thank you for your support, Mark.' The vicar was the last to leave. 'Why it always has to be such a battle I'll never know.'

'Village politics. Jostling for position is everything when your influence is fading. Don't let it get to you.'

Julie knew the perfect antidote to a morning of committees. Thirty minutes later she was crossing the cobbled yard to the stables at the rear of the Manor. Blackmore snorted a greeting.

'Hello boy. Sorry I'm late.' Julie saddled up the chestnut, led him out of the yard and swung easily up onto his back. She turned across the sweep of the driveway beneath the front façade. 'What do you think? Hoar Oak or Doone valley?' She looked to the west where the rain-clouds always gathered before overflowing onto the Chains, the wettest part of Exmoor. There was some high cloud but nothing threatening. 'Let's go.' She pushed him on, up beside the rippling Farley Water to Shilstone Hill.

For a town girl she had adapted well to country life. With Hugh's patient tuition, swathes of anonymous flowers had resolved into individual personalities like the forever frazzled ragged robin or the magical eyebright. But today she preferred not to stop, urging Blackmore on across the open moor and finally back to the Manor; not to the imposing public rooms but to the Victorian conservatory, a space that cosseted with its warm, sultry air.

With half closed eyes, Julie surveyed the orchids, flowering freely from pots scattered across the chequered floor. They'd been Hugh's passion, the only thing he had felt passionate about after... She shivered. She was alone now, but in truth she'd been a widow a lot longer than five years. 'Far too long, damn you.'

'The meeting wasn't that bad was it?' The vicar appeared at the doorway. 'Sorry to make you jump but there wasn't any reply at the front.'

'Come in, Mark.'

'Anything I can help with?'

'Sorry?'

'Whoever or whatever it was you were damning.'

'Oh you know, life, nothing really. Have a seat.'

'Thanks.' He pulled a wicker chair closer. 'Went as well as it could I thought - the meeting.'

'I suppose so.'

'You don't sound convinced.'

Julie smiled. 'Makes you wonder why we bother sometimes; when you've got the likes of Frank Williams deliberately blocking you all the time. I mean, it's the same year in, year out.

Wears you down eventually.'

'Especially when there's no-one to share it with.'

'Yes.' Julie stood. 'Tea?'

'Thanks.' He followed her along the oak floored hallway into the kitchen. 'Was that a throwaway line or are we in danger of losing our Parish Council Chair?'

'I don't know.' She turned the tap on, filled the kettle and placed it on the elderly Aga. The sound of knocking pipes followed her round the room. 'It's not just the Council. It's this place... everything really.' She opened the central doors of a dresser that filled the end wall and took down a teapot. 'China or Indian?'

'Wouldn't know the difference. Whatever you're having.'

Julie warmed the pot, measured out some leaves from an octagonal tea caddy and poured the boiling water.

'I can understand you feeling isolated up here on your own - without your husband.'

'Yes.' She paused. 'Actually, no. No, it hasn't been so different since he died.' She looked at him. 'Sorry, have I shocked you?'

'Not at all; the truth never shocks me.'

'Anyway, it's not worth dwelling on. Let's go through.' Julie picked up the tray and led the way back to the conservatory.

Mark said, 'I don't know much about orchids but these look pretty specialised to me.'

'Yes, Hugh collected them. They seem determined to live despite my hit and miss care. Which is more than you could say for Hugh.'

'Oh?'

'You must have heard... he took his own life.' She glanced sideways at Mark. 'Five years ago. And for ages before that he was too wrapped up in his own misery to help me. Seemed to think he had a monopoly on guilt. Every day for twenty-five years...' Julie stopped. 'I'm sorry. I'm being unreasonable. He was a good man. And it's all in the past isn't it?'

'Maybe. But the past can overshadow the present no matter how much we try to ignore it.'

Julie blinked rapidly and turned away.

'Want to tell me about it?'

'What's to tell? My husband committed suicide. That's all there was to it. He didn't consider his family - didn't share anything - just did it.'

'The misery and the guilt? What was that about?'

'The children.'

'And he suffered all that time?'

'It's best forgotten,' she said brusquely. 'Nothing will bring the children back so what's the point in going over it.'

'Do you?'

'What?'

'Keep going over it?'

Julie gazed out across the lawns. 'He'd sit there. Day after day. The men would come for orders and he'd just sit. Staring. As if he was the only one grieving! Was it really too much to want one day when I could stop having to understand, when my husband could be there for me?' She stopped abruptly. 'Oh, what's the point? How can you ever make sense of the deaths of two innocent children?' She searched in her pocket, pulled out a handkerchief and pressed it against her eyes. Why? Why was it still so painful? After all this time why couldn't she smile at their memory? She tucked the handkerchief in her sleeve. 'Sorry about that. As I said, probably best left in the past.'

'No apology necessary.'

'More tea?' She poured another cup. The perfect hostess. That's what Hugh had always said. 'How about you?' She said quickly. 'Do you regret giving up city life to bury yourself down here?'

'Honestly? The wilds of North Devon weren't my first choice but now I'm here... no I don't have any regrets.'

'You were a lawyer before weren't you? That's quite a change.'

'Yes...'

'Sorry; tell me to mind my own business,' Julie interrupted.

'It's okay. I don't expect my parishioners to be the only ones baring their souls. It did throw me for a while, moving from a world of suspicion and mistrust to the absolute trust placed in me here... though in my wilder moments I sometimes imagine it's the other way round.' He smiled. 'But please don't quote me.'

'Wouldn't dream of it,' Julie said. 'And your family...?'

'None yet. So I'm not going to pretend I understand. But I do know about grief. And the damage it does when it gets locked up inside.'

'Damage?'

'It locks us into the past, with emotions we keep shoving down until they poison us.'

Julie's hand trailed absently over a winter jasmine covering the wall behind them, picking off the dead leaves. 'I dream about how it might have been, if I hadn't taken them to the dance.'

'Dance?'

'In the hall down by the river. They were having such a great time; all of them were.' She looked at him. 'Do you know about the floods in '52?'

'A bit.'

'When the water came we had to get the children out of the hall, up the hill. Only when we got to the top Alistair and Michael weren't there. I'd have gone back for them... but this friend was closer. I know she found them, I heard her calling - only she wasn't calling, she was shouting. They were six years old!' She almost flung the words at him. 'They were frightened; needed comfort, reassurance, someone to guide them out of there. But she drove them to their deaths.' Her body was rigid.

'Did you talk to her?'

'She died too.'

'I'm sorry.'

'I wasn't. Oh God, what a thing to say... Sorry, vicar, I didn't mean... I guess I saw it as some kind of justice, her dying too.'

'Doesn't help though does it?'

'No.'

Mark paused. 'I noticed the stone was leaning as I came through the cemetery this afternoon. Shall I get it seen to?'

'Please,' she said eventually.

'And there was a visitor at the grave. She left a bunch of chrysanthemums.'

'Who was it?'

'Didn't see her to speak to, and she was too wrapped up against the mizzle for me to describe her.'

'She put flowers on the twin's grave?'

'Yes.'

'I don't understand. Who...?'

'She spent a long time looking for the headstone.'

'Did she stay long?'

'No. Knelt down, said a few words and left. I think she walked back along the coast path.'

'What did she say?'

'Wasn't close enough to hear, though she seemed distressed. Any idea who it could've been?'

'No. None.' Julie finally broke the silence. 'Anyway, how can I help?'

'Sorry?'

'Your timing was perfect but I'm sure something brought you all the way up from the village.'

'We forgot to mention security for the "Shakespeare at the Manor" performance. It's kind of you to offer the grounds but we can't have everyone assuming they've got free access to the house.'

'I suppose not. I'll get Hugh's folder; might be something there from the last time he organised it. Are you all right here? I thought it might be warmer in the sun than huddling by the fire in the sitting room. Stone mullion windows might look impressive but I wouldn't recommend sitting near one.'

Ingrid was relieved to be free of the mist as she made her way along the Strand from the bus station to Barnstaple record office. The clock in the square chimed three. Just two hours to closing and the last train back to Salisbury. She requested the North Devon Journal-Herald for August 21st 1952. There would

103

be eyewitness accounts of the floods; people with the proof she needed. It had to be here, somewhere.

Practically the whole paper was devoted to the tragedy. Unbelievable images and testimony of stunned onlookers filled page after page. She'd read most of them before. Many filled a file she'd kept hidden away for almost thirty years. But now she knew what she was looking for, everything was different. Anger was replacing guilt: a white-hot anger that they could allow this to happen. Anger that it was all the result of mindless experimentation with no thought for the consequences, and worse, with no accountability. Well that was about to change.

She scanned account after account until one fixed her to the page: a description of a strange light in the sky and '*this horrible smell, a strange sulphurous smell.*'

'Sulphur, sulphur,' Ingrid whispered to herself. 'Think!' she almost shouted out loud. Where had she read about sulphur?

She was interrupted by the records clerk. 'Excuse me, but we're closing now. We open again at nine thirty.'

Ingrid gathered her notes and wandered out into the square. It was five o'clock. Her train left at five thirty; she had to start walking across the bridge if she was going to catch it. But her feet wouldn't move. Not yet. She stood by the riverbank watching a couple of ducks.

'All along the backwaters, through the rushes tall

Ducks are a dabbling, up tails all.'

Great. She could conjure up ridiculous rhymes but the stuff that mattered stayed lost. A young man brushed past her, balancing a bag of charcoal on his shoulder, on his way to join a group of friends grabbing the last few moments of dry weather for a barbecue. She doubted they would worry even if the heavens opened.

Charcoal. It went with something; saltpetre, that's it... and sulphur. Charcoal, saltpetre and sulphur was used at WAECO to power the rockets. Would the sulphur linger in the air? Could that have been the horrible smell reported in Lynton? As well as using planes could they have been cloud seeding by shooting silver iodide up from the ground? She had to get to a phone.

Ingrid raced across the traffic to the boxes outside the Lion. Her shaking hands misdialled the number. 'Come on, come on.' But then she was through. 'Guy this is... Moira. Listen, I've got something... from the paper...'

'Not on this phone,' he interrupted. 'Give me your number. I'll call you back.'

Ingrid repeated the numbers, barely visible beneath the heavily scratched plastic covering, and replaced the handset. She turned away from the door, ignoring the gesticulations of an elderly woman wrestling with an armful of packages. The phone finally rang.

'Where are you?' Guy's voice was strained.

'Barnstaple.'

'What have you got?'

'Sulphur. I've got a report of a sulphurous smell on the morning of the floods.'

'So?'

'Sulphur was used in rockets.'

'To do what?'

'To cloud seed with silver iodide from the ground.'

'It fits. I think I know how we can prove it too.'

'How?'

'I'm coming down. Meet me in Lynmouth tomorrow. It'll need to be early, say nine thirty.'

'Tomorrow? But I have to get back.' It was a knee jerk response to twenty-five years of being accountable for her actions. But Jack would have no idea of when she returned to their empty house. 'Where?'

'Somewhere the water reached but hasn't flooded since would be perfect - for a sample.'

'The West Lyn was the worst. We can get to it easily; they've made paths along the banks for visitors. You can't miss it.'

The West Lyn River was quite different to the East, dropping steeply down from the Chains through Barbrook to Lynmouth. Along the way it had carved out a dramatic valley, part of the privately owned Glen Lyn Estate. Ingrid paid her fee at the modest wooden hut and entered the gorge. The river was deafening after a night of heavy rain, although still far below the level reached on the night of August 15th 1952, marked by an old, weather-beaten sign way above Ingrid's head.

A board next to the path announced that as much water came down the river in that one night as flows along the Thames in three months. Ingrid shivered.

She walked on past the Seven Stairs Falls, taking a zigzag path up the hillside. It was forcing her away from the river but instinctively she knew Guy would press as far up the valley as possible, away from prying eyes. Once this path levelled out it would take her to the very top of the gorge. But as she approached the ravine Ingrid realised her mistake. She was surrounded by vertical walls of rock. No chance of finding any sediment here.

She retraced her steps, back to the tree and fern covered hillside. Moss-covered trunks led her eyes upwards. The trees were bursting with vibrant pale green leaves, forming a dense canopy. Damn, she hadn't realised the trees were so far on. She would have to drop down to spot Guy.

It was slippery beneath the carpet of last year's leaves but by clutching at the trunks, leaning out almost at right angles, she was able to inch her way down. Then, through the spray thrown up by the waterfall to her left, she sensed, rather than saw, a figure beneath her.

Suddenly the hillside gave way. She grasped for a tuft of grass, a rock, a root, anything to break her fall; but they came away and she landed awkwardly a few feet below. Her vision narrowed to a black tunnel of pain. She pressed back against the wet earth, willing it to pass. If she stayed absolutely... completely... still... maybe everything would stop spinning.

Her watch slowly came into focus. It was nine forty. How long had she lain there? Five, ten minutes? She had to get up. But her arm was twisted awkwardly. Dislocated maybe? Taking a deep breath, she rolled to one side and eased her hand towards a gap in her coat buttons. Pain shot through her body. She began to tremble. 'It's just the shock. Breathe... breathe. Get a grip, for God's sake.'

Slowly, her vision cleared. The roughly dug walls of a crude quarry came into focus. Checking her arm was still supported she rolled on to her knees. There were rocks jutting out of the quarry side. Using her good arm, she grasped at one within reach and pulled herself to her feet. Seconds, maybe minutes passed. The sounds of the wood were unnaturally loud, echoing through her mind, compensating for her pinhole vision. But slowly the pinhole expanded to encompass crooked branches stretching across in front of her, every now and then resting on the earth like a weary traveller. But she wasn't high enough to see more. Using a foothold in the earth wall, she eased herself up through a crevice until she lay amongst the moss and ferns on the hillside.

Where was Guy? She scanned the riverbank. He was still there, or at least a figure she took to be him, standing with his back to the river. No point in shouting; with the river in full spate the roar would drown out her words. She had to get down there.

But as she pulled herself upright, a tall figure emerged from up-river, striding towards Guy. They talked; as two friends catching up. Did they know each other? Suddenly Guy gesticulated wildly then backed away, shaking his head. The stranger grabbed his arm. This was no friend. She could sense the threat.

For a moment they were locked together, then Guy broke free and stumbled away through the undergrowth. The stranger pursued him, gaining ground, forcing Guy back towards the river until he was trapped, balanced on a rock at the water's edge. This was madness. What was going on?

The stranger closed in, blocking her view. She crept along the slope using the trees as cover. But there was no sign of Guy. A voice inside her screamed. No! Had he fallen? Been pushed?

She held her breath, willing him to surface. Hopeless: he'd have been battered against the rocks and carried downstream with the force of this torrent.

Ingrid looked at the stranger. He was standing alone on the riverbank, staring. She followed his gaze to where the morning sun was catching spray from the river, now slowly changing from white to a deepening shade of blood red.

Chapter Ten

Ingrid paused at the door to check the address she'd hastily written down. The receptionist at Earthshield had been surprisingly helpful. 'Weather modification? Yes, Mrs Clarke, we have someone who can help. I'll give you the number.' And that was that. This impressive property, within sight of the Cathedral spire, didn't fit her image of an environmental activist's home though. Its sleek, modern lines and half acre plot wouldn't have come cheap.

'Hello. Do I have the right house for Alex Carmichael?' Ingrid paused, nervously gripping her coat where it hung loose over her still aching shoulder.

'Err... yes, please, come in.' The man who had answered her ring stepped back.

'Ingrid Clarke.' She held out her one good hand. 'Thank you for agreeing to see me at such short notice. I'm getting a bit out of my depth with this and the person I spoke to at the office said...'

He interrupted. 'I'm sorry; I'm Steven Carmichael, Alex's father.'

Ingrid dropped her hand. 'Oh, I just assumed...'

'Not a problem.' His gaze took in the abrasions to her cheek and neck. 'Alex isn't back yet but I'm sure he won't be long. Please, come in.' He led the way into a vaulted sitting room. 'You look like you could do with a drink. What can I get you?'

'Whisky, thanks.'

'Please, sit down.' Ingrid took in the stylish interior. Polished wooden floors, modern art on the walls, an open staircase up to a mezzanine floor; this was no Barratt's house. She opted for a low leather and steel armchair. He handed her a glass. 'You look like you've been in the wars.'

Ingrid's arm was held tight against her chest by a sling. 'Just a fall. Shook me up at the time but I'm on the mend now, thanks.'

'I'm sorry Alex isn't back yet. He knows you're coming?'

'Yes. I rang yesterday.' Ingrid was instinctively drawn to the massive wall of glass that allowed this space to flow seamlessly into the gardens. 'What a beautiful room.'

'Thank you. It changed a bit along the way but we were pleased with the end result.'

'Did you design it?'

'Yes, bit of a hobby of mine. Although the wall of glass was my wife's idea.'

'It's beautiful. It makes me feel...' Ingrid paused, '...free. I can breathe here.' She watched a squirrel hesitate, bound across the lawn and disappear behind an oak tree. 'Your wife must be delighted with it.'

There was a pause. 'Unfortunately Martha died before it was completed.'

'I'm sorry.'

His lips formed a smile that failed to reach his eyes. 'But you haven't come to talk about house design. I'm sorry punctuality isn't one of my son's strong points.'

'It's not a...'

The door burst open. 'Sorry I'm late.' The young man went up to Ingrid and held out his hand. 'Alex Carmichael.'

Ingrid tried to get out of the low-slung chair, but with only one free hand and muscles still sore from the fall, she kept slipping back.

Steven stepped forward. 'We shouldn't leave you to struggle. They're a pain to get out of at the best of times,' he said, placing his hand around her back. His touch was gentle, responsive.

'Well, it's a while since I've made such a fool of myself,' Ingrid said. 'First I mistake you for your son and now I get stuck in your furniture!'

'Don't worry about it. At least my ridiculous chairs have brought some colour back to your face. And now, I'll leave you in Alex's capable hands.'

'Thanks for the drink.'

'My pleasure. If there's anything else I can do don't hesitate to ask.'

Ingrid had the distinct impression he meant it.

'The office said you wanted to talk about cloud seeding,' Alex opened as soon as they were settled in the study.

'Yes, I'm out of my depth. I need some...' What? What exactly did she need from this young man? He seemed nice enough but so young. And restless, like a puppy, constantly shifting his position in the leather chair, yet never quite fitting into it. Now if her appointment had been with his father...

The facts seemed a safe enough place to start. She retrieved Private Dean's photograph from her briefcase. 'It all started with this.'

A couple of hours later any doubts she had about Alex were gone. He listened intently, asked intelligent questions, grasped the science much quicker than she had and displayed an unexpected passion for the subject. He had also stopped squirming.

He turned to Ingrid. 'What have you done with this? Who knows about it?'

'There were four of us; myself, Nick, my boss at the Post, and Guy - I never knew his surname - from the Met Office. And someone Guy knew at the MoD.'

'That's where all this comes from, your contact at the MoD?'

'Yes.'

'Anyone else know about it?'

'Yes, but I don't know who. Maybe someone at the MoD. Guy,' her voice shook, 'Guy thought they were on to us. He... he must have been right.'

'Explosive stuff about the bomb - sorry about the pun.'

'And the Lynmouth floods.'

Alex shifted in his chair. 'It was a tragedy but I can't see them going to the same lengths...'

'I know someone was cloud seeding. If they caused all those deaths they have to be held accountable.'

'Just because they were seeding doesn't mean they caused the floods. No proof - where, when, how far away, whether it reached Lynmouth.'

'But you saw... it was here somewhere.' Ingrid scattered the papers. 'Look. Seeding three hundred miles away could have been to blame.'

'It's circumstantial. Don't see how you'll make it stick.'

'I know. That's why I need your help, to prove it.'

'I don't think I'm the right person...'

'They said you'd jump at this.'

Alex hesitated. 'Proof could be difficult to get. It all happened ages ago.'

'Not everything.'

'I thought you said the floods were in '52?'

'Yes. But someone's trying to shut us up now.'

'How?'

She couldn't speak. Not without unleashing a flood of tears.

'Can I get you something, some water?' Alex asked.

'No... no,' she gasped. There was going to have to be a first time she said it; and it had to be now. 'Guy... Guy is... dead.'

'Dead! What... how?'

'I... I don't really know.' She paused. 'I'd arranged to meet him by the river at Lynmouth. On the way I fell and did this,' she nodded at her shoulder, 'so I didn't get to him. Maybe if I had things would have been different... At first I thought they knew each other but then Guy backed away, like he was afraid. He got trapped by the river. I couldn't see but I knew the water was dangerous; it was in flood after all the rain. One minute he was there... the next, he'd been swept away.'

'What did the other man do?'

'Stood and watched... just watched... then walked away.'

'Hang on - are you saying it was murder? That he was pushed?'

Ingrid turned her back on Alex and stared out the window. 'I don't know, but the man didn't get help, didn't do anything. What would you call it?' she said, her voice steadier now.

Alex was silent.

She turned back. 'Don't you think it's all too much of a coincidence: just as he was about to prove they were seeding? So you see it isn't all in the past. You have to help Alex. Please. I can't do this on my own.'

'What do the police think?'

Ingrid stared at him.

'You've reported this?'

'I... No-one knows I was there. If they did... if it was murder...' Ingrid stuttered.

'It's okay,' Alex said quickly. 'I understand. You're right. Poor bloke's dead. No point in taking any risks.' He folded his legs into the chair. 'Conspiracy to murder... even if it was manslaughter...' he said under his breath. He looked at Ingrid. 'Can I hang on to all of this?' He pointed to the sheets strewn across his father's desk. 'And if you've anything else I'd like to see it. Otherwise, hold fire until I catch up with you. It'll give us time to think. But if anything else happens call me.'

'Thank you, Alex, but please, be careful. I don't want any more young lives on my conscience.'

Elliott Grigg looked at his watch and groaned. It was only 7.30pm - he still had the buffet and official presentation to survive. When Steven Carmichael had proposed a full-blown leaving "do" he'd protested as politely as he knew how but politeness was misread as modesty and Glenda was presented with a pile of invitations to send out.

Elliott knew he was difficult to pigeonhole. He had the looks of a university don - immaculately turned out with old school tie, handkerchief, brogues, bespoke suit, cufflinks, a well trimmed beard and brushed white hair. Strangers automatically addressed him as "Sir", gave way in queues and held doors open for him. It wasn't an appearance he'd deliberately cultivated. He was constantly surprised when he caught sight of himself in the mirror, but it kept acquaintances, troublesome relations, colleagues and the like at arm's length. Glenda, of course, took absolutely no notice.

'You look like you could do with this.' Glenda handed him a glass of punch.

'Thank you, but one is usually my limit.'

'Dutch courage - won't do you any harm for once.'

'I guess not. And I don't mean to sound ungrateful. I really do appreciate everything they are doing but...'

'You'd have been happier with a quiet drink down the pub.'

He smiled. 'Precisely. You couldn't organise an urgent call could you, maybe from Elizabeth?' His wife was at home in bed with a cold.

'Sorry. Love to help but I'm stuck with these two,' she nodded in the direction of Powell and Carmichael having yet another heated discussion as they strode through reception, '...for now at least. I don't think they'd be best pleased if I sabotaged things. They think you'll be eternally grateful for this display of their respect, gratitude... whatever.'

'Of course; forget I mentioned it.' Elliott smiled. This young woman was half his age yet had more self-confidence than he'd ever know. Maybe it was to do with living alone, taking charge of her life. But he didn't envy her returning to an empty house at night, solitary meals, and one-sided conversations with the cat. He and Elizabeth were coming up to their ruby wedding. Forty uneventful years, just the way he liked it.

'How about a compromise?' Glenda took hold of his hand and led him towards Powell's office on the other side of reception. 'A bit of time out before the speeches.' She pushed the door open. 'Whoops.' She backed out 'Not such a good idea. Let's try admin.'

'...So we wash our hands of it and carry on as normal, is that your plan?' Steven Carmichael was pacing back and forth wielding a fax in his hand, oblivious to the door closing.

'Quit the sarcasm, Steven.'

'How do you expect me to react? Hoskins was meant to buy him off - not stand there and watch him drown. We could be charged with conspiracy to murder! We could lose the company, our freedom, everything. Think yourself lucky it's only sarcasm you're getting.'

'Where's the risk? Hoskins is days away from the biggest payout he's ever had so he's not going to say anything. There were no witnesses, and even if there were, what did they see? A man losing his footing on the riverbank. With the river swollen like that, what could Hoskins have done without ending up drowned himself?'

'Raise the alarm. Get help. Anything other than strolling off in the opposite direction.'

Powell leant against the desk. 'You'd do well to remember he was acting as we agreed.'

'I didn't agree to this.' He waved the fax at Powell.

'Maybe not, but like it or not you're involved. And if your memory needs refreshing I have it all on tape. Just a little habit of mine you understand.'

Steven met his partner's stare. 'I don't take kindly to threats.'

'Threats? Who mentioned threats? Just keeping my business associate up to date with my paperwork. Relax, Steven, we're ahead of the game. Thanks to our colleagues at MI5 the Museum boss is out of it, the Met office guy is no longer an issue, so that just leaves the woman.'

Steven sat down, his head in his hands. 'This is just another negotiation to you isn't it? Weigh up the risks, devise the strategy, keep your cards close to your chest. How did I ever let it get this far?'

'Give it up, Steven. You've been happy enough to enjoy the benefits. And you know damn well you're not going to throw it all away now. So concentrate on the woman.'

'She's hardly a threat.'

'For fuck's sake, open your eyes. She's not a little old lady looking for something to pass the time. She's got a reason for doing this. We just don't know what it is... yet.'

'You could have sabotaged everything; everything.' Steven looked up. 'Is LYRE signed yet?'

'No. So we have to keep the lid on this.'

'But once LYRE is signed and sealed the company will withstand anything.'

'Get your head out of the sand, Steven. For a start it doesn't deal with the liability issue; the bigger the assets, the bigger the payout they'll be after.'

'But we could still make it.'

'Make it!' Powell hissed. 'Make it! I'm not interested in making it. We've done enough of that - all through the seventies with papers headlining, *Cloud seeding over-rated; No proof artificial rainmaking works*. Company profits fall through the floor, my house celebrates its second mortgage and I'm taken to the cleaners with a divorce. Don't talk to me about making it.'

'It's throwing your money around that's left you skint. This business has seen me all right.'

'I'm not about to have everything sabotaged by some interfering amateur. We do whatever it takes to sort it.'

'Great, found you.' Alex Carmichael stuck his head round the admin. office door. 'Sorry, Glenda but the caterers need you. Something about where you want the buffet.'

'I've told them half a dozen times. Come here and keep Elliott company until I get back. And he could do with a top up.'

'Sure. Pass your glass, Mr Grigg.'

'Elliott, please.'

'Back in a minute.' Alex refilled the punch glass from the bowl in reception then diverted to his desk before returning.

'So, it's one out, one in,' Elliott said. 'How are you enjoying being SkySearch's newest recruit?'

'It's okay. How do you feel leaving it all behind?'

'Do you know son, I haven't a clue.' He smiled to himself. It wasn't a response he gave very often. 'I'm ready to take things easier but I'll miss it.'

'What will you miss?'

'The work; right from the beginning it was all about the work.'

'What were you doing in those days?'

'Cutting edge stuff at the time.' He looked straight at Alex. 'I shouldn't really be talking about it...'

'It's okay, I've signed the Official Secrets Act.' Not a complete lie. He'd have to sign, as soon as they got the paperwork sorted.

Elliott took a gulp of punch. 'Powell can be such a pain but no-one could beat him at getting contracts.'

'Government stuff?'

'Yes.'

'I guess that meant the MoD.'

Elliott gazed at his drink.

'What did you work on?' Alex asked.

'Cloud physics mostly. We did a bit of seeding with the Met Research flight; they had a programme going from the late forties. Then POLEX came along.'

'POLEX?'

'Polar Experiment of the Global Atmospheric Research Program,' he said, pronouncing the words with exaggerated care. 'Americans and the Soviets were experimenting with melting the ice caps. What do you think about that?'

'They were co-operating? How? Why?'

'Global warming. Warm up the frozen north and "hey presto", Siberia and Alaska get to be worth a bob or two. But that was nothing compared to what this came up with a couple of years back.' He pointed to his brain. 'Pure gold. I should be getting a Nobel prize not a clock.'

'Oh yes?' Alex held his breath.

Elliott shook his head. 'Can't tell you boy, not that one. Cutting edge stuff - did I say that before?'

'Yes, but I'd say it's doubly true for you, Sir. I'm studying some of the work that's being done now; amazing it's taken so long to take notice of Tesla isn't it?' he fished.

Elliott's eyes lit up. 'Clever lad, just like your father. Shame the Soviets got there before us on the electromagnetic transmissions. Tweaking the weather on the California coast was my favourite - them and their all surfing, all swimming, all outdoor life. Well they deserved it.'

'Deserved what?'

'The drought of course.' Elliott fixed his eyes on Alex. 'Studies not got you that far eh? Nothing more than playing though; so much more they can do with it.'

'Like what?'

'Defence communications of course. Take out everyone else's, keep their own. But they won't have it all their own way, not now we've got LYRE - not that I'll ever get the credit for it.'

'Why's that?'

'Too hush hush. Perfect defence weapon. Lot more work to be done though; got to be sure about the consequences. Can't go messing about with low frequencies on this,' Elliott touched his brow. 'Got the potential to make us all go loopy. They'd better make sure they keep it away from the idiots...'

'Sorry.' Glenda burst into the room. 'All sorted, and you're on in ten minutes, Elliott.'

'Oh God, no.' He pushed himself off the desk and slid to one side.

Glenda and Alex reached out to steady him. 'Better get some food and a coffee inside you first I think.' She held his arm and guided him out the door.

Alex flicked a switch in his pocket and removed the tape.

Chapter Eleven

'So you see, Mrs... Mrs Clarke shall we say,' the shorter of the two continued, 'you have a decision to make. A decision on which a great deal depends. Choose wisely won't you.'

They hadn't said much, these men who had finally stepped out of the shadows into her present and, much worse, into her past. Ingrid reached for the mantelpiece. She should react, deny everything, but no words came. Perhaps she hadn't the energy for deception; not any more. The horror of Guy's death had changed all that.

'Please don't delay your decision, Mrs Clarke. We'd hate to see you experience any personal loss.'

Ingrid stared through the patio door to where Jack lay on a recliner, enjoying a rare burst of sunshine. He'd come round two days after she'd returned from Lynmouth. It was strange. She'd been absent for three days and no one had missed her. No contact from work, and the hospital thought it perfectly normal she hadn't been near her husband for so long. 'It gets difficult after a while doesn't it?' they'd all agreed.

A bullfinch landed on the bird table. Jack turned, keen to share the moment with her. She knew she should smile, but any reassuring gesture was already too late. His glance had moved, just a fraction, to take in the two figures behind her.

Jack stumbled into the room. 'Are you all right love? What's happening here?'

The visitors turned their backs on Ingrid, still standing motionless by the fireplace. 'Just some incomplete paperwork,

Mr Clarke,' the man responded. 'Nothing to worry about.'

'I'll decide what I concern myself with in my own home thank you.'

'We'll be in touch, Mrs Clarke.' The short one held her eyes for a few moments, turned and followed his colleague out of the room.

Jack put an arm around Ingrid's shoulders. 'What is it? What's wrong?'

'It's all right, Jack. Sit down, you're meant to be resting.'

He guided her to a chair and knelt awkwardly beside her. 'What's going on? Who are they?'

How could she answer? What could she say about the anonymous representatives of Her Majesty's Government who'd invaded her home, her life? *They're government officials who don't like some private research I'm doing. If I don't stop they're going to destroy our life together.* It wasn't exactly the news to deliver to a recovering invalid.

'Don't lock me out, Ingrid. What is going on?'

Silence.

'I'll make a cup of tea. Then we'll talk.' Leaning heavily on the chair, Jack got to his feet.

Ingrid heard cupboard doors opening and shutting as he searched for cups, water running as he filled the kettle, the rattle of the teapot lid being removed. How could things be so normal?

She began to cry, silently at first, and then in uncontrollable sobs. She pressed a tissue over her eyes. This was no time to fall apart. She had to think. Whatever she did someone was going to get hurt. It had to be true. Lynmouth was destroyed because they were cloud seeding over Exmoor. Why else this visit? Why else should Guy have been...? Ingrid shuddered. She hadn't slept in days. Perhaps she should be grateful they'd only chosen to blackmail her.

But they could destroy her life as completely as a bullet - her life with Jack. She laughed. A couple of weeks ago she'd considered throwing it all away and now, now that it wasn't her choice, her life with Jack felt so precious. But if she stayed silent they would get away with it. All those needless deaths...

Jack carried the tray through. 'Here, drink this.' He handed her a cup of strong, sweet tea.

'Thank you,' she said softly.

'What's all this about? Is it to do with your retirement? Problems with your pension? Because you've no need to worry on that score.'

'No. It's nothing like that.' If only it were. Then she could lean on him, look to him to make everything right.

'What is it then?'

'Give me a minute.' She snapped. 'I'm sorry, it's just that... I need...' More than anything she needed him to understand. To put his arm around her and hold her together like he always did. Without him the untidy threads of her life would start to unravel. Leaving what? What was left beneath the façade of the last twenty-five years?

Jack dropped his arm and turned away. 'This can't go on, Ingrid,' he said, his voice sounding strained. 'I've tried, really tried, over these last few months, to cope with your... your antagonism... distance, call it what you will. I've invested everything in us, Ingrid, I don't want to lose you, but I can't go on like this, with you keeping things from me. Not anymore. I need you to think about... about whether we have a future together.'

Ingrid was stunned. He'd never, ever spoken of anything being wrong. Never, in twenty-five years. She had always been the one with grievances, not him.

'I didn't know you felt so badly...'

'That's not what I said. I'm simply not prepared to go on as we have.' Jack gazed out at the garden.

'I'm sorry, Jack. But I've been distracted, by... things.'

He turned to her. 'Don't you see, that's exactly what I mean? Things! What things? And why can't you discuss them? Or should I say discuss *him*?'

'Him? That's ridiculous. There's no-one else.'

'So the lunch dates, phone calls, private sessions are all in my imagination are they?'

'Yes.'

Jack stood up. 'Why all the lies, Ingrid? You called him when we were in London. And I saw you, together, at the office.'

'Nick?'

'Is there anyone else?'

'No, of course not. And Nick and I aren't... involved. We've been collaborating on a project. You know about it. The cloud seeding. Nick had contacts. He was helping me.'

'Was?'

'He hasn't been involved for weeks. It was just a project we got interested in.'

'Obsessed with don't you mean? No other project has given you nightmares.'

'This one became personal. Something happened, years ago. I've never spoken about it.'

'Lynmouth?'

'Yes. How...?'

Jack sighed. 'I heard... at the hospital. So many lies.'

The decision had been made for her. 'I won't be a minute.' She disappeared upstairs. A few minutes later she reappeared with a black metal box, placed it on the polished dining room table and unlocked it. Inside were two manila folders, the first old and tattered, the second almost pristine. She put them side-by-side in front of her, as if unsure which to open first.

'I always meant to share this with you, only it's not easy. You've every right to be angry. But I never meant to hurt you.'

'You're frightening me.'

'Please, Jack. Please promise that you'll hear me out.'

'I always have, haven't I?'

Ingrid had been fiddling with the elastic band around the older file; it was already perished and now it gave way, allowing the yellowing contents to spill out across the table. They were press cuttings, old, crumpled, and all covering one event. Jack picked up a piece of faded newsprint.

'Do you remember the Lynmouth floods?' she said.

'Came out of the blue didn't they, in the middle of the summer? Some tourists lost their lives as well as locals.'

'Yes. Thirty-four people died that night.'

'And you were there?'

'Yes.'

'But you never said, never gave any hint...'

'Don't you see... I couldn't.'

'No I don't. I don't see at all.'

Of course he didn't. How could he? 'We were used to the streams changing, from a trickle in summer to raging rivers after a storm but that night... The rain had been torrential and the rivers just didn't stop rising. I couldn't believe it. Massive boulders, whole trees carried along, crashing into people's homes, sweeping everything away - roads, bridges, cars washed out to sea, everything... destroyed...'

'I can't begin to imagine how you felt, being there, walking amongst all that debris...'

'I didn't,' she said, too sharply. He was doing his best with her drips of information. 'I wasn't there... not afterwards.'

'I still don't understand. Is this all about the boys who died?

'Yes. They... Their bodies were washed up a few days later.'

Jack reached out and pulled her close. 'That's enough, love.'

'More than enough, but not everything.' She pointed to a name in the paper, under the heading, *Missing presumed dead*.

'Moira Williams?' Jack read. 'Did you know her, this Moira?'

'Yes. She was swept away, behind the dance hall.'

'Oh my love. It could have been you.'

'Yes. Moira died that night.' Her voice faded away. Jack was in familiar territory again with a scenario he'd often played out of the solid, reliable husband providing reassurance and comfort. He was constructing a picture of some trauma that had been too much for her to bear, let alone tell him about.

'Stay home today, Ingrid.'

'But you don't...' she stopped. Perhaps he didn't need to understand it all. Perhaps this was enough - for both of them.

'I'd like that, Jack.' She'd been thrown a lifeline: she caught hold of it.

'Good morning, Mrs Clarke. You decided to use up your leave then.'

'Only a day, Mr James, I won't be making a habit of it.'

'There's not long to go now anyway is there?'

Ingrid wasn't in the mood for chapter and verse on her movements. She sank into her office chair and gazed at the desk, still covered in papers that obstinately refused to organise themselves into any kind of order. Just like her life. She understood what Guy meant now, about Nick. He'd been bought off. He had too much to lose to stay involved. But she desperately needed to talk to him about Guy. Reaching for the phone, she noticed the manila envelope. She prised the flap open and read. *Notification of early retirement. I can inform you that your application for early retirement has been successful. As agreed your employment will cease from the end of the month. Your pension details are as follows...*

What application? She loved her work. She'd given years to the paper; the last thing she wanted was to leave. She looked at the bottom of the letter. *Yours sincerely, Nick Pearce, Editor in Chief.* So his daughter's care was only part of the deal. They were out to take her life apart, piece-by-piece. And they knew about Moira. Ingrid reached for her inhaler.

She knew the truth now, wasn't that enough? It wasn't her fault. The floods, the deaths - maybe none of them would have happened without whoever it was cloud seeding that August. 'Whoever it was,' she whispered to herself. She still didn't know, not really. Who ordered the experiments? Who carried them out?

Her stomach leapt at the thought of the figure standing by the river... She pressed the heels of her hands into her eyes. It was a scene her mind replayed night after night. 'Why? Why kill him? It's madness.' Ingrid looked at the cathedral spire for inspiration. 'So buy Nick off, blackmail me, but murder...' Her mind was spinning. None of it made sense.

Maybe it didn't need to make sense. Why not let it go, forget all about it? They could have a fresh start somewhere - abroad maybe, leave all this madness behind. 'Like before.' The words were out before she could stop them. Well it had worked hadn't it? For twenty-five years she'd been happy.

'No!' Ingrid flung her arms out, scattering the contents of her filing tray across the floor. 'Not again,' she sobbed, pushing her clenched hands against her head, trying to erase the memory. 'How could it happen again?' All she'd wanted was to be free of the nightmare of their death and now... now there was another nightmare. Was she going to have to spend her entire life running away?

'There.' Jack was looking pleased with himself. 'Go on, read it.'

'What is it?' Ingrid asked, still muzzy from the tranquillisers she'd finally agreed to take.

'The evidence you're after. This cloud seeding thing of yours is quite interesting when you get into it.'

Ingrid looked up. Jack had been painfully eager to please since her outburst, intent on making Nick redundant.

'I've been looking up a few contacts from my RAF days. It seems the Met Research Flight was active in the early 1950's, flying out of Cranfield mainly. They did all kinds of sorties, looking at cloud physics - so they said - but that can cover a multitude of sins. Anyway...'

'Jack,' Ingrid interrupted, 'I didn't ask you...'

But Jack was well into his flow. 'According to this,' he pulled out a sheaf of papers from his briefcase, 'they were...'

Ingrid's mind was racing. They'd made it painfully clear. She stopped nosing around cloud seeding right now or they would expose her and drag her through the courts. It was no idle threat. Yet Jack had been blatantly working all his old contacts, some still employed by the MoD.

Jack paused. 'Are you taking this in?'

'Why are you doing this?'

'I understand why it's so important now. I don't pick things up as quickly as I used to,' he smiled at her, 'but you think the tragedy at Lynmouth, the loss of those children, your friend, that it all had something to do with cloud seeding don't you?'

'Yes, but...'

'I should have listened to you, supported you more. But it isn't too late is it? I've got contacts from my flying days Ingrid, very informative ones as it happens. We can get to the bottom of this and then you'll be able to move on. Take a look.' He spread a collection of documents in front of her. 'Court cases about rain being stolen, people in the colonies requesting experiments...'

'Jack, please stop.'

'And there's this man called Powell, worked at the Air Ministry for a while then left to set up his own private rainmaking company,' he leafed through the papers, SkySearch UK I think it's called. There were loads of them making a commercial business out of cloud seeding. I can't see anyone giving up a well-paid job and a pension for something that didn't work.'

Ingrid caught hold of his arm. 'Jack, please, this must stop, right now. I appreciate it, I really do, but you mustn't go asking around about cloud seeding.'

'Why ever not?'

'Because...' What could she say? 'Because I need to put everything to do with Lynmouth and the floods behind me. I'm sorry I kept it from you, I truly am, but it's over and done with now. That's how I want it to be. Please, let it go.'

'But it's not over and done with, is it, Ingrid? What about the nightmares, the sleepwalking and the times when...'

'When what?'

He paused. 'When I know you're still keeping something from me.'

'It's not like that.'

He shrugged off her hand. 'So let me be clear about this. When Nick was helping you with your research it was all closet meetings in the pub but when I get involved suddenly it's "stop, I don't want you doing this". And that isn't keeping something from me?'

'Things are different now. Your heart attack changed everything. It made me realise how important you are to me;

gave me the chance to say all those things that I'd kept from you, to wipe the slate clean. I don't need to go there anymore, with Nick, with you, with anyone. The life you've given me is everything, Jack.' She could almost believe it.

'Is this what you really want; to leave it?'

'Yes, it is.' She wrapped her arms around him. 'Can we get away for a bit, in the plane?'

'Maybe, after the next check up. Where do you want to go?'

'Let's go abroad, away from everything.'

'So that's it? No more digging up the past, no more talk about the weather?'

Ingrid smiled. 'Definitely no more talk about the weather.'

Chapter Twelve

Alex surveyed the impressive amount of material on weather modification scattered across the sitting room floor. Together with everything Ingrid shared with him, he had plenty to work from. Now all he had to do was find out exactly what was going on. The answer was right under his nose - in SkySearch files; but there was a problem. He knew how to bend the rules, how to get at stuff companies wanted to bury or how to expose corrupt politicians, but he was a novice when it came to betraying his father.

Maybe there wasn't a link; maybe there were two cloud seeding outfits - two loads of amateurs. Maybe. Maybe not. But even then, surely it was all above board, scientific work done in good faith but with tragic consequences? But then there was Powell. And what looked very like murder.

Alex was sick of the voices raging inside his head.

The front door slammed. Alex hastily shuffled the papers into a box file and pushed everything under the sofa. He looked up. 'Hi, dad, how...' It was a long time since he had seen his father looking so rough. 'What's wrong?'

'Leave it, Alex.' Steven disappeared into the study.

There had been something seriously wrong ever since Elliott's leaving do. Alex could hear his father, night after night, pacing his room. His heart began to race. Suddenly he was ten years old again caught in the middle of one of their rows. His mother accusing his father of selling himself - to someone or something - shouting, begging, pleading that something must change. And his father, storming through the house, holing up in his study for hours on end.

Alex stood outside the study door. 'Dad.' Silence. He opened the door. Steven Carmichael was staring out the window. 'What's going on, dad?' There was no response. 'If mum was here she'd get it out of you.'

'And give me grief for months on end.'

'Probably, until you saw it her way.'

'Yes, well, she never doubted did she? It made decisions simple for her. But sometimes it's not that clear cut. Especially when there's so much at stake. Things get in the way.'

'What kind of things?'

Steven slumped into his leather office chair. 'Leave me alone, Alex.'

'Don't shut me out, dad. You never know, maybe I can help.'

'I don't need help from someone barely out of school.'

'Great. Okay.' Alex retreated to the settee and scooped up the remote control.

'I'm sorry.' His father was standing in the doorway. 'I didn't mean to push you away. It's just... I don't want you caught up in this.'

'In what? Is this about the liability thing?'

'Leave it.' Steven snapped.

Alex held his father's gaze. 'No! How about you try seeing an adult here instead of a child?'

Steven hesitated. 'I'm sorry, you're right.' He walked across and sat opposite Alex. 'You know I was telling you about these amateurs looking to blame some floods on cloud seeding? Well there's more to it. One of them wasn't such an amateur. He was linked with a group of fanatics who are convinced that the weather is being manipulated to hold countries to ransom. The possibility that cloud seeding caused the destruction of a North Devon village was too good to miss.'

'How do you mean?'

'He planned to use it to prove the government were lying about their involvement with weather modification. Great tactics - blow it up out of all proportion, scare the living daylights out of the public and make sure no-one touches weather modification with a barge-pole - until something else knocks it off the front page.'

'Was? Past tense?'

'Powell decided he was too much of a liability. I thought he was just going to buy him off but...'

'But?' Alex had to know. 'What did Powell do, dad?'

'It's... complicated, but I didn't stop him. I did what I always do, made a noise and let him get on with it. But I swear to you, Alex, it never occurred to me that Powell had something more permanent in mind.'

'Something more permanent?' Alex looked at his father.

'It went wrong. The man... he's dead.'

'Did Powell kill him?'

'No, he paid someone - but not to kill him. It was an accident. It had to be.'

'Have you got proof?'

'It's my word against his.'

No more maybes. One group of amateurs, one dead man, and his father right in the middle. 'If you didn't have anything to do with it you've got more on him than he's got on you.'

'There's a tape; it could be misinterpreted.' Steven paced back and forth. 'And it's not over yet. There's this woman.'

Light reflected on the waves, no, not waves, they were leaves, fresh, new, transparent leaves catching the light for a second before scattering it onto the ground all around her. She could almost reach out and gather it up, filling her entire life with beauty, tranquillity, peace; it was such a wonderful peace, surely she must have died and gone to heaven.

Ingrid relaxed against Jack's back as the dream worked its magic.

The light caressed her face. Though her eyes were closed, she knew the sky was a powdery blue, a blank canvas for the few soft flecks of white floating lazily from here to there. Was 'here' East or West? Was 'there' the other way around? Did it matter? Somehow it did. But not just now. Now was all there was, one perfect endless moment of peace when all was still. But they were moving, the billowing clouds. Why were they moving? She wanted perfect stillness, perfect peace. Why wouldn't they be still? Maybe they had somewhere to go, some mission she was witnessing. Yes, that was it. These towering clouds had a mission - and all she had to do was observe, how easy was that? But it would be easier if they'd decide on a direction. With some going this way and some that it was too confusing, and she'd lost sight of the beautiful blue. Why were they hiding the beautiful blue from her? What was it they had to hide? The truth, was that it? Of course, the truth. They were holding it for her. All she had to do was take wing and fly up, up into the clouds.

She could feel the dampness against her skin as she disappeared inside the blackening mass, and the prickling, then pain as ice crystals stabbed at her body. And something pushing her, ever higher and colder, a massive face with pursed lips blowing her upwards, away from her perfect peace. 'No, stop.' The crystals were clustering around her, encasing her, and together they were becoming heavy, so heavy... she couldn't hold herself up any more. She was plummeting down, cold and wet, and transparent, then holding a pale diffusion, a pink sheen, a deeper pink, a red stream, pulling her back to the earth, to the river bed, to his dismembered body...

Jack sat on the dressing table stool, watching Ingrid toss and turn, drenched with sweat. This was the third night this week. Whatever daytime resolutions she might make, this was their reality; a reality that demanded a response.

Julie stared at the refreshment quotes. They ranged from outrageous to unthinkable. It was the usual cartel in operation and it would have the same inevitable conclusion. She would bring in someone from outside and the local suppliers would play victim - bemoaning the lack of support from their own community. She could already hear Frank Williams whingeing. 'Locals will know who to blame when their shops close down and they end up having to drive miles for supplies.'

The phone was a welcome diversion. 'Julie Davenport,' she said.

'Good morning. My name is Jack Clarke. I apologise for disturbing you but I wonder if I might have a moment of your time. My name won't be familiar to you but I'm married to a friend of yours from way back.'

'Oh yes, who's that?'

'Ingrid, Ingrid Clarke.'

Julie paused. 'I'm sorry but the name doesn't mean anything.'

'No, of course, she wasn't Clarke then and it has been a long time since you saw each other, around thirty years I believe.'

'I usually pride myself on my memory, but no matter. How can I help, Mr Clarke?'

'I wonder if we might call to see you. It's a rather sensitive matter, for both of you I believe, but a reunion may be helpful.'

'Go on.'

'I'd prefer to discuss this in person rather than over the telephone.'

'And I would prefer to be put in the picture, Mr Clarke.' Julie didn't understand why she was being so sharp. He was perfectly polite, a complete gentleman in fact, yet something was making her uneasy.

'It concerns a difficult time for both of you, a time when you lost touch.'

'Oh yes, when was that?'

Jack was regretting his uncharacteristic impetuosity. Why didn't he sleep on the idea as he always did? What on earth had possessed him to think that ten minutes with a psychiatrist he was barely acquainted with at the flying club made him into an expert on trauma?

'We are going back quite some time.'

'So you said, thirty years wasn't it?'

'Yes, to 1952.'

Julie was silent.

'Hello?'

'I'm still here, although I don't know why, Mr Clarke, after all...'

'I know, Jack interrupted, 'this call is terribly insensitive. I apologise. I know it was a time of great loss for you, but I'm desperate. My wife is... is in a bad way. I have to do something you see.'

Julie had the distinct impression this man wasn't accustomed to speaking with such feeling. 'I still don't know how I can help, Mr Clarke,' she said, a little more softly.

'My wife, Ingrid, has told me about your sons. I am dreadfully sorry for your loss. It's a loss she also took very hard, along with that of a friend. I don't know the detail but I think she may have had some kind of breakdown. In any event she left Lynmouth and never returned.'

'I'm sorry, that must have been difficult for you.'

'Oh no, my apologies, I haven't explained this very clearly. I didn't know my wife at the time. In fact it's only recently that I've discovered anything about this. It was the shock of course, that made her lie to me all these years. But now she's told me it's the first step isn't it? I can help her come to terms with what happened. I know it will bring us back together.'

Now Julie understood. This man had rung a complete stranger about a time of great personal tragedy because he was desperate to save his marriage. The silence lengthened.

'Please accept my apologies for having troubled you. This was a totally inappropriate call to make. I can't imagine what possessed me to disturb you in this way. I am sorry,' he said.

'Wait.' Instead of giving up and checking out, this man was prepared to go to any lengths to save his marriage. Julie had the feeling he would always be there for his wife, supporting her, easing her burdens. She steadied her voice. 'If you think it would help then... bring her here. Perhaps we can help each other.'

'Thank you,' Jack whispered.

'Hello, Ingrid.'

Ingrid scanned the crowded street. 'Nick.' She felt a curious mixture of pleasure and pain at seeing him.

'How are you?'

'Oh, rushed off my feet with knitting and the W.I., you know how it is. But then you don't do you? How is the new job?'

'It's not so bad is it, having more time? How has your health been?'

'Nick, we both know you forced me out of a job I loved and had no intention of leaving. How do you think I am?'

He took her arm and guided her into a doorway. 'I wish I could explain, it wasn't my decision. There were... other considerations.'

'I'm sorry,' Ingrid's voice softened a little. 'How is Ellie?'

'She's had a transplant. So far so good.'

'That's great news.'

'But why bring up Ellie?'

'She is the other consideration isn't she?'

'What do you know?'

'Enough. I had a visit too.'

'What happened?'

'I was lucky. They just threatened me. Not like poor Guy. He's dead, Nick. They as good as killed him.' It sounded ludicrous even to Ingrid, standing there on a Salisbury Street talking about what amounted to murder.

'What! Why would they do that? I know I said he was treading on thin ice but I meant he might lose his job, maybe get prosecuted, but killed! Where? How?'

'Lynmouth, by the river.'

'How do you know?'

'I was there. I'd arranged to meet him. He said he could prove they were cloud seeding, but I fell into a quarry and dislocated my shoulder so I didn't make it.'

'Thank God, it probably saved your life.'

'It might have been an accident, I couldn't really see. This walker appeared. They talked, Guy seemed to back away from him and then... then he was in the river.'

'And the other man didn't help?'

'No, just watched... then walked away.'

'Did anyone see you?'

'I don't know.'

'Think. It's important. If they know you're a witness they might come after you.'

Ingrid slumped against the wall. 'I don't think so. I was lying in the ferns.'

'Why the hell did you carry on with it? I told you to let it go. You've got to destroy everything; it's not worth risking your life for.'

'Oh, Nick, when did this get so unreal? Did I dream it all, about Guy and the river? I'm beginning to think I must have. Private Dean's got a lot to answer for.'

'Too right!' He paused. 'But it hasn't all been bad has it? We got to work together.'

'Yes, it was fun.'

'So why don't we take up where we left off?'

'But you said...'

'Not with rainmaking, with us. Get yourself a pass and let me take you out for dinner. How about Thursday?'

'I... I don't know. There's Jack.'

'Come on, it's time to start putting yourself first. You deserve some pleasure. It's all been about Jack for weeks now. Think of it as time off for good behaviour, your reward for doing such a great job.'

'It wouldn't be fair.'

The pause was too long to be comfortable. 'And what about me? All I'm asking is the chance to make it up to you. Do you think it's fair to throw my attempt at an apology back in my face?'

'I'm sorry, I didn't mean to... I suppose I could make it.'

'Only if you're sure.'

'Yes... yes, I'm sure.'

'Well you could sound a bit more enthusiastic. It's not every day I offer to treat my favourite lady to a night on the town.'

Despite herself, Ingrid was smiling. 'Just dinner, between friends.'

'If that's how you want it, then yes.'

'Okay, but I'm not sure about Thursday. Next week sometime. I'll call.'

'You mean it?'

'Yes.'

'It's time we were leaving,' Jack called up the stairs.

Ingrid closed the bedroom door. 'Will this be enough?' she asked, holding up a thin summer coat.

'It's fine. We're only going for a ride.'

'So why the panic?'

'There's no panic. I simply wish to get going before we lose too much of the day.' Jack held out her coat. 'Let's get on and enjoy it.' He ushered her through the front door, checked it was locked and scanned the house for any open windows. Then it was a race to get the passenger door open, to hold out a helping hand, to settle her into her seat.

Here we go, Ingrid thought. Check gear stick is in neutral. Jack checked it. Now the handbrake. Ditto. Adjust the mirror. He did. Now tune in to radio four. Jack paused, and looked at her. 'I'm a bit of a creature of habit aren't I? You choose.'

Ingrid leant over and kissed him. 'Thank you,' she said, and then tuned in to radio four.

'But that's...'

'As they say, it's the thought that counts,' she said.

Jack laughed, rechecked the mirror and reversed the car out of the drive.

'Where are we going?' Ingrid asked, an hour or so later.

'Sit back and enjoy the ride.'

'I'd prefer to talk.'

'We haven't really talked... about that night, about Lynmouth, have we? If it would help I'm happy to listen,' Jack said.

'What's the point?'

'It would help me understand, to be there for you when the

nightmares come. I'll always be there for you Ingrid, whatever you tell me. You do know that don't you?'

Ingrid returned his smile. She was surprised how much she wanted to believe it.

'Tell me about Moira. Were you close?' he asked.

'I guess you could say no-one knew Moira better than I did.'

'How did you meet?'

'We were all land girls, having a lark together. Only after Julie moved out things weren't half so much fun.'

'Was that to marry Hugh?'

'Yes.'

'What happened to Moira then?'

'A meal distributor, Frank Williams, used to call at the farm for orders. They got talking one week, then it was a trip to the pictures, then a dance and before she knew it he was kind of a habit. He was very persuasive and manly in an old fashioned kind of way. Always told Moira when they would be going out, what they would be doing, that sort of thing. Poor Julie despaired of her. Said Frank was undoing all her good work.'

'What did she mean?'

'Oh nothing. Anyway, they got together. He was gorgeous to look at, kind of drew you in until it was too late to do a U-turn when you realised what a dictator he was. Poor Moira had no say in anything. Frank was accustomed to being master in his own home. It was like living with father all over again, Moira never stood a chance.'

'So Moira wasn't happy?'

'If familiarity makes you happy then perhaps, for a while. As long as the blinkers stayed in place Moira could just about survive. Julie did her best to dislodge them, to get her to tell him where to go, but some habits stick.'

'What did she do?'

'For a long time, nothing. Anyway, it's all water under the bridge now. Oh God, what an awful thing to say, with the floods and everything.'

Jack placed a comforting hand on her knee. Ingrid knew she was receiving it under false pretences, but it felt so... reassuring.

She smiled and placed her hand over his. 'You've told me about Julie and Moira but you haven't told me anything about yourself yet,' he said.

'I wouldn't say that.' She looked down as they crossed a long low bridge over the motorway. An unending stream of cars and lorries stretched away to the horizon. Where were they all going? South to the coast or north to Bristol, the Midlands, London maybe? Everyone going somewhere.

'Jack, where are we going?' She suddenly realised they were heading due west.

He hesitated. 'Lynmouth.'

'Stop the car. Now!'

'No. This horrible event has stolen too much of your life. I'm going to show you it's possible to face the past and then let it go. Trust me. I know what I'm doing.'

Ingrid laughed; a harsh sound that ricocheted around the car. 'But you don't. You have no idea.'

'I do, Ingrid. I've taken advice. This is the best way. Please, trust me.'

He wasn't asking but telling. Suddenly her lifeline was starting to feel like a noose, a noose that tightened with each passing mile.

Despite herself, Ingrid couldn't suppress a rush of excitement as Jack drew into the car park by the National Park office at Dulverton. The tree-covered valley sides were so beautiful, softly enfolding and embracing this charming little town. She smiled. Such an old-fashioned word, but Dulverton was charming, totally suited to her life with Jack.

It was a beautiful day; perfect for strolling up to the café. They selected a round gingham-covered table by the multi-paned bow window and settled down to watch the flow of residents and visitors. There was activity, but it was softened, as though the town had passed a by-law eliminating stress, rounding off the edges of every voice, smoothing people's features, bringing them to a deep appreciation of life.

Ingrid watched as a middle-aged couple stretched after their long drive then paused, letting the atmosphere seep into them.

But it was all a mirage, a brief glimpse of another life where people knew exactly who they were. Ingrid shuddered.

'Shall we move on?' Jack asked.

'Take me home, Jack.'

'It will be all right. Trust me.' He opened the door and, as they stepped onto the pavement, gently took hold of her hand.

A few minutes later they were driving out of Dulverton, following the river Barle up towards the moor. Then breaking free of the trees out onto the rolling, bracken and heather covered ground leading away to the slopes of Dunkery Beacon. It was exhilarating. But they weren't going past Dunkery today. At the next junction, Jack turned left towards Simonsbath. The high beech hedges fringing the lane began to close in. Ingrid's chest tightened.

She focused on the world outside the window. Simonsbath church appeared high up on the right, the walk alongside the Barle away through the trees to the left, the roads to South Molton and Bratton Fleming, the long stretch out of the hamlet, across the cattle grid out onto the open moor again, the sea up ahead, the imminent drop down to Hillsford Bridge...

'Would you like to stop?' Jack asked, unusually sensitive to her mood.

'Yes... please.'

He pulled into a small quarry. 'It's okay love, take your time.'

Time; that was it! All she had to do was get through today and it would be over. She wasn't facing a personal hell, remembering the unthinkable, looking for absolution; she was just getting through a day, minute by minute; a day with a definite, tangible end. She looked at Jack, his face creased with worry, and smiled. 'Let's go.'

Eric Fairweather closed the door of the stone faced cottage behind him. It was one of a row of twenty or so that occupied a narrow strip of land between the steeply sloping valley sides and the East Lyn River. A few hundred yards further down, where the East and West Lyn joined before making their final run out to sea, the valley widened to accommodate the rest of Lynmouth. But here it held the cottages close. Hikers taking this scenic route were gently funnelled up past the brightly coloured front doors and along the riverside path to Watersmeet, Rockford and Brendon until they emerged onto the moor: a beautiful walk when the sun reached the valley floor but a different story in winter. Then the valley was cast into deep shadow.

From his bedroom, Eric marked the sun's progress as it inched its way towards him. By the end of March it would teeter outside his window before bursting through sometime at the beginning of April. Today he walked down the path in full sun, between the doll's house lawns and through the gate. Age had gifted him a slight stoop and a faltering gait but with the help of a stick, neither interfered with his daily vigil by the river; although he'd recently given in to his landlady's entreaties to stay in out of the rain. 'What good will it do,' she'd said, 'getting yourself laid up just for the sake of missing a day or two?' She'd been right of course. What was a day or two after thirty years? 'Maybe the day or two that matters,' the voice in his head nagged. But not today. Today was fine.

He crossed the narrow road separating the cottages from the river, conscious of the roar echoing across the valley. Rainwater running off the moor had turned a somnolent stream into something uncomfortably different. For the first few weeks, months even, the noise had kept him awake at night: either that or the pictures the dreadful power of the river evoked in his mind.

'Morning, Mr Fairweather,' the young postman greeted him as he leapt off his bike, dropped it against the wall and rifled through his bag. 'Looks like a nice one.'

'It does. Makes a change after all the mist.'

'You'd better get a move on if you want to bag your bench.' He nodded towards the coaches creeping down the steep hill from Lynton. 'You'll have competition soon.'

Eric Fairweather turned his head in the direction of the car park at the bottom of Countisbury Hill. 'How many today?'

'Just two... no, three that I can see so far but we're getting into the season now; the rest won't be far behind.'

'I expect not. Anything for me, Andrew?'

'Couple of official looking ones. Nothing exciting.'

Eric took the envelopes, hesitated, then folded and secured them as best he could in the gaping pocket of his tweed jacket. He held them with his elbow, an arrangement that worked well enough as he shuffled along the narrow pavement towards the grassy bank overlooking the river. He stopped behind the bench positioned closest to the path. Dropping the envelopes onto the seat, he pulled a large white handkerchief from his pocket and leant over the back. A few moments later the brass plaque was shining as bright as new. *For Moira, who loved this place.*

'You've made a good job of that.'

Eric turned towards the voice. 'Thank you vicar. I usually bring some Brasso but this will do for now.'

'Here, let me help.' Mark Forrester took hold of the stick and Eric's elbow and eased him down on to the seat. 'Mind if I join you?'

'Please.'

'This is more like it,' Mark said, taking in the sun. 'After last night I thought I'd get drowned today.'

'Yes.'

Mark paused. 'We haven't seen you at church lately. Let me know if you need transport won't you?'

'Thank you, I will.' A coach pulled into the car park opposite. Eric extracted a pair of binoculars from his other pocket. There was no need to adjust the focus; it was always set for the same distance.

The vicar took the hint. 'Good... Well... I'll leave you to it then.'

Lynmouth was busy, a reflection of the late morning sun casting a rosy glow over the village. With her eyes fixed on the ground,

Ingrid made the path alongside the East Lyn without catching a glimpse of the river spilling out of the Glen Lyn Gorge. At Jack's suggestion they were going back to where the hall had stood, just a few hundred yards up the valley. Ingrid's gaze swept from face to face as they passed others on the narrow path. It was a long time ago and she'd changed, hadn't she?

Across the water an elderly man sat on one of the raised benches overlooking the river, watching the day trippers as they spilled out from the tour coaches lined up in the new car park. Did he live in one of the tiny stone cottages alongside the river that had survived the floods? Maybe he'd even been here that night. She paused to look; there was something about him... He had a curious way of moving his head as he followed the stream of walkers striding along the path.

Then they were there, in the gardens, at the very spot... And she felt nothing. Jack guided her to a bench at the top of the garden away from the water's edge. That's so sensitive of him, she thought. He delved into the rucksack and produced some sandwiches. Jack, thinking about and making sandwiches?

She settled back, enjoying the food, the shaded slope, and the sounds of children playing in the shallow pools at the water's edge. It was lovely to hear their rippling laughter... their whoops of delight... the light-hearted teasing... their screams of excitement... growing louder, echoing back and forth across the valley, magnified a hundred-fold, searing in to her mind. It was enough, more than enough.

The village plunged into darkness. Girls screaming, starting to run. Forming a human chain, passing them one by one up the slopes, so slippery, everywhere so dark and the rain, thundering down, terrifying, children losing their way, walking back into danger, the water, tugging at her legs, pulling her under, suffocating her...

'It's okay: let yourself remember. I've got you, you're safe.' Jack was whispering in her ear. 'Let it go. I'll hold you for as long as it takes. I'm here for you. That's right my love, let it go.'

The tears finally tore themselves free.

Quiet returned as the last of the holidaymakers drifted back to their hotels and guesthouses, leaving the elderly man the sole sentinel over his valley. 'Time to go?' Jack asked, masking the strain of the last few hours.

'Yes please; take me home, Jack.'

Jack held the car door open. Ingrid sank gratefully into the leather seat, closing her eyes. Thank God it was over. Perhaps now they could get away. Start again.

Jack balanced a hand-written note on the dashboard to read the brief directions he'd taken down over the phone. 'Are we going back over the moor?' Ingrid asked, as he took the road towards Simonsbath.

'In a while; we're calling on someone first.'

Ingrid sat up. 'Who?'

'You'll find out in a minute.'

'This isn't the time for games. Where are we going?'

'Up to the Manor.'

'No, I can't go back there. Please, it's over, you have to take me home, away from here.'

'Julie is expecting you.'

'What!' Ingrid turned to face him.

'Your friend, Julie Davenport, she knows you're coming. You haven't had a decent night's sleep since I've been home. The nightmares are getting worse. I had to do something.'

'And you have. You've helped me, Jack. Don't ruin that.'

'But don't you see my love, it won't ruin anything. This was just the first step. Things will get even better and I'll be there for you every step of the way.'

'So I'm expected to go along with your plans as always, is that it? You didn't think to ask if I wanted to meet someone I haven't seen for thirty years, someone you don't know the first thing about?'

'Trust me, Ingrid.'

'No, Jack, you have to trust me. I know you mean well but please, take me home.'

They had reached the junction at Hillsford Bridge. Turning left would take them back across the moor to Dulverton, Taunton and home, back to their life together. Jack hesitated, but the driver behind was getting impatient. He pulled across the road and through the gates to the Manor. 'A compromise then,' he said, before she could react. 'I'll wait outside; leave you to catch up on your own. It might not be as awkward as you think. Trust me.'

Ingrid slumped in her seat. What a waste; all the effort she'd put into believing everything was going to be all right. If only Jack hadn't brought her back. Poor misguided Jack, still doing what he thought was right and getting it so, so wrong. It was over, and he had only himself to blame. All he had to do was drive away. But he wasn't going to, was he? Because Jack was programmed to 'do the right thing'.

They turned the corner and for the first time in thirty years Ingrid found herself staring at the Manor's imposing facade.

'Stop the car. I'll walk.'

'It's all right love, I'll take you right up, you'll get soaked in this rain.' The sun had become obscured by storm clouds and rain was driving across the valley.

'Stop the car,' she shouted, then instantly regretted it. These might be their last moments together. She didn't want them to be scarred by anger. 'Please.'

He pulled up. 'If that's what you want.'

She sat quite still, then reached over and gently kissed him. 'Thank you, Jack.'

'What for?'

'For some of the happiest years of my life.'

Chapter Thirteen

The raindrop gathered speed as it slid down the window of the summer house. It was swiftly followed by others until Julie's view of the river was obscured, as though she was viewing it through barely open venetian blinds.

It had been a while since the compulsion to come and sit here had been quite so strong. But ever since the phone call... the mention of 1952, of her loss...

'No, Alistair, you can't go until you've finished your toast. You'll both be hanging around while Moira and I get everything ready and I don't want you deciding you're hungry then. Michael's finished. It's not fair to keep him waiting.'

'I won't get hungry.'

'And pigs won't fly. Oh, all right. But I don't want a peep out of you when we get there.' There wasn't time to argue. Moira would already be at the hall and there was still so much to do before the children arrived. And the band... Julie looked at the clock. Oh no! She'd forgotten the band. Thunder rumbled round the valley. They'd be soaked waiting around in this weather.

'Boys, get your coats on and into the car. Now.' It wasn't far to the hall; no more than five minutes. And Moira might be early. Did she have a key? Julie couldn't remember.

'Mummy, when's daddy coming?'

'Soon, Alistair. He promised he'd be here didn't he?'

'Can I take my marbles?'

'No, Michael. Now get in the car. Both of you'

Serviettes, washing up liquid, tea cloths, tea, coffee... what else was it she'd said she'd bring? Too late now.

They were a few hundred yards down the drive when Alistair called out. 'Mummy, stop.'

Julie twisted round. He had his face pressed to the window. 'I can't stop now, darling, we're late.'

'Mummy, you must. Something's hurt.'

'He's right, mummy, look,' Michael pointed.

They didn't often cry wolf. Julie stopped the car and followed their gaze into the woods. She could just make out a deer lying on its side in the undergrowth. Alistair was right; it looked distressed. She held her coat over her head and opened the door. 'Stay here.'

She edged closer, sensing the deer's tension at her presence. Something was stopping it fleeing. An injury?

The deer heaved, its whole body straining against some invisible force. Julie smiled.

'Is it hurt, mummy?'

'Why is it making those sounds?'

'Come under here.' Alistair and Michael pressed closer, the three of them finding shelter from the rain under her coat. 'It's fine. She's just giving birth. Look. You can see the legs.'

'Wow,' Michael said. 'Daddy will be so jealous.'

'Yes. You're very lucky to see this.'

The deer strained as another contraction exposed the tip of a nose.

'I don't like it,' Alistair hid his face against Julie. 'It's hurting her.'

'She's all right. As soon as the body starts to come it will all be over.' They sat in silence as first the head and then the body appeared. 'Look, here it comes.' With a final heave the fawn fell to the ground.

'It's not moving. It's dead. It got squeezed.'

'Look,' Julie said. The deer turned to nuzzle the fawn. Stimulated by her tongue, it shivered and stretched its head.

Alistair peered out from Julie's coat, tentative at first, then with all hesitation forgotten as he was drawn into the magic of birth. Julie was mesmerised by his face. Such wonder; pure childlike wonder. The same as she'd felt when her children were first placed in her arms. She knew then that nothing would ever mean more to her than protecting and caring for these precious lives.

'Come on you two. Miracle it may be but it won't wash with Moira if we're much later...'

Her tears fell. Even after all this time... the memories were too precious to leave behind but when would the pain ease? If she'd only known what had happened. Would it help? Maybe not. But nothing could be worse that the scenarios she conjured up for herself. Of them falling, perhaps being knocked unconscious, lying there for someone, for Moira, to see and carry to safety. Being trapped by debris that stronger arms than theirs could have lifted to free them.

Something prompted her to look up; perhaps the movement on the drive. This must be her mystery visitor. She watched as the figure lifted her arm and waved. Had the woman seen her? No, she was waving at the magpies. None of her usual visitors did that. She watched as the stranger reached the door, hesitated and looked back down the drive, to a car in the distance. If she'd come by car why leave it there and get drenched walking to the house?

Julie lifted her coat over her head and stepped out into the rain.

Chapter Fourteen

Jack was right. She was soaked by the time she reached the house. She wanted to turn, to run, but with Jack sitting there where could she run to? A single magpie flew across her path. 'One for sorrow,' she whispered and waved.

The door opened. 'Good morning.'

Ingrid hesitated. 'Julie?'

'Mrs Davenport's slipped out for a minute, but she's expecting you Mrs Clarke. Come in.'

'Sorry, only we haven't met for a long time.'

'Not a problem. I'm Christine. I clean for Mrs Davenport. Have a seat. I'll tell her you're here.'

Ingrid walked into the formal sitting room. Nothing, absolutely nothing had changed. 'Thirty years,' she whispered. 'Almost half my life.'

'Mrs...' Julie hesitated at the door. 'No... he can't have meant... it can't be you.'

'Hello, Julie,' Ingrid said. The silence lengthened.

'No, no; it can't be...' Julie grasped the door. Very slowly, her gaze moved from the ghost standing before her through the window, to the magpie perched in the oak outside. 'You waved. Moira was the only person I ever knew who waved at magpies. But they didn't find you... after the floods. We all thought... thought you were dead.'

'I'm sorry... turning up like this. It must be a shock.'

'I don't understand. All this time... you've been...' Julie stopped. 'Was it you? Did you put flowers on their grave?'

'Yes.'

'Why?'

'I don't know, I just felt I...'

'Why come back now? Why not before?' Julie said.

'It's complicated. I know it's a shock,' Ingrid stammered. 'It wasn't my idea. I didn't know Jack was bringing me here.'

'And that makes it all right?'

'No. Nothing will ever make it right.' Ingrid turned her back on Julie. 'It's just... I haven't had time to think.'

'No time! You've had thirty years. How long do you need?'

'I'm sorry, I'm so, so sorry. If I could turn back the clock I would... but what happened, with Alistair and Michael, it wasn't my fault, you have to understand that.'

Julie stared at her. 'You shouted at them... shouted at two terrified six year old children you'd gone back to rescue!'

'Don't, please don't,' Ingrid strained to catch her breath. 'It was all so confusing. You know what it was like - the rain, the noise, the children screaming; but even if I'd managed to hold onto his hand...'

'What! Whose hand? Alistair's? Michael's? Whose?'

'I don't know. I'm so sorry, Julie. His hand was there one moment, then I lost my footing and he was gone...'

'But you weren't. Apparently you are very much alive.'

'The water swept me away - I don't remember anything until I came round the next day caught up in trees. Even if I'd led the boys out of there, there's no way I could have hung on to them.'

'They searched those banks for days; they didn't find you.'

'I... I moved on. I was battered and bruised but it was like I'd been thrown into another world. No identification, no ties, nothing.'

'You had amnesia?'

'In a way. It's as though I'd been washed clean, empty... like a shell; I could go anywhere, be anyone... You know how it was, Julie. You know,' she pleaded. 'Something inside snapped and yes, I ran. I didn't know where I was going; it didn't matter, as long as it was away.' Ingrid steadied her breathing and glanced up. Julie was leaning against the window sill, tense but listening.

'It was such hot, sultry summer weather. I slept out under the stars...'

'When I was at the makeshift morgue identifying my son's bodies you were gazing at the stars.'

Ingrid stared at Julie. That's exactly why she was gazing at the stars, why she could never be who she was again. 'Lynmouth didn't exist, I didn't exist. It must have been the shock, I don't know... I remember walking off the moor at Dulverton. I bought some clothes at the charity shop - I'd been in my stuff for days - and some food. I can't really remember; nothing made sense.'

'You bought food and clothes. What with?'

'What?'

'You'd been swept away by the river and left with nothing. How did you buy food and clothes?'

'I don't know.'

'It's all a pack of lies isn't it? You didn't have amnesia. It was a calculated plan. While everyone else was searching the river and the bay where were you? Sneaking back to your house to pack your stuff? You ran all right, but from what you'd done. Nothing else.'

'No, that's not how it was.'

'So how was it?'

'I don't remember.'

'How convenient.'

'All I had were the clothes I was wearing at the dance... the dress and jacket - the jacket.' *Running back to the hall, seeing the takings on the table in the entrance, scooping them up, zipping them into her jacket pocket.* 'I remember now. I had the dance takings in my jacket pocket.'

'You took the money? While my boys were drowning you stopped to pick up the money!'

'I didn't know how serious everything was then. And later... the money was just there. It paid for clothes, food, the bus... to Taunton and then Salisbury. When the coach pulled into the bus station something made me get off. I remember walking into the Cathedral: it was so calm, so peaceful.' Ingrid suddenly became aware of Julie's tears.

'In thirty years I haven't had one day of peace yet so soon after you'd...' She couldn't say it again. 'And not one word to us. Do you realise how much I needed to know... to know how they died?'

'Yes,' Ingrid whispered. 'I can't ask you to forgive me... but please, I beg you, please try to understand. You know how things were for me at home, with Frank. When I realised everyone thought I was dead it seemed the best way. You accused me of escaping. Well, I did.'

'Oh, Moira.'

'Moira?' Jack's voice cut through the room. 'Who is Moira?'

Both women turned towards the doorway. 'This is Moira.' Julie said, nodding toward Ingrid. 'Moira Williams.'

'And Frank?'

'Frank is her husband.'

'Is...?'

Jack looked at Ingrid, standing motionless. 'But you're mistaken. This is Ingrid, my wife. We've been married for twenty-five years.'

'Moira?' Julie stared at Ingrid.

Ingrid looked from Jack to Julie, caught between her present and her past. 'When... when I left the Cathedral I found myself in the graveyard. So many lives gone, just gone; some far too soon. There was one, still in her twenties, so young... It seemed right she should have a second chance at life. That we both should.'

'You stole someone's identity?' Julie gasped.

'Yes.' Ingrid thought she'd spoken aloud but couldn't be sure.

'The quiet wedding, no documents, no family - all because you were living a lie, you never were Ingrid.' The colour drained from Jack's face. 'You didn't want me, just an identity, a roof over your head, a future. What a blind fool... flattered that you'd fallen for someone like me.' He gripped the back of a chair.

'No, no, it wasn't like that.'

He turned to Julie. 'And this Frank Williams, he's still alive?'

'Very much so.'

Jack looked at Ingrid. 'Why? Why all the lies? Why couldn't you trust me?'

'It wasn't you I didn't trust, Jack. It was me. I couldn't allow myself to remember. But everything else was real. I wanted to be with you.' She put a hand on his arm. 'Please... you have to believe me.'

'I want to Ingrid... Moira... damn it, whoever you are!' He brushed her hand away. 'Do you have any idea what it's like to look at the woman you've shared the best part of your life with and not even know her name?'

'I'm sorry, Jack. I'm so sorry.'

He shook his head. 'Twenty-five years and every day a lie.'

'No, that's not how it was.'

'How can it possibly be anything else?' He turned towards the door. 'Ingrid is dead.'

The sound of Jack's car disappearing down the drive gave way to silence. 'Who are you now then?' said Julie. 'Ingrid is dead and according to the flood memorial so is Moira.'

Ingrid's head was in her hands. 'I've blamed myself every day of my life for the boys' death - but there was nothing I could do. It wasn't my fault; I know that now.' She looked up. 'You've got to listen to me, Julie. They were rainmaking.'

'What?'

'The Ministry of Defence, they were manipulating the weather, experimenting with increasing rainfall. I know there were flights up that day. I don't know where yet but seeding anything up to three hundred miles away could have affected us here as long as the wind was strong enough and in the right direction...' Ingrid knew she was babbling. 'Don't you see? It wasn't an Act of God; it was the government's doing, interfering with the weather. They have to be made accountable. With your help we can...'

'We! After everything that you've done you dare talk about "we". I want you to leave.'

'But...'

'Get out!' Julie shouted.

Ingrid stumbled into the hallway, through the heavy oak door and across the gravelled driveway, disappearing through a curtain of rain.

Ingrid could just make out a dipper bobbing up and down on one of the boulders that interrupted the river's flow. Bobbing up and down, up and down, up and down, up and down...

'Good afternoon,' a tall figure greeted her. 'Time to get out of this weather I think. Another hour or two and the river will become quite nasty. Just as well to watch your footing in conditions like these, Mrs Williams.'

She wiped her eyes. 'What?' She hadn't been Mrs Williams for over thirty years. She looked up, but he was well on his way up the path beyond hailing distance. And what would she have said anyway? She was nothing, nobody. She had been Ingrid; Ingrid who lived a quiet, dignified life in Salisbury with her quiet dignified husband. But Jack had made it clear. Anything they had was over, gone. Ingrid was dead. Ingrid, Ingrid, Ingrid, Ingrid... she rolled the word around inside her head until she'd rendered it meaningless.

Words. What were they? Vibrations in the air, that's all. But a few choice vibrations had just destroyed her life. Although it never was her life was it? She'd stolen it, and the parts she hadn't stolen she'd conjured out of the air and built into a fiction of a life. A family history full of tragically early deaths; likes and dislikes woven into the patchwork at appropriate places to give colour and interest, along with a few of life's ups and downs. Ups and downs. Her brittle laugh disturbed the dipper. A life like a pop-up book. With people popping up out of their graves. Ingrid popping up...

'Stop!' she pressed her hands to the sides of her head and rocked backwards and forwards. 'No, no, no, no, no, no, no, no. no...' The movement and mantra began to work, numbing thoughts and feelings. Was this how it felt to be dead?

Nothingness? She held her hands out. So whose hands were they? Not Ingrid's. Not Moira's. Whose?

The rain blurred her vision and a familiar noise rushed in her ears; not inside - out there, a few feet away. The roar of water rushing towards its destiny; no hesitation, no doubts, falling over itself in its hurry to reach the oblivion of the ocean. 'Freedom... freedom... freedom,' the water whispered, drawing her closer, ready to throw its arms around her. The faces of all those it had already embraced smiled up at her. They needed her, Michael and Alistair. She'd let them go and they needed her.

She moved to the water's edge, into a shallow eddy, gripping a slender trunk for support. Then slid into the next pool, her shivering body sending tremors along the overhanging branches. The tree was urging her to loosen her grip; to become one with the torrent's embrace. But her hands held fast. Ingrid caught a glimmer of light reflecting off her wedding band. Moira's hand, Ingrid's band, bonded till death do them part. Her hands, fighting for all they were worth to save her life. Suddenly the river tore at her numbness, thudding in to her chest and taking her breath. She was drowning, and this time there would be no reprieve, no soft canopy where she'd wake in the sunlight. Well maybe that's how it should be. Perhaps her only talent was for running away.

'No, it's not true,' something inside screamed. Maybe before but not now. Ingrid wasn't an act, someone she could shake off like an old coat. The name was borrowed but the person was real. Ingrid had changed her. She wasn't going to run any more. But the river was rushing past with such force, tearing her arms from their sockets. Why had her body taken so long to wake up? Seconds ago she could have scrambled to safety but now, when every cell in her body was screaming for life, it was impossible. The current was too strong, dragging her under.

Chapter Fifteen

Alex cut across Kew Bridge to the south of the river, turned left and swung himself, two at a time, down a flight of steps, landing at the door of Earthshield UK. He'd been to the office a couple of times since his interview but the brunette who answered the door was new to him.

'Hi, I'm Alex Carmichael. I'm meeting Madeline at ten.'

'You're a braver man than me, Alex Carmichael,' she responded, smiling broadly. 'Ms. Cox appreciates a bit of respect from her new recruits.'

'Then Ms. Cox shall have it.' He wasn't too concerned about how his boss liked to be addressed, but if it kept this conversation going... 'How about you?'

'How about me?' She folded herself back behind a desk and began stuffing leaflets into envelopes.

'Been here long?'

'In this house? Or with Earthshield?'

Peculiar answer. 'With Earthshield.'

'I guess since it was formed. I help out from time to time.'

'So you're a volunteer?'

'You could say that.'

Alex checked his watch. He was ten minutes early. 'Can I help?' He pointed at the pile. She pushed a handful across the desk. 'So tell me about Ms. Cox.'

'What do you want to know?'

'What's she like to work for? Will I get a rough ride with the stuff I've sent in?'

'Difficult to say. She had over forty applications for your job, lots from campaigners with years of experience, yet she chose you. Why do you think that was?'

'She's obviously a very perceptive lady; able to spot natural talent and disarming good looks a mile off.'

'A word of advice. If you want to keep the job, lose the attitude. She's more interested in honesty, integrity, loyalty, intelligence...'

'No problem.'

'And did I mention modesty?'

'Did I mention dinner?'

'Focused, single-minded, quick off the mark - there's a strong chance you'll do very well, Mr Carmichael.' The voice from behind made him jump. 'Come through.' Madeline Cox held the door open for Alex.

Madeline placed her tortoiseshell glasses on the desk. 'This is good, very good.'

Alex relaxed. He'd submitted the report days ago - it had been an anxious wait. 'Thanks. I know there are holes but I'm working on them.'

'How did you get hold of this information?'

'A couple of sources; I'd prefer not to be specific.'

'I don't make a habit of allowing the reputation of this organisation to rest on the shoulders of young, inexperienced employees going out on a limb.' She fixed him with her grey eyes. 'As I said, this is good. But for it to go any further than this office I need it substantiated: signed witness testimony, copies of official documents, recordings. Verifiable evidence, Alex.'

He should stay focused, but those eyes... piercing, insightful eyes illuminating someone totally dedicated to her cause - just like his mother. 'There is someone, a woman...'

'Ingrid Clarke,' Madeline interrupted, 'yes, we put her in touch with you remember?'

It was a long time since he'd felt so foolish.

'So this,' Madeline nodded at his report, 'is all based on her information?'

Alex hesitated. 'No.'

'Why am I thinking "blood out of a stone" here, Alex?' She scrutinised him. 'Do you want this job?'

'Definitely.'

'Good. Because you have something here I'm prepared to put at the top of the agenda at our next meeting.'

'Fantastic...'

'On two conditions. Firstly, you supply concrete evidence to back up these allegations and secondly,' she paused, 'you tell me who you're working for.'

'I don't understand.'

Madeline stared at him a moment longer then reached into a drawer. She placed a SkySearch report in front of him, with his father's name prominently underlined in red. 'When were you going to tell us about this, Alex?'

'I don't see...'

'What conclusion would you reach in my place?' she interrupted. 'That this intelligent young man with a first class honours degree is actually unbelievably dumb, or that he's playing out of his league.'

'I still don't...'

She pointed at the SkySearch report. 'This is your father, yes?'

'Yes.'

'And your father's business is weather modification, yes?'

'Yes.'

'And you didn't think it relevant to mention that at your interview?'

'I guess...'

'I'm interested in facts not guesswork. Even more interesting is that you're actually an employee at SkySearch. Correct?'

'I wasn't at the time.'

'Let's suppose I give you the benefit of the doubt.'

'About what?'

She leant back. 'You turn up, fresh out of university, with no previous campaigning experience, claiming to be able to get us information on government involvement in weather modification. We're curious so we take you on, give you a bit of rope. We even hand you Mrs Clarke - interesting coincidence that, her turning up so soon after you - but let's not get side-tracked.' She stood and walked round the desk, stopping behind Alex.

Should he turn round? What the hell was going on?

She continued. 'Then I hear you're a bona fide employee of your father's company. That gives me something of a dilemma.'

'I don't see why.'

Madeline's hands weighed heavy on his shoulders. 'Do I berate you for being less than honest with me or congratulate you for infiltrating an organisation to get us the information we're after?' She paused. 'Nothing to say, Alex?' She spun his chair round. 'Just one more question then. Which organisation have you infiltrated, Alex?' She flung the words at him. 'SkySearch or Earthshield? Exactly who are you working for?'

The penny dropped. 'Earthshield. You. I persuaded my father to give me a job to get the information you want. This is important - I don't want to stuff up. Getting what I needed from my old man was the obvious way to do it.'

Madeline sat down. 'How long have you been with us, Alex?'

'A few weeks.'

'And how old are you?'

'Twenty-three.'

'Have we made such a fundamental impression on you that after a few short weeks your loyalty to us, to Earthshield, is stronger than your twenty-three year old loyalty to your father? Is that what you're telling me, Alex?'

'Yes... no - it's not like that.'

'So what is it like?' She waited.

'I'm an investigative journalist. I'm not interested in reporting village fetes, charity shows or... domestics. I want to prove myself, and this is how I can do it.'

'But if this is true,' she waved his report at him, 'to prove yourself here you'll have to betray your father.' She looked straight at him. 'I don't see you hanging your father out to dry. I need employees I can trust; people who are a hundred per cent behind the cause.' She paused. 'I think this is where you and I part company Alex, don't you?'

'No,' he blurted out. 'No, I don't. Give me a chance, a trial period, at least until I've found out what's going on.'

She picked up his report and read. '*There's evidence to indicate that a programme of ionospheric experimentation, code-named LYRE, is about to be commissioned by the Ministry of Defence. These experiments may have a catastrophic impact on human behaviour.* Sounds pretty clear-cut to me. These experiments can't be allowed to go ahead.'

'You need me. I'm inside the company. Elliott knows me...'

'Elliott?'

She was playing him and he'd fallen right into it. 'If you want information, I can get it.'

'There can't be any half measures, Alex, not with something like this.'

'But my father wouldn't be part of anything destructive.'

'I imagine the guys who split the atom were loving fathers too, but once the technology is out there people will always use its destructive potential. Always. We can't allow that to happen. We have to find a way of stopping it, and that's going to mean shutting your father's company down. His life's work, his pension, his future, all shattered - by you. How does that make you feel, Alex?'

How did he feel? His father was sucked in so deep who knows what he might do? Powell had to be stopped. Maybe this was true loyalty.

'Take your time Alex.' Was it his imagination or was her voice softer? Sounding so like his mother.

'There are things... I didn't include.' He nodded at the report.

'Yes?'

'My father's partner...'

'Richard Powell?'

'Yes. He's got a hold over my father because of the cloud seeding scare.'

159

'Ingrid Clarke's story?'

'It's not a story. They were involved, and liable if it can be proved. Powell did something to stop it coming out. He can't risk the company being investigated before LYRE is signed.'

'And this "something" is the hold he has on your father?'

'Yes.'

'If your father had any backbone he'd stand up to Powell, whatever the consequences.'

'Would you... if you could be charged with conspiracy to murder?'

'Christ. Wait here.' She left the room.

Alex leant on the desk. How the hell had they got here?

The door opened. 'I want Sophie in on this.' Madeline ushered in his potential dinner date. 'I gather you haven't been properly introduced. Alex this is Sophie, my daughter.'

He didn't usually put both feet in quite so emphatically. 'I guess dinner's off?'

'Definitely.'

'Thought so.'

'But lunch is good.' She turned to her mother. 'What's the plan?'

'If it can be proven SkySearch were liable for Lynmouth that deals with the first problem - and possibly the second too.'

'Okay,' Sophie handed Alex his report and opened the door. 'Let's get a strategy sorted. Pizza or pie?'

Mark Forrester didn't usually visit Lynton Cottage Hospital on a Saturday, but these circumstances were anything but usual. He nodded a greeting to the elderly parishioner sitting in the waiting room but his eyes were scanning the beds for the stranger that, after a long visit with Julie, he felt he knew intimately. He found her in a small private room off the main ward.

'Good morning.' There was no response. 'You've had a lucky escape by all accounts.' He pulled a chair closer. 'Almost swept away according to the young couple that found you.'

Silence.

'So how are you? Still a bit battered and bruised I expect. Sister tells me this is your second stay with us in as many weeks. How is the shoulder?' Ingrid closed her eyes. 'I know...' he paused. 'I know a little about why you're here.' She turned her head away. 'If it would help to talk that's what I'm here for.'

Was she shutting out the reality of the ward, the events that had brought her here or an entire lifetime of deception? How did anyone cope with guilt they'd denied for over thirty years? 'I'll come back tomorrow. Maybe you'll feel like talking then.'

He stood, replaced the chair and walked down the ward to the office. 'Morning, Sister. Are you planning on keeping your patient in the private room for long?'

'I don't expect so. We'll probably move her into the general ward tomorrow.'

'Any chance of tonight? Be easier to keep an eye on her.'

She smiled. 'Why don't you just come out with it, Mark? I've a medicine round to attend to.'

'Might be wise to keep her under observation. She's struggling, emotionally, and may take things into her own hands.'

'Suicide risk?'

'Maybe.'

Ingrid hated being exposed to this inane world. From dawn to dusk the cackling women on the main ward never tired of their symptoms. One more mention of enemas and she'd slit her wrists. Saying it like that, in a perfectly ordinary sentence, made it sound quite acceptable. They were only words after all. Those good old vibrations. 'Slit my wrists,' she muttered. 'Slit my wrists.' What was a 'slit' anyway? Peculiar word. 'Slit. S...l...i...t.' That was better; dragging it out reflected the action more.

And why wrists? How on earth did anyone come up with the word wrists for a bendy bit between the hand and the arm? It didn't make sense; nothing made sense. Probably because she was dead. Jack had said it. 'Ingrid is dead.' That's what he'd said. Julie had said it. Everyone wanted her dead, and she had always done what everyone wanted. Best not to go there. Best not to. 'Best not.'

'Best not to what?'

Despite herself, Ingrid opened her eyes. The vicar was sitting beside her. 'How long have you been there?'

'Long enough to know you might appreciate sharing the load, while you recover.'

'Why should I want to do that?'

'I don't know. Why should you?'

What kind of crazy response was that! Where was the sympathy, the encouragement to keep her going? Not that she wanted any of it.

'So what's the answer?' he persisted.

'To what?'

'To why you should want to recover.'

'I don't.'

'But if you did, what would the answer be?'

'What kind of a question is that?' Ingrid shut her eyes.

'Tell me tomorrow,' he said, placing his chair back against the wall.

'Sod off,' she hissed under her breath.

'Mind if I come in?' Twenty four hours later Mark was back.

'Do what you like,' Ingrid responded, staring at the ceiling.

'I'll take that as a yes.' They sat in silence. 'Sister says you're okay to be discharged in a couple of days. Will you go home?'

Silence.

'Is there someone I can contact for you?'

Silence.

'Sister tells me you haven't got up yet. It's a lovely day, why don't we go and sit outside for a bit?'

'Why don't you leave me alone?'

'Because I think you're quite alone enough as it is.'

'It wasn't a question.'

'Sounded like one. I'm not leaving you alone because you're struggling and I can help. Did you think about the question?'

'What question?'

'About why you should want to recover.'

'I'm sick to death of should's.'

'That's your choice.'

'What is?'

'Being sick to death. If that's what you really want, then your body will oblige. Is that what you really want?'

'Be easier.'

'Quite probably, and is it what you want?'

'How the hell do I know?'

'Being in hell is often a great place to be. Sometimes we start to see through all the baggage of our lives and get a clear view of what we want and what we'd rather leave behind. What do you want to leave behind?'

'Everything. There's nothing left.'

'You're left.'

Ingrid pulled herself up. 'What bit of me exactly? You've obviously been talking to Julie, so what bit of me do you think is still here? Anything of Ingrid left? According to my husband, only of course he isn't my husband, Ingrid is dead. Worse than that, Ingrid never existed - not past the age of twenty-two anyway. So maybe these bits that are left are all Moira. But she's dead too, Julie said so. The memorial says so. So who exactly is left? Can you tell me that?'

'Yes, I can. The woman who fought for life in the river is left. Look at your hands.' The heavy bandages had been removed leaving the wheals across her palms covered by light gauze gloves. 'The branch cut deep into the tissue but your hands refused to let go. Why? Why endure such pain if you didn't want to live?'

'Maybe I thought I deserved to suffer. Maybe letting go was the easy way out.'

'So the easy way out was there but you chose not to take it. There's still some suffering for you to do so you hung on to life.' He paused. 'That gives me a dilemma. I help you release the suffering - you give up on life. I'm not too comfortable with that. So maybe I'll leave you with your suffering.'

'You think I choose to suffer!' Ingrid threw the words back at the infuriating figure by her bedside.

'Not consciously perhaps.'

'I want to rest.' Ingrid slumped back beneath the bedclothes. There was only one pain in her life and he was sitting right next to her.

'Where will you go?'

'What?'

'When they discharge you. Where will you go?'

Where would she go? She'd chosen to ignore talk of recovery and release. This anonymous hospital ward suited her, it held her life in suspension; there was nothing to think or feel in here.

'Physically there's nothing keeping you in this bed. They'll have to discharge you. But there are options that will keep the world at bay until you're ready for it. Would you like me to arrange something?'

A curt nod was all Ingrid could manage. Anything to get him to go away and leave her in peace.

'Okay.' He squeezed her arm. It took Ingrid a while to numb the area sufficiently for his touch not to matter.

'The car's waiting for you.' It was the second time the nurse had come for her.

'Yes,' she said, meaning no of course. She wasn't ready at all.

'I've put a case of things in the boot for you. People have been so generous; I hope you like what we've selected.' She paused. 'Well, enjoy your stay at the Abbey.'

The vicar had arranged it. She was going to a local community for rest and recuperation. Some rest. It was filled with holidaymakers. Ingrid looked towards the fire door at the other end of the ward. Her whole body ached but surely to goodness she could make it to the bus and freedom. She hauled herself out of the chair and across the room. The bar was stiff but the door eventually gave way, opening out onto a metal fire escape.

'I won't stop you running. But are you sure that's what you want?' Mark was standing behind her.

'I'm not running. Anyway, what's it to you?'

'The car's waiting out front. Shall we go?'

Ingrid slumped against the wall. It was always the same. Always would be. Her wishes counted for nothing. She walked back up the ward, refusing his arm.

The sun was blinding. She could hear voices but there were no pictures to go with the soundtrack. Mark guided her towards the car.

'Stop.' There was one sound she couldn't ignore. It had been a long time, but there are some things you don't forget. She put a hand up to shade her eyes and looked across the street, straight into the face of Frank Williams, berating the woman standing beside him. 'Who is she?' Ingrid asked.

'His wife.'

'Oh.' This was too good to miss. Ingrid walked awkwardly across the road. 'Hello, Frank,' she said.

'Morning,' he grunted.

'Some things never change do they?'

'What?' He stared at her.

'I apologise for my husband.' Mrs Williams smiled nervously at her.

'Please don't apologise. I know exactly what he's like.'

'Do we know each other?' he said.

'Oh yes, we know each other very well.'

'I'd like to know how because...' he paused, half turned away then looked back at her.

'Penny starting to drop is it, Frank? If I said that this lady isn't your wife, that she can't be, would that help?'

'What does she mean?' The woman tugged at his arm. 'Frank?'

He shrugged her off. 'Nothing. Nothing... doesn't know what she's talking about.' But his hands were trembling.

'Because dead women can't talk. Is that right, Frank?'

'Moira? What the hell? Where have you...' he stuttered.

'It's been a long time but some things don't change do they? You're still the ugly bastard you were thirty years ago when I decided being dead was better than putting up with one more day of your bullying.' She turned to the woman. 'I was young; what's your excuse for letting him walk all over you?'

They were attracting a crowd. 'So what if you are Moira,' he hissed, recovering himself. 'What's it to me? Crawl back where you came from and leave us alone.'

'You bastard. You destroyed my life and you're going to pay for it.'

'How do you work that out?'

'Do you know how long bigamists get?' Ingrid's voice was becoming shrill. 'I can tell you.'

'Come on, Eileen,' he took his wife's arm and steered her along the pavement.

Ingrid called after him. 'I'm alive, so we're still married, and that makes you a bigamist - several times over.'

He turned, stared at her and began to laugh, softly, bizarrely. 'You stupid cow. Come back after all this time to threaten me have you? You're dead. It's official. I'm free to marry who I bloody well like and you can't do a thing about it.'

Frank Williams strode off. The crowd of onlookers began to drift away - all but one. The elderly man standing by the vicar hesitated then took a step towards Ingrid. 'Excuse me but...'

'Enjoy the show did you?' Ingrid interrupted, barely seeing him through the tears filling her eyes. She pushed by him and slumped into the back of the waiting car.

It was three minutes past eleven. He was late. Ingrid walked to the window of the Abbey's garden room. Any other time she'd have been transfixed by the view across the tended grounds to the sheep pasture and the sea beyond. But not now; the path through the long grass to the beach would have to wait.

'Morning.' Mark, as always, was irritatingly upbeat.

'You're late.'

'It's good to see you too.'

'They want me to stay another week.'

'That's great.'

'Why? I've been here two weeks already and I'm not getting anywhere.'

'Where do you want to get?'

'Out of this.'

'Out of what?'

'Stop tormenting me with questions. That's all it is, questions, questions, questions. I've had enough.'

'Okay.'

'What do you mean, okay?'

'You've had enough. That's fine.'

'How can it be fine? Aren't you meant to care about saving people like me?'

'Saving people... that sounds a bit like banking them. Saving them for a rainy day,' Mark laughed. 'I've never thought about it that way.'

'You think my life is something to laugh about do you?'

'I do actually. All life is meant to be something we can laugh about, something to enjoy, something to celebrate. And you will again, when you're ready.'

'When I'm ready! So as far as you're concerned, this nightmare is down to me being uncooperative is it? "Oh don't worry, Ingrid will come to her senses soon enough".'

'I'd never have used those words but you may have put your finger on it. When you're ready you will find your senses, and everything else that makes you who you are.'

'Oh yes, and how do you suggest I do that?'

'Let us in. Let the people here hold you until you're ready to hold yourself. When we resist something it's like pulling on a chain that's hooked into an eye. The more you pull the tighter it gets. Release the tension in the chain and you have some slack to slip the hook out of the eye.'

'Meaning?'

Mark smiled. 'Let me ask you this... what do you want?'

'I don't know. I don't want to live with this awful weight.'

'That's great, and that's what you *don't* want. Now tell me what you *do* want.'

'I never get it right do I? Never give you the answer you want.'

'I hope not. It's what *you* want that's important.'

'What I want...' Ingrid repeated. They were only words. But they were suffocating her. She wanted to scream.

'I want it to be over, I want to be free of them, free of their eyes, their words, their fear, their... Oh, what's the point? It's all too long ago.'

'How long ago?'

'Way back, forever, I don't know.'

'So go way back, see young... Moira. How is she feeling? What is she feeling? It's time she was heard. Tell her you're listening. Tell her it's okay to let the feelings out. Tell her it's time to let it go.'

Didn't he know that she couldn't let go, that she had to keep it all inside, that it would destroy her? But suddenly the familiar voice wasn't alone. There was another one, whispering that maybe this was the time, this was the place. The cry started somewhere way, way back, breaking through childhood days filled with fear, through all her trapped and cowering adult years, reaching its climax on the banks of the East Lynn River. It was a deep shuddering cry that released a stream of tears.

Mark held her until the crying finally ceased. 'Tell me,' he said.

Ingrid shook her head. 'What's to tell?'

'The truth.'

'About what?'

'The pain you've lived with all these years.'

The tears welled up again. She pressed her hands against her eyes. 'What's the point? You can't change anything.'

'No, but you can.'

'But it's not as if they were violent or threw me out on the streets or anything. It was the kind of childhood anyone has. You do as you're told. You survive and you get out.'

'Were you happy?'

Ingrid stared at him. 'Happy?'

'As a child, were you happy?'

'At times, when I was down the woods, on my own.'

'And when you were home?'

Ingrid shuddered. 'I don't remember.'

'But perhaps young Moira remembers. Reassure her that she has you, a loving, adult, you at her side. She isn't alone. Tell her it's safe to remember. Tell her you love her and she's safe.'

'Oh God,' Ingrid sobbed, 'Moira never heard those words. Why couldn't he ever say them?'

'He?'

'My father.'

'No father wants to cause his beautiful daughter such pain.'

'So why did he? I could never get it right. Why wasn't I enough? Why couldn't he love me?'

'I'm sure he did - as best he could. But perhaps his parents were never able to love him as he needed to be loved. All he could do was love as he'd been taught to love, which sadly wasn't enough for either of you.'

'I don't understand.'

'With time you will. But the only love you need right now is your own.'

'That's just as well; I've made a mess of finding it with anyone else.'

'How was it with your husband?'

'Suffocating. There was only room for one "I want" and it wasn't mine. The first time anyway.'

'And the second?'

What of Jack? Surely he had loved her, cherished her. But where does cherishing end and possession begin? 'He's a good man, but...' Ingrid paused. It was time for honesty. 'He's like my father, deciding what I want, who I am.'

'So what do you want?'

'To be free... I want to be myself.'

'Of course. So now we begin.'

Chapter Sixteen

There was a tap at the door. 'I'm off, Mr Carmichael. Will you be long? Admin are waiting to close the files.'

'I'll take them through myself, Glenda,' Steven said, his attention fixed on the papers covering his desk.

'But they...'

'Thank you, Glenda.'

'Night then,' she said.

Steven was only vaguely aware of the door closing. It was a shock to see how close to the wire they were trading. They needed the LYRE contract signed, and quickly.

It took him more than an hour to find it - the hefty petty cash payment Powell had withdrawn for expenses. Expenses! Bad enough when he thought it was bribery but now he knew it was blood money... 'Bastard!' he shouted in the direction of Powell's office. 'Damn you! Damn your deals.' Deals made without his knowledge or sanction. Signing away their liability...! He was shaking, the trembling of a trapped prey, powerless to do anything but react moment by moment. It had always been that way. Powell acted, he reacted. Now he was in so deep there was no way out but Powell's way.

Unless...

He pushed his chair back and began to pace. Five minutes later he picked up his pen and scribbled a note. 'What do you think, Martha?' he muttered. 'Sanest thing I've done for years or utter lunacy?' He shook his head and walked through to Powell's office. The private line was ringing.

'SkySearch,' Steven answered, vaguely aware of the clicking of the machine on Powell's desk, automatically recording the call.

'About time.' The voice was harsh, abrupt. 'I want more.'

'More?'

'For the woman.'

'What are you...?'

'My minders are getting curious. You've got a day. No money, no deal.'

'Wait! I'll have to talk with my partner.'

'No. I deal with you. Just you, Powell. Like always.' The line went dead.

The security checks seemed to take even longer when Steven arrived at SkySearch the following day.

'Have you seen Powell, Glenda?'

'Mr Powell's in his office, Mr Carmichael. Shall I tell him...?'

Steven was already on his way through the door. 'What was the last contact you had with Hoskins?'

'Last week, when I paid him off,' Powell said.

'What did you tell him?' Steven said.

'With Guy out of the picture his instructions were to keep a watching brief on the woman.'

'A watching brief. That was it? You didn't give him any further instructions?'

'No.'

'Is this what you call a watching brief.' Steven pushed a newspaper headline in front of Powell. *Lynmouth river almost claims its second victim. Middle-aged woman, Moira Williams, admitted to hospital.*

'This Moira Williams, she was the woman you paid him to watch, yes?'

'What if I did? You were so bloody cavalier about it. Just because she was a woman she wasn't a threat. Hoskins called me. He heard it all. Apparently Mrs Moira Williams, missing presumed dead after the Lynmouth floods, reincarnated herself as Mrs Ingrid Clarke of the Salisbury Post. Our delicate little journalist from Salisbury was a bigamist and double murderer!'

'What?'

'You heard.'

'Say it again - her name.'

'Names don't you mean. Moira Williams alias Ingrid Clarke. It was her husband that blew the whole thing wide open. It was classic!'

'Ingrid Clarke?' Steven struggled to concentrate.

'Husband walks out on her, friend chucks her out of the house and according to Hoskins, she's wandering by the river looking like she's going to end it all. Only,' he pointed at the paper, 'it looks like she ballsed it up.'

'No,' Steven shouted. 'You ballsed it up. You ballsed it up when you drafted that contract thirty years ago. You ballsed it up when you started negotiating with Hoskins. You ballsed it up when you briefed him to intimidate that woman. She doesn't deserve any of this.'

'Your sudden concern is very touching.'

'I didn't know who it was...'

It was Powell's turn to look amazed. 'And you do now?'

'I've met Ingrid Clarke, yes.'

'Does she know? About you and SkySearch?'

'No, I don't think so. It was through my...'

'Your what?'

'It doesn't matter.'

'It does if she's put two and two together.'

'She's already in a hospital bed; isn't that enough for you?'

'Shut up and let me think.'

'No. You shut up. I've let this go far enough. Much too far,' Steven said.

'Oh, the worm has turned has it? Do what you do best and crawl back in to the woodwork. I'll sort this.'

'No! Not anymore. There's got to be another way.' He paused. 'When are they going to sign up to LYRE?'

'A couple of weeks, three at most.'

'Can they get out of the contract?'

'Are you kidding?'

'No liability resting with us then?' Steven's voice was heavy with sarcasm.

'Get to the point.'

'I'll keep her out of the way until then.'

'How exactly do you plan to do that?'

'That's my business.'

'Going to hit her with the full force of your personality are you, Steven? Ask her nicely not to say anything?'

'I'm not going to hit her with anything - that's your speciality.'

Powell scowled. 'And afterwards? When the shit hits the fan and we have to hand over every penny in compensation? What brilliant plan are you going to come up with then?'

'I don't know, but I'm telling you I can buy us time now.'

'Not good enough.' Powell lifted the handset of his phone.

'What are you doing?'

'Fixing it.'

Steven wrenched the phone out of Powell's hand. 'No. No more.' He reached into his pocket and waved a tape in front of Powell. 'And if you argue the toss I'll send this to the police.'

'What the fuck's that?'

'I'm very impressed with the way you tape all your calls Richard. Came in very handy when Hoskins rang last night. Very emphatic he was about dealing just with you. And all neatly recorded on this - well when I say on this, of course I mean the original that I've deposited with my solicitor.'

'You're bluffing.'

'Be my guest.' Steven held out the tape.

'You stupid bastard. Well if you think I'm going to stand back and watch every cent I've got invested in this miserable business handed over on some compensation gravy train think again.' Powell walked round the desk to face Steven. 'One way or another I'm taking my money. This partnership is dead in the water, Carmichael. Watch out you don't end up the same way.'

'I agree. This partnership *is* over. And I'm going to make it easy for you.'

'What does that mean?'

'This.' Steven held a memo out to him.

'What the fuck's that?'

'My offer to buy you out.'

Powell grabbed the piece of paper. 'You must be kidding. My share's worth double this.'

'Okay, I'll raise my offer.' He placed the tape on the desk. 'The money, and the original.'

'Anybody home?' Alex shouted. 'Dad?'

'In here.'

Alex threw his coat on a chair, kicked off his shoes and walked through to the sitting room.

Steven was standing by the glass doors, his hand tracing the engraving in the panes. 'Took me three weeks to decide on this. Seemed so important at the time. Crazy to think I wasted so much energy on it now.'

Alex folded himself on to the settee and scooped up the remote control.

'For Christ's sake, Alex,' his father said. 'You've only just walked through the door. Can't you survive five minutes without television?'

'You've never objected before.'

'Well maybe I should have. Anyway, I need to talk to you. I'm selling the house.'

Alex pressed the mute button. 'You can't.'

'I'm buying Powell out of SkySearch. It's the only way I can raise the money.'

'There must be some other way.'

'There isn't. I've been through it too many times.'

'But this house was for mum...'

'You don't need to remind me of that!' Steven turned away. 'I couldn't do it for any other reason. She wanted me to break up the partnership years ago; said Powell was dragging the company the wrong way, going against everything she stood for. I was so stubborn, arguing the toss even when she was right.'

'You're going to pay him to walk away and leave you to carry the can! It doesn't make sense.'

'He's not getting anything like market value.'

'But something's better than nothing - which is all you'll be left with when the compensation claim hits and the business folds.'

'So I need to make sure it doesn't.'

'Face reality, dad. SkySearch is as good as over. You're going to need every penny you've got in this house for yourself.'

'You don't know that.'

'I do.'

'I just need some time.'

Alex sighed. His father wasn't listening.

'If I can keep Ingrid Clarke quiet until this last contract is signed...'

'Ingrid; how do you know about Ingrid?'

'...then maybe I can persuade her...'

'Hang on a minute. What do you mean, persuade her...?'

Steven paused. 'Convince her that the seeding couldn't possibly have caused the tragedy.'

'But the evidence...' Alex stopped. Madeline was right. Right now he had no idea where his loyalties lay.

'I'm leaving for Lynmouth as soon as I've got a few things together. We got on pretty well. After everything she's been through she might welcome some company.' Steven was thinking aloud. 'Yes, I mean, I'm just your father, bumping into her while I'm up there on business. Maybe I should take the file...' Steven walked through to his study.

'What file?' Alex asked from the doorway.

'What? Oh, the cloud seeding file. Powell wanted to destroy it but I got to it first. It will prove our seeding had nothing to do with Lynmouth. Because it didn't, Alex. It was nowhere near enough to have had that catastrophic an effect.'

So it was here, at the house. Everything he needed. 'You'd better tell me where it is, just in case.'

Steven hesitated. 'No. I don't want you involved. It'll be safe enough.'

Chapter Seventeen

Ingrid leant back on the bench in the conservatory, losing herself in the scent of a jasmine.

'You've a visitor, Ingrid.' The Abbey administrator was at the door.

'Ann, before you go, I'm sorry I've been such a pain. Thank you, for everything.'

'It's been our pleasure. Glad you're feeling more yourself now.' She stood aside to let someone through.

'I wasn't expecting you today Mark... Oh.'

'Not Mark I'm afraid,' Steven said.

'Mr Carmichael. What are you doing here?'

'Steven, please. I guess this is a bit of a surprise. I should have called first. I'm sorry.' He shifted uncomfortably.

'No. *I'm* sorry. Please, sit down.'

'Thanks.' Steven pulled a cane conservatory chair over. 'I imagine you're wondering what I'm doing here.'

'Well, yes.'

'Alex tried to contact you. He rang your home. Your husband said you'd gone away and he didn't expect you back...'

'He said that?'

'Or something like that. I wasn't paying too much attention to the exact words.'

'No, why should you.' Ingrid stared through the glass. Being in this protective cocoon had lulled her into a false sense of security. It was going to be a while before she could face the reality of Jack.

'Alex seemed to think you might be in some kind of trouble. Serious trouble. He didn't say what but as I was up this way on business I offered to look you up.'

'That's kind of you, both of you, but as you can see, I'm fine.'

'I gather you've had a rough ride.'

Ingrid looked at him. There was something about his presence here, in her sanctuary, that made her uneasy.

'I asked after you at the hospital - because of Alex's worries. I know staff shouldn't talk but...'

'What did they say?'

'Nothing confidential. Just that you'd had an accident in the river and were convalescing here.'

Ingrid's attention wandered to a butterfly beating against the glass. A Red Admiral. Amazing how something so fragile could fight like that.

'I've come at a bad time.' Steven stood.

Ingrid half smiled. 'No, please, stay. I've spent too much time on my own. Maybe you could get us some drinks, from the lobby. A coffee would be good. Weak, one sugar.'

'What is this place?' Steven asked a few moments later, handing her a mug.

'A retreat centre. Perfect after my little moment of drama. I seem to make a habit of being battered and bruised whenever we meet,' Ingrid said.

'How is the shoulder?'

'It aches, but nothing like as bad as it was.'

'If you'd rather not say anything that's fine, but if you want to talk... well, I'm a good listener.'

Ingrid paused. Did she want to talk? After her sessions with Mark she was all talked out, but this felt different. 'I... it's...' She paused.

'Only if you feel like it. Or we could talk about the weather.'

'What do you mean?' Ingrid shot back at him.

'Nothing... nothing at all. Just a figure of speech. You know, weather's looking bad today, bound to rain, yes bound to rain. Meaningful stuff like that.'

'Sorry. Guess I'm still jumpy. Things have been difficult recently.' She paused. 'There's been a family trauma; my husband and I... we've separated.'

'I'm sorry.'

'That's why Alex got the response he did. Jack's still angry. But that's...' She drifted off.

'And how about you? How did you end up in hospital?'

'I took it badly.' This really wasn't the conversation to be having with someone you barely knew. But there was something about Steven Carmichael. He wasn't trying to control her like Jack, full of himself like Nick or relentlessly focused like Mark. He was simply there. 'Anyway, I ended up in the river, hypothermic and in shock when they brought me in.' Maybe next time she'd tell him more. Yes, Ingrid suddenly realised, she'd like there to be a next time.

'Do you fancy a walk? I'm told there are some paths through the woods round here. And it is a lovely day,' he said.

Ingrid looked beyond the glass walls of the conservatory. A peacock was displaying on the lawn, its tail feathers vivid in the sunshine. She walked through the door.

Sophie sank effortlessly into the steel and leather chair in the Carmichael's sitting room. 'You were a long time returning my calls. I was beginning to wonder.'

'Had a lot to think about,' Alex said.

'And?'

'I called didn't I?'

'Yes.' She reached out and touched his arm. 'I'm glad you did.'

'It's good to see you. Thanks for coming over.'

'I'm in Andover tonight anyway - same direction.'

'Business or pleasure?'

'Both.'

'What is the day job?' he asked, handing her a tonic water.

'More of a night job really. I'm a costume designer for a small travelling theatre company.'

'So Earthshield is...'

'My mother's passion and mine when I'm within hailing distance. No, that's not fair, it's my passion too. But she'd swallow me up if I didn't have my own life. I'd like to move out, but theatrical salaries don't allow for private residences in central London with direct access on to the river.'

'That's why I'm shacked up with the old man.'

'Is he around?' Sophie asked.

'No. He's gone... away for a bit. Why? Would it be a problem?'

'Possibly. This project has enough emotional time bombs; I don't particularly want to discover that he's like his son, utterly charming.'

Was that a come-on? 'But all we're doing is watching his back, right?'

Sophie shrugged. 'You do understand my brief is to find a way of stopping LYRE - and that means destroying SkySearch.'

'Do you have to be so brutally honest?'

'Yes.' She sat in silence, refusing to soften the blow.

'Only...'

'You're not having second thoughts are you? You made a promise to my mother.'

'I know. I won't let you down.' He paused, allowing her presence to ease his conscience. 'So how are you going to do it?'

'You tell me.'

Alex was being reminded of his commitment to deliver. 'It's here somewhere.'

'What is?'

'The SkySearch file on cloud seeding, with a report on Lynmouth.'

'Did you get to read it?'

'No, but it's definitely here.'

'Where?'

'I don't know; in my father's study somewhere.'

'Has he got a safe?' she snapped.

'I don't know.'

'You don't know!'

'It's my father's study; I respect his space.'

'Well right now you're an investigative journalist, not a son. Think.' She was already searching the massive beech desk that filled the centre of the room. 'What's moved? Furniture, clocks, papers... anything?'

Alex looked around. 'Nothing obvious.'

'When you were here with your father, where did he stand? Was he obscuring anything?'

'I don't know...'

'Close your eyes, picture it. Where was he?'

Like mother, like daughter, Alex thought. This woman would make a great interrogator. 'He was standing in front of the desk.'

'Here?' She stood between the chair and the desk.

'No, in front of it, here.' Alex moved to the opposite side. Sophie sat on the desktop and swung her legs over until they were resting beside his.

'Budge over.' She ran her hand along the underside of the lip at the back of the desk. 'Yes,' she exclaimed. She threw herself onto the floor and edged underneath, leaving her long slender legs exposed.

'Is this it?' she asked. Alex forced himself to look at the red folder she was pushing in his direction.

'Where did you find that?'

She placed the file in front of them. 'I came across a desk like this at an oil company I was - well, what I was doing is irrelevant. It's a clever design. So what have we got?' She flicked through the pages. Statistics on cloud seeding, research conclusions, costings, flight plans, meteorological charts, personnel... 'Have you got a photocopier?'

'I can use the fax.'

'Start with this.' She handed him a flight plan for August 15th 1952.

'Good Morning,' Steven called through the car window. 'You're up bright and early.'

Ingrid had been perched on the wall outside the Abbey for at least fifteen minutes, alone except for the solitary figure sitting on a bench on the hillside opposite; too far away to see clearly but unmistakable. He was there most days, but never inside the Abbey.

'I didn't want to miss my chauffeur,' she said, smiling at Steven. She opened the door and settled herself into the passenger seat. He'd turned up every day for the past week, happy to wander down to the beach or play scrabble in the Abbey library. He was such easy company, the perfect antidote to her sessions with Mark. She needed them, she knew she did, but Steven offered pure escapism. Nothing cluttered their days; no shadows from the past, nor from the future come to that. 'Where are we going?' she asked. This was the first time he'd suggested going out in the car, away from the Abbey.

'Wherever you want.'

'How about Hunter's Inn?'

He turned right, onto the narrow winding lane that clung to the coast. It was slow going, constantly pulling in to let other cars go by. 'Will you be going soon?' Ingrid asked.

'I might stay on for a bit.'

'Can you do that?'

'Maybe. Would you mind?'

Ingrid smiled. 'No, I'd like it.' She paused while he negotiated a hairpin bend. 'You never did say what your business is up here.'

'Oh, it's to do with my company - supplying information to farmers. I've been looking for more contracts.'

'What kind of information?'

'New technology, that kind of thing. But I've got some leave owing. And I can't think of a better place to take it.'

'You like it here?'

'Love it.'

'Don't you miss the city?'

'Not really. I've been thinking for a while that I should move on. Since Martha died it's not been the same. Time for a fresh start. How about you?'

'I don't know. My life's been more of a series of false starts.'

'Not with you.'

They had been climbing steadily through the trees, soft sunlight breaking through here and there, creating a kaleidoscope on the rough surface of the lane. But now they had reached the tree line, emerging onto a sea of purple heather-covered moorland stretching ahead towards Holdstone Down. 'Can we stop? I love this view,' Ingrid said.

Steven pulled the car over to the edge of the cliff, spread a rug out on the ground and lifted out a cold bag. 'What would you like? Salad, sandwiches; a glass of wine?'

'I'm feeling spoiled.'

'That was the general idea.'

Ingrid settled herself on the rug next to Steven. It was a beautiful day, clear all the way to the Black Mountains across the Bristol Channel.

'I'm not surprised you don't understand, about my false starts I mean. Not sure I do. The vicar here, Mark, has helped a lot but I guess I'm still trying to make sense of everything.' She took a sip of wine. 'When I told you I took it badly, with Jack, that was a bit of an understatement. I tried to commit suicide.'

'By the river?'

'Yes. Things hadn't been right for a long time but then Jack... well he did something that brought everything to a head. There are things in my past that were too painful. I ran... sort of started again. When Jack found out, well, that was it.'

'I'm sorry.'

'Please, don't offer me sympathy; I don't deserve it. You know how you can be so fed up with someone all you want to do is get away, but when you risk losing them suddenly it's the worst thing you can imagine? Maybe you don't, but I felt as though I had no-one left. No family, no friends.'

'No-one?'

'Not that mattered. I tried to ask an old friend's forgiveness for something, to explain that it wasn't my fault, that someone else was to blame, but she wouldn't listen.'

'To blame for what?'

Ingrid paused. 'Do you know anything about the Lynmouth floods?'

'A bit. Back in '52 weren't they?'

'Yes. Something happened that I thought was my fault, only now I know it wasn't, it wasn't me at all.' She paused. 'It's amazing what goes on that we haven't a clue about.'

'Like...?'

'Like what caused the floods.'

'No mystery there, it was a natural disaster wasn't it? A tragic one but just the result of too much rain.'

'Precisely. Too much rain. More than could be created naturally.'

'What are you saying?'

'Did you know that the Government commissioned experiments in artificial rainmaking? They were doing it just before the floods.'

'How do you know?'

'I just do.' She shuddered and bent her head.

Steven rested his arm around her shoulders. 'Maybe some things are best left in the past. Maybe whatever haunts you was left behind at the river.'

'I hadn't thought of it like that. All I could think about was ending it.'

Steven placed his other hand gently over hers. 'One thing I do know,' he said, his voice unsteady, 'I thank God you didn't succeed.'

She leant back against him. 'How do you do it, Steven?'

'Do what?'

'Make everything okay. Sitting here with you I can't imagine how anything could possibly be wrong.'

'You've had a lot to cope with. It's hard doing that alone.'

'Yes, it is. I guess I'm still getting used to being on my own.'

'Not completely I hope.'

Ingrid smiled up at him. 'No. But there are some decisions I have to make for myself.'

'Yes?'

Ingrid pulled her hand away and leant forward.

'Sorry, none of my business,' Steven said.

'I don't mind. Really.' She topped up her wine glass, and walked to the edge of the cliff. Steven half rose. 'Only it's not that easy. Sometimes we have to take the right decision even if we stand to suffer. Then again, maybe it's not that hard either. I don't have much to lose.'

'Don't say that.' The words were out before he could stop them. 'Others may feel there's a great deal to lose.'

Chapter Eighteen

King Lear adjusted his costume and stepped out onto the heath provided, for one night only, by the gravelled terrace outside Julie Davenport's drawing room. The Twin Town's Literary Festival was in full swing and the crowds had been piling along the driveway since early afternoon for this year's 'Shakespeare at the Manor'. A collection of garden chairs and improvised tablecloths covered the lawns as a convivial mix of locals and holidaymakers settled in to enjoy the performance. Weaving between them were volunteers wielding bright yellow buckets inviting contributions to the church roof fund. Even the weather was playing along. It was a beautifully still, summer's day - until the actors stepped out for Act III when the prop man's thunder roared and lightning flashed as King Lear raised his voice above the storm.

'Blow, winds and crack your cheeks! Rage! Blow!
You cataracts and hurricanes, spout
Till you have drench'd our steeples, drown'd the cocks!
You sulphurous and thought-executing fires...'

'What do you think of it so far?' Julie whispered.

'Great night for the church roof,' Mark replied. 'The play's good too.'

'Can't believe how lucky we've been with the weather.'

'And the forecast is good for the last couple of days so it looks like we've got away with it.'

'Got away with it?'

'Not having the wet weather insurance.'

Julie smiled.

'So what happens now?' Mark asked.

'What do you mean?'

'Well, you've spent every waking hour, and a good few sleeping ones, making a success of this festival. So now you're either looking forward to a well-deserved break with nothing more than long rides on Blackmore to worry about or...'

'Or what?'

'Or you'll be looking for something else to stop you thinking about Moira.'

Julie flinched.

'She's still here,' he pointed to his head, 'isn't she?'

'No... I don't know. I mean, it happened. You can't change that. But I'd almost managed to forget, hardly thought about her.'

'Until she turned up on your doorstep, very much alive.'

'Yes.' Julie paused. 'I've tried to push her back into the past, where she belongs but... it's not that easy.'

'No.'

'So what do I do?'

'Talk to her.'

'No! No. I can't.'

'She's been through a lot. Might not be as difficult as you think.'

'You're asking me to feel sorry for her?'

'No, but compassion maybe, for both of you. How are you going to move on until all of you, including Hugh and the boys, are at peace with this?'

She pressed her hand against her forehead. 'I can't... I can't forgive her.' The words caught in her throat.

'So she's to blame?'

'Of course she is.'

'Of course?'

'Well, if she isn't, who is?'

'Maybe you think you are, for not looking out for your

children. Maybe Hugh because he wasn't there when you needed him. Maybe having someone else to blame, someone not too close to home, eases the pain.'

'No... I don't know.' She clasped her arms across her chest. 'How can I live with myself if I'm to blame? Look what it did to Hugh!'

'Maybe no one was to blame. Maybe it was just a terrible accident.'

Julie stood. 'I can't do this, Mark. I have to get on.'

'Call me... anytime.'

Julie circled the audience and the tented area set aside for the actors, and entered the Manor through the kitchens. Why did Mark have to keep bringing it up? She'd almost forced Moira out of her mind again. Hadn't she?

She looked along the corridor to the hallway, to the magnificent oak staircase and the cellar door, normally perfectly concealed in the panelling. Only today it was ajar, almost inviting her... Julie crossed the flagstones and switched on the light. The steps were worn, but not by her. She'd only been down a handful of times in the last thirty years, with the things that were too painful to see but too precious to let go.

She edged her way down into the gloom, just able to make out the two brown leather cases lodged high on the metal shelving, their straps tightly fastened. 'I'll never open them again, never even look at them,' she'd said to Hugh. 'I just need to know they're there.' A stepladder hung on a hook at the end of the shelving. Strange. Forward thinking hadn't been one of Hugh's strong points, but Julie was grateful for it now. She opened the steps.

It was a struggle getting the heavy case down and it slipped out of her grasp. But neither the fall nor her efforts to slide the catches worked - they were rusted shut. Maybe the other one would be easier. She moved the steps along, climbed up and reached for the second case. But her hand brushed against something else, another handle. She pulled it towards her. It was an official document briefcase, the leather hardened, cracked with age. And it was locked. 'That's curious.'

She carried the briefcase upstairs, to Hugh's study, chosen because of the view the deep sash windows offered of the parkland. Julie smiled. He'd loved to watch the deer grazing their way down to the river; such a wonderful combination of grace and alertness. When he died she couldn't bring herself to change anything and somehow, as the years passed, didn't feel the need. With seventeen rooms she was hardly short of space.

Where to start? If it was Hugh's case he must have had a key. His desk was the obvious place to look, a fine mahogany roll-top he'd discovered in an auction at Dunster just along the coast. The price went far too high but Hugh had wanted it so much. She pulled out the small drawer at the centre of the pigeonholes; perfect for the small, important things that regularly get lost. She was right. There were keys, several, but none that fitted this lock.

The drawers below were filled with Hugh's files - on his restoration of the stables, work for the festival, the estate farms, the Manor, Air Crew reunions and goodness how many on orchids. But there was no sign of a key. 'So where is it, Hugh? You may as well tell me because by hook or by crook, I'm going to get into it.'

She pulled out the Air Crew file. He hadn't been to any reunions since the early '50s when he stopped flying, retired sick with depression. It wasn't a risk the RAF wanted to take. No, it wasn't the RAF by then was it? Julie searched her memory. He was transferred to some other outfit, but whoever it was couldn't take the risk of putting up a pilot who'd lost sight of the value of life. He retreated into estate routine, living a half-life until that too lost all meaning for him.

But still no sign of a key. 'What the hell,' she declared, trying to prise the catch apart with her beautifully manicured nails. Three casualties later a laughing fit overtook her. It came from nowhere as Hugh's voice, as clear as if he were standing beside her, rang through the room, horrified. He'd loved her slim, delicate hands. They were the reason his father had decided to give their marriage his blessing. 'That girl's hands show breeding,' Mr Davenport senior had said.

Julie smiled; how lovely to be thinking of Hugh with laughter. It was like stumbling across an old movie and finding it wasn't grey and faded after all, but flooded with colour.

'Ready for coffee?' Julie asked, wrapping her arms around Hugh as he leant over his desk.

'I'll say,' he replied, turning to place his hands on her hips, drawing her close.

'It's wonderful to have you back. Are you home for a while?'

'Should be. Only a few sub-contracts for a research firm in hand, nothing exciting.'

'Doing what.'

'You know I can't tell you.'

'Why not? The war's over. What's so secret?'

'Stop fishing.' He turned back to his desk. 'Isn't it time you fetched the children?'

'I'm not giving up.'

'I know. But it won't get you anywhere.' He looked at his watch. 'The children?'

'Moira's collecting them.'

'What are you two doing this evening?'

'A bit of ballroom dancing maybe. We're getting good. It's time you took me somewhere to show off.'

'We'd better take Moira along - I've got two left feet.'

'Sounds good to me. She could do with a night away from that bully of a husband.'

'You shouldn't interfere Julie.'

'I can't stand to see him treat her like that.'

'You can't make her leave him.'

'I know, but I'd like to offer her the Lodge, if she ever needed it. Is that all right?'

'As long as Tom's happy in the stable flat.'

'It won't be long-term; just a bolt-hole. Anyway, I'd love to have her closer. It would be company when you go off. When's the next one?'

'Next what?'

Julie threw a cushion at him. 'Don't play ignorant with me, your next trip away.'

'Next week.'

'Oh, no! It's the twins play at school. They've got bigger roles this year and they've been rehearsing so hard to impress you.'

'Might not come off; it depends on conditions. I won't disappoint them without good reason.'

'And there's the dance in the evening. Moira's coming but we could do with some help with the heavy stuff, setting up the stage, that kind of thing.'

'I'll see what I can do.'

Julie kissed him. 'Thank you, you gorgeous man.'

'Mummy, daddy?' The child's voice came from the hall.

Julie opened the door. 'We're in daddy's study.'

'Mummy, Aunty Moira says it's the best drawing of the Valley of the Rocks she's ever seen, look.'

Michael burst into the room, followed by Alistair, both competing to get to Julie with the results of their afternoon's art trip. Michael spotted his father first.

'Daddy! Look mummy, daddy's back.'

'Yes darling. Isn't it great?'

'Look what I've done, daddy. Aunty Moira said it's the best picture she's ever seen of the Valley...'

'Are you there, Moira?' Julie called.

'Just coming,' Moira puffed from halfway up the stairs. 'They started running as soon as they saw your car Hugh.' She slumped onto the couch.

Julie reached out to Alistair. He was always hanging back, letting his brother grab the limelight. It used to upset her, but she'd learnt to accept their differences. Michael had one gear - full speed ahead. His brother was more sensitive, taking his cue from everyone around him before committing himself. 'Where's your picture darling?'

He reached into his bag and took out a crayon sketch. It was very good considering he was only six. 'We'll put this up on the wall, Alistair.'

'No, Michael's is better, Aunty Moira said so.'

'No I didn't Alistair,' Moira said. 'I said Michael's was good, but so is yours.'

'It is, you know it is.' Alistair bolted out of the room. Michael dropped his picture, squirmed out of his father's arms and rushed after him.

Julie turned to Hugh. 'Go after him will you? He's fed up that Michael got to you before he did.'

'What's on the agenda for tonight?' Moira asked as Julie joined her on the couch.

'Ballroom dancing at eight but how about a ride first?'

'That depends on...'

'I know. Just a gentle walk, possibly trotting, but absolutely no gallops.'

'Maybe.'

'No need to be nervous. You're really good when you trust Blackmore to lead you.'

'Ah, trust. That's a tricky one. I'll stick to relying on myself if that's all right.'

'I wish you'd rely on your friends a bit more, let me in sometimes... like when you need to talk, about Frank.' She picked up Moira's hand and tucked it under her arm.

'I waste enough of my life on that lay-about. I'm not going to let him spoil our time together.' She pulled away. 'Come on.'

Julie collided with Hugh at the door. 'We're going for a ride. Is Annie giving the twins their tea?'

'Yes, they're all organised. She's managed to get Alistair out of his shell too. How long will you be?'

'I don't know, an hour maybe. Does it matter?'

'No, not at all, have a good time.' He kissed her and closed the door behind them.

Halfway down the stairs Moira stopped. 'Just a minute, Julie, I've left my bag.' She ran back up into Hugh's study.

Julie heard Hugh's voice. 'What do you want?' he asked sharply.

'Sorry, forgot my bag. I didn't think to knock. Sorry if I disturbed you,' Moira blurted out.

'No, I'm sorry. Please, get your bag... and have a good ride.'

Moira backed out of the room, closing the door behind her. She turned and mouthed at Julie. 'What did I do?'

'Nothing. He had no right to speak to you like that.'

'Oh well, I hope he finds what he was looking for. Come on. Before I change my mind.'

Julie picked up a photo of Hugh from inside the drawer, wiped her sleeve across the glass and placed it on the desk. The briefcase could wait.

Chapter Nineteen

Ingrid walked across the Abbey's tended grounds, over the stile to the sheep pasture and down towards the sea. The sun had broken through the mist, casting a brilliant sheen across the water, inviting holidaymakers in to bathe. She paused at the top of the beach. The small pebbly bay was sheltered by two headlands; to the east high green cliffs pitched downwards and then, in a bull-nosed way, rounded off before meeting the sands. To the west the drop was more precipitous, plunging to a row of layered rocks, jagged edges all pointing out to sea.

Picking her way across the pebbles, Ingrid settled herself against a rock and lifted her face to the warmth. She was alone. Steven had gone, but she still felt his presence. When had she last felt so at home in her own skin? Ever? The tight band of tension that had gripped her all these years was easing. She could breathe again.

Ingrid shielded her eyes with a hand. An elderly couple were heading for his and hers fold up chairs, separated only by a woven picnic basket and two walking sticks. He helped his wife to her chair; she helped him to a sandwich. Perfect harmony could exist, couldn't it?

Beside her, a stream of children poured onto the beach, laughing, shouting - they were making such a noise! Ingrid smiled, remembering a long sandy beach, her mother in the chair, herself and her father together... playing. Playing: the word sounded wrong but how else to describe the absence of boundaries drawn so tight they suffocated?

A child rushed by, clutching his treasures - a bucket full of razor and crab shells; a faded green fisherman's float tied to the handle and blue plastic netting trailing behind. It caught under a boulder beside an elderly man hovering at the top of the beach. He'd probably been a lot taller once but hunched shoulders and natural shrinkage gave him a shrivelled appearance. Ingrid watched as he scanned the beach, his head constantly moving from left to right as though following a one-sided tennis match.

Eric Fairweather supported himself with his stick as he watched the boy release his booty. At least this was a small bay, not like Woolacombe, a massive strand stretching further than his eyes could see or legs could carry him now. In his younger days he'd been glad to haul the windbreak, chairs and picnic basket as far as it took to find space to play without disturbing anyone else's peace. He smiled at the memory. Their painstakingly constructed sand-boats were the best; complete in every detail, with seats they could settle into as the tide swirled back to lift them off, away on a fantasy voyage. They'd travelled all over the world, he and his daughter, in those precious minutes before the sea undermined the walls, sucking their dreams back beneath its waves.

It was a bittersweet experience, their annual week by the sea; wonderful to be free from the production line and the pressure to complete his allocated actions before each metal carcass moved out of reach. But he wasn't free was he? Now he was responsible not just for the weekend, but all day, every day. Decisions to make, dangers to watch for. And then, when his job was done, when he thought he had brought her safely through, she was gone; leaving himself and Sarah going through the motions - until Sarah died of a broken heart. Thirty years ago, all but a month or two.

He'd known. All these years he'd known. That was why he'd moved to Lynmouth, to watch and wait. But now... Maybe it would be easier to turn around, to forget. He'd managed, working all the shifts he could get, then volunteering to keep the parts manuals up to date when he retired. He'd still be doing it if his eyesight hadn't deteriorated so quickly. Glaucoma they said. Something to do with pressure damaging the eyes. He had lots of blind spots now but if he moved his head a certain way he could make things out well enough.

The excited shouts of a group of children clustered at the water's edge distracted Ingrid. They were pointing towards rocks away to her right, calling their parents to share in a discovery. Looking towards the sun made her sneeze. She grabbed a tissue, dislodging a piece of card from her jacket pocket. Only it wasn't card but folded sheets of paper that had got soaked and dried together. Peering at the blurred print she could just make out *sulphur* and *August 15th*.

A few short weeks ago these hastily scrawled words had consumed her. Yet now? Sitting on this beautiful beach, at peace, looking forward to seeing Steven again - what was the point of this scrap of paper? She threw it towards the sea. Let the water come in, take it, wash away the words and the memories.

She looked back at the mother sharing her children's excitement at spotting a seal basking on the rocks. The message was semaphored up the beach to where granny was happily guarding the water wings, buckets and spades at base camp. 'The children have found a seal.'

'Found an eel; do you want the bucket?'

The mother shook her head.

'Excuse me, I believe you dropped this.' The voice was thin, tentative; that's what threw her. If it had been strong and forceful she'd have recognised it in an instant.

Ingrid looked up at the elderly man, holding out the pages she'd thrown to the wind. She took them from his shaking hand. 'Thank you.'

'It is you, Moira, isn't it?' His features were cast into shadow by the sun. 'I imagine I've changed,' he said. 'I'm sorry. I should have asked the vicar to say something. After everything you've been through it was wrong of me to expect...'

'Yes,' she interrupted. 'So how are you?'

'Oh, I have my off days but not so bad considering.' He looked around. 'It's quite nice here isn't it?'

Quite nice! After thirty years her father had appeared out of nowhere... and was talking about how it was "quite nice" here! 'How did you find me? What are you doing here?'

'I asked at the Abbey.'

'Not now, how did you know I was in Lynton?'

'Perhaps he shouldn't have said, but I'm sure he thought it was for the best...'

'Who? What?'

'The vicar.'

'Mark! I don't understand?'

'He knew about the bench, about why I came and...'

Ingrid interrupted. 'Outside the hospital, with Mark. Was that you?'

'Yes.'

Ingrid stared at a small girl trying to launch a kite, her father beside her, gently encouraging but not interfering. She couldn't do it. She couldn't hear this.

'Could I sit down? I'm not so good on my legs these days.' She made room for him. 'I never really believed it, that you were gone. I kept looking for you, at home, down here, scanning the faces, the news, the papers. It broke your mother's heart.'

Ingrid began to gasp. No more collisions please. Push them away, block them out, this wasn't happening. She wasn't sitting on a beautiful North Devon beach with her father, a man she hadn't seen for more than half her lifetime. She took a deep breath and looked at the old man sitting next to her, perspiring with the heat, or perhaps emotion. 'NO,' a voice cried from inside; he doesn't have an emotional bone in his body.

'I missed you so much, Moira, we both did. Your mother refused to go out for weeks on end after the floods in case there was news.'

'I can't hear this; please... don't.'

'I'm sorry. I swore I wouldn't show my feelings. I don't... I don't want to drive you away again.'

'What are you talking about? It wasn't *showing* your feelings that drove me away.'

'I don't understand.'

'No, you never did.'

'All I ever wanted was for you to be happy Moira.'

'That's not how it felt. You never listened, not to me. It was always "don't do this", "don't do that".'

'I was your father. I had a job to do - to keep you safe. His voice faltered. 'What an absurd thing to say. I didn't keep you safe did I?' He paused. 'Why did you go, Moira? What was it? What did I do wrong?'

'Nothing.' Ingrid stared out to sea. It was calm, untroubled. Maybe now was the time. 'Why... why couldn't you love me?'

'But I always loved you. How can you doubt that?'

'You never hugged me or anything. Or told me.' Despite a wave of compassion for the man, if not the father, Ingrid couldn't keep the anger out of her voice. A family eating their picnic lunch on the bamboo mat next to them edged a little further away, reluctant to have their day sullied by a relationship squabble.

'It wasn't my way to hug and kiss but I always loved you. I still do.'

Ingrid pushed herself off the boulder. 'I'm sorry. I'm really sorry; maybe another time. I know you've made an enormous effort, and I really appreciate it,' - did she, or were they just words? - 'but I need more time to... well... just time. A lot's happened. I don't even know who I am, not really...' her voice faded.

'I'm staying here,' he handed her a card for a small bed and breakfast by the river in Lynmouth. 'When you've had the time you need, please... call me.'

Ingrid walked up the beach, she wouldn't look back: she looked back. He was so small and insignificant sitting there, hunched up against life. Surprisingly the sight didn't take her breath away. He'd never stopped looking for her. Wasn't that love? It was a thought that carried her back to the Abbey.

'Ingrid,' Ann called to her from the office window. 'Can you come through?'

There was a policewoman waiting in the corridor. 'Mrs Clarke?'

'Yes?'

'Would you like to sit down?'

'What is it? What's wrong?'

'It's your husband. I believe he had a serious heart attack a few weeks ago.'

'Yes...?'

'He was admitted to Salisbury General on Tuesday after another attack. He recovered and was thought to be doing quite well. Sadly he had another one last night and the hospital was unable to revive him.'

'You're saying... he's dead?'

'I'm afraid so.'

'No. He was doing okay. They'd given him the all-clear. He can't be dead.' Not before she'd apologised. No, that word wasn't anywhere near what was needed. After everything she'd done, he deserved, and was going to get, so much more from her. She had it all planned. She was going to let him know that she was totally at fault, that this was none of his doing.

'No, he'll just be in a coma, like last time. He can't be dead.'

The house was cold. Ingrid stepped over the unopened letters on the mat and walked through to the sitting room. Jack's empty chair was perfectly positioned, as always, to the left of the fire. A book was splayed open on the side table: she picked it up and replaced it on the bookshelves, its spine perfectly aligned. Through the window she could see a fork standing upright in a bed that only a few weeks ago had been filled with the most beautiful azaleas, her favourite flower. Now it was an expanse of newly dug earth. Bare. No, not bare, barren. Just one bush survived, but its flowers lay scattered on the ground, crushed as Jack fell... He'd lain there all night because there was no one to notice, no one to care...

Ingrid forced herself to focus. If only she'd been here; come back sooner instead of hiding away at the Abbey, spending time with Steven, being so selfish. What had she been thinking of? But the second attack had been in hospital. They were with him in seconds. 'When they decide to go there's nothing we can do,' the nurse had said. That was her real crime. She'd destroyed Jack's life and he'd decided to go. She had killed him.

'Oh, Jack, I'm so sorry,' she sobbed. What had happened? Just a few days earlier everything had been so right and now... now it couldn't be more wrong. She sank to the floor, staring at the fork, willing it to move, willing Jack to look back at the house and smile, anxious to share some pleasure with her.

Darkness came and went and still she sat, hunched on the floor. She had no idea how long someone had been knocking before the sound finally registered. Ingrid pulled herself to her feet and stumbled to the front door. It was the young nurse from the hospital who'd given her the anonymous white plastic bag containing Jack's things.

'I'm so sorry to disturb you at a time like this but when you collected Mr Clarke's personal effects something was missed out: only it was marked urgent and addressed to you so I thought I should bring it round; it was only an hour or so before the end of my shift and no trouble to drop it in on my way home; I suppose that sounds a bit strange when it's morning, only I've been on the night shift; I'm just on my way to bed after I've had a bit of dinner; well I suppose it's breakfast really, only it doesn't feel quite right having breakfast before you go to bed does it? Not that I'll get any sleep, my brother's home from school today and he doesn't know how to close a door; every time it slams I'm awake again and...'

Ingrid took the envelope the young nurse held in her hand and gently closed the door. Gathering up the other letters scattered across the mat she returned, this time to the comfort of the settee. She turned the envelope over to see her name in Jack's handwriting. With a trembling hand, she slit the top open and pulled out one sheet of white hospital paper.

Dearest Ingrid

I hope and pray that you will be able to find it in your heart to forgive me for what I've done. My selfish anger blinded me to what really matters - what you share with someone, not what they keep from you. I love you, always have and always will. I was crazy to act as I did. I've taken steps to undo it. I pray that Mr Jackson will arrive in time.

I miss you my love. I've asked them to try and find you. I bitterly regret my words and hope they won't be our last. Mr Bridges has been very frank with me. I kept it from you - yes, I am guilty of having secrets too - but after the first attack he told me I was living on borrowed time. Maybe that's what you and I have in common, both of us borrowing time.

It's strange but I don't regret taking you to Lynmouth. There is nothing as important as the truth and if my actions have helped you to find yours then I am content. My father always used to say, 'the truth is like a compass, it shows the way we want and need to go.' Don't give up until you have found your truth, Ingrid.

With my love, always, your devoted husband, Jack.

After everything she'd done he was asking for *her* forgiveness?

It was a long night, alone in their bed. As a grey light finally brought definition to the bedroom she crept downstairs, wandering from room to room. She paused at the door to the sitting room. For years she'd wanted to take Jack's books out of those damned symmetrical bookcases and replace them all higgledy-piggledy. But now that she could...

She stretched her arms, she needed to breathe. 'Maybe I'll make it one big room.' After all, she could do whatever she liked now; this bungalow was hers and hers alone. She waited for a reaction. Surely there should be one? Only it wasn't her home was it? It was Jack's, and she'd gained access under false pretences so what right did she have to do anything with it. 'Maybe I'll rent it out,' she said, 'go away somewhere, start again.' That's something she was good at, starting again.

The front door bell rang. 'Morning Mrs Clarke,' Mike said, handing her the morning's post. 'I didn't want to leave these without saying how very sorry I am. Mr Clarke was such a gentleman, always ready to ask about the family.'

'They told me you found him, Mike.'

'Yes, in the garden.'

'Did he... was he suffering?'

'No, not then. It's funny but I think he was almost expecting it. He kept saying he had things to sort out before he went.'

'Did he say anything else?'

'Not that I can remember.'

'Thanks Mike.'

She thumbed through the envelopes. One was stamped with their solicitor's logo. Ingrid whispered, *'I pray that Mr Jackson will arrive in time.'* She tore the letter open.

Dear Mrs Clarke

May I express my condolences to you on the passing of your husband. I realise this must be a difficult time but as your husband's executor it is my duty to convey his wishes, as expressed in this, his last will and testament.

In summary, the terms of Mr Clarke's will are as follows. He leaves all his assets to the Heart Foundation, those assets to be realised within the next three months. For those three months all costs incurred by yourself at the marital home will be covered by Mr Clark's estate but thereafter you will be required to make your own arrangements for accommodation and financial support.

The two assets not to be realised are the Rover car and the Voyager caravan. These are bequeathed to yourself. With this bequest I am required to pass on the following words exactly as spoken to me by Mr Clarke.

'I leave you the car and caravan so that you can run away any time you want...'

'The Heart Foundation.' She looked at his photograph. 'So that's what you meant, Jack. Well, there's nothing to forgive. I deserved your anger, I still do.' She not only deserved it, she wanted it. 'I'm glad Mr Jackson didn't arrive in time. I don't deserve your beautiful home; I can't live here without you.'

But what would she do? No home, no job; the familiar struts holding up her life were collapsing one by one, leaving what? She smiled, hearing Mark's voice. 'When life brings you to your knees that's exactly where you'll find God waiting for you.' She struggled when he brought God into it - but Jack believed. Ingrid picked up the leaflet from the funeral director. There was one last thing she could do.

Ingrid walked into the church behind the coffin. Faces turned as she passed, many of them familiar from Rotary and the flying club but so many others... she had no idea Jack was held in such affection. Even Mike was there.

The vicar took her arm and led her to an empty pew. The sound of people straining to keep a respectful silence bore down on her, intensifying the oppression she'd always felt in church. But not Jack. He was a warden here, in his element surrounded by tradition and ceremony.

She forced herself to look at the coffin, just a few feet in front; struggled to picture him lying there. They'd asked if she wanted to see him. She'd said 'yes', but when it came to it she couldn't; just couldn't.

Someone's hand was under her elbow encouraging her to stand as the organist played the introduction to the first hymn. It happened twice more, before and after the vicar's address, and then she was outside, standing beside the open grave. It rained as the bearers lowered him into the ground. Large raindrops drumming on the coffin, beating out the mantra – rain on the plain, rain on the plain. Her tears fell as she remembered rose coloured chairs, marble tables and breathing easy with Jack's arm around her.

They said all the right things at the house afterwards but Ingrid was relieved no-one insisted she join them for a day or two or that they stay to keep her company. She was happy to be alone; wanted to be alone. Jack was a private man. He wouldn't have told anyone what had happened between them. But there had been the occasional look...

She wandered around, picking up crumb-filled plates and empty cups. There was comfort in a mindless task that clearly set the agenda for the next few moments. But what then?

She slid Jack's letter from behind the clock and re-read his words. *The truth is like a compass, it shows the way we want and need to go. Don't give up until you have found your truth, Ingrid.* 'What truth, Jack? The truth about us, about me?' She looked at the file lying on top of the bureau. It was the one he'd tried to give her, on cloud seeding. 'Of course!' Jack wasn't referring to some deep and meaningful journey of self-discovery. That wasn't his style. He meant the truth about Lynmouth, the truth about the floods.

She opened the file. It was full of information about something called the Meteorological Research Flight. What was it he'd said? Something about research being done out of Cranfield, people setting up commercial companies. 'Is this what you meant, Jack?' she whispered. 'Is this your signpost to the truth?'

Chapter Twenty

Ingrid sprawled on the sitting room floor surrounded by photocopied papers, hand-written notes, pizza wrappings and dirty crockery. She threw down her pen and re-read her notes.

FACT   *Project Popeye continued for seven years so it must have worked.*
FACT   *Seeding in August '49 produced rain thirty minutes later.*
FACT   *They were rainmaking on Salisbury Plain in the early 1950's.*
FACT   *They were seeding in the middle of August 1952.*
FACT   *Cloud seeding is capable of creating rain up to 300 miles away.*
FACT   *Seeding from the ground uses rockets powered with sulphur.*
FACT   *Sulphurous smell reported in Lynmouth on August 15th 1952.*
FACT   *Programme on controlled rainfall was pulled after the Lynmouth floods.*

The sound of the paperboy cramming the newspaper through the letterbox distracted her. She levered herself up from the floor and reached the front door in time to catch it. He'd excelled himself. Not only was the paper a crumpled mess, it was covered in mud. 'Nice one, Jamie.' Ingrid laid it on the boiler to dry, suddenly conscious of the rain lashing against the window.

They'd forecast the weather would break this week. 'But did it break itself or was it broken, that is the question?' Was it nobler to suffer the slings and arrows of outrageous fortune or should she take arms against a... sky of troubles and by opposing end them? 'What do you think, Jack?'

She'd talked to him a lot over the past few weeks. His answers were always there, in her mind. Even the irritatingly pedantic ones were comforting, like a coat that was too shabby to wear but too familiar to discard.

Ingrid wandered back to the papers scattered across the sitting room floor and picked up her file. Did she really have any facts or merely a collection of interesting thoughts? Where was her proof; proof that seeding had actually affected Lynmouth? 'What does it all mean?' She flung the file across the room. 'You bastards! Come out here where I can see you.'

She stared at her hands, rubbing her fingers where the mud had dried. Mud. She walked through to the kitchen and looked at the mud-stained paper, drying to a powdery dust. Was it possible? She hurried up the stairs. 'Damn,' Ingrid scratched her arm as she hauled herself into the loft. The pencil torch was useless but the battery was dead in the bigger one. She edged her way through Jack's stuff to the corner where her few possessions were neatly stored. Or used to be. The box was upended, its contents strewn across an old carpet - all except for her diary. Her mud-stained Keepsake Diary was resting on top of a packing case. Could it really hold any clues after all this time?

Back in the sitting room she went through the papers again. Air Ministry, Meteorological Research Flight, Guy's faxes, Schnectady, SkySearch... SkySearch? Ingrid didn't remember that one. She leafed through the pages, twisting her head to read Jack's notes in the margin. SkySearch had undertaken cloud seeding research for the government, in conjunction with the Meteorological Research Flight, from the early 1950's onwards.

She glanced at the address. SkySearch was based just outside Salisbury, at Old Sarum. Was that how Jack found them? Two names were highlighted, the company directors: Richard Powell and... Steven Carmichael. The words swam on the page. Steven Carmichael - a director of the firm that was responsible for cloud seeding research!

He couldn't be. It didn't make sense. How could he have spent all that time with her, been so... if... 'Oh my God.' The thought tore through her. Could he have been responsible for Guy? 'No, no, he can't have...'

But he knew where to find her. He'd asked about the research. And - she struggled to recall his exact words - hadn't he suggested she leave it all behind? But he'd seemed so sincere, so kind. Always there for her. Always there. Watching her? Her chest tightened. 'Of course,' she gasped. She'd trusted Alex, told him everything. And he'd told his father. And Steven Carmichael had come looking for her.

The phone had been ringing for a while by the time Ingrid reached it. She blew her nose and grabbed a fresh tissue.

'I didn't have you as a woman who broke her promises.'

'Nick. I'm sorry. I forgot.'

'You forgot! Could do a lot of damage to a chap's ego with words like that. But I'm not one to hold a grudge. How about I whisk you off for that dinner this evening - or are you tied up?'

'Tied up?'

'With Jack...' Silence. 'Ingrid?'

'I'm still here... Jack had another heart attack... they couldn't revive him.'

'Oh you poor girl. And you're coping all on your own. Stay exactly where you are, I'm coming over.'

'No I...' He'd rung off.

He was right about one thing. She was feeling very alone.

'Come here.' He wrapped her in his arms. 'My poor Ingrid,' he whispered, stroking her hair, kissing her forehead.

She hardly knew what she wanted any more, but it was so good to be held.

'It's okay. I'm here.' It was several minutes before Nick released her and they moved into the sitting room. He stopped at the edge of the paper-strewn floor. 'What's all this?'

'Jack wanted me to carry on.'

'What? There are people out there threatening blackmail,

murder, God knows what and your husband wanted you to carry on!'

'It wasn't like that; he didn't know.'

'But if he had known, would he want you to put yourself at risk?'

'I don't know...'

'Of course he wouldn't. All this is going, permanently. But first, I'm taking you out for that dinner.'

Nick dropped her at the restaurant entrance. The waiter guided her to a table with a view of the cathedral spire; her friendly spire. The candlelight made it quite magical and wonderfully normal at the same time. She'd forgotten what normal was like. While she'd been fighting for her life in the East Lyn River, people had been sitting here, deciding between a prawn cocktail and whitebait. She could hear them, talking about holidays, children, houses, jobs, their future... No, that was Nick.

'What do you think, Ingrid? Could we make a go of it?'

'What? I don't know... No, it's too soon.'

'I'm not talking about marriage; who cares what anyone else thinks. We're old enough to make our own decisions.'

Was she? Where had all the peace and presence she'd found at the Abbey gone? Wasn't there anything she could bring back with her or had Steven stolen it all? She looked at Nick. He was talking about something, his eyes flashing, hands all over the place. She smiled. He always managed to make her smile. That couldn't be so bad could it?

They never discussed whether he should stay the night. There was simply never a right time to separate, to relinquish the comfort his familiar presence brought to her empty house, empty life, empty body. His touch was all it took for numbness to give way to sensation. Their lovemaking felt like a confirmation of the life still in her. She wanted to shout at fate, destiny, 'them' that she was alive and kicking. It felt wrong for Nick to be beside her, where Jack had lain - but a part of her wanted it to be right.

Like staying the night, she never actually agreed that Nick should move in. He simply returned to the same door he left each morning, to eat the meal Ingrid prepared for him, to share her bed, to sit in the leather armchair by the fire, to start talking about alterations they could make to the house, to plan a room for Ellie.

But she hadn't shared the detail of Jack's will with him. It was easy to arrange the house viewings when he was at work and if they did stay together, well, a move would be good anyway; a fresh start.

Awake in the early hours, Ingrid sat at the kitchen table drinking tea. 'What would you say, Jack? About Nick; about SkySearch; about everything?' He was strangely silent. She walked through to the sitting room, making a mental inventory of the furniture. They'd bought a few pieces together over the years but most of it was Jack's. The table and chairs, standard lamp, sideboard and the bureau, crammed full of official papers, all the stuff on Jack's family tree - and the Lynmouth file. She pulled it from the drawer where she'd hidden it out of Nick's sight. Sitting on top was Jack's note. *'The truth is like a compass, it shows the way we want and need to go. Don't give up until you have found your truth, Ingrid.'*

'Is that Alex?'

'Ingrid? Good to hear from you. I was worried.'

'I need to see you.'

'I'm at home today so how about here?'

'No. Not at your house.'

'Where then?'

Ingrid hesitated. Maybe meeting him alone anywhere wasn't a good idea. 'I'll come up to Earthshield. Maybe we can meet with some of the others?'

'It depends how they're fixed.'

She sensed the hesitation in his voice; it was all she needed to know. 'I'll be there at twelve.'

At exactly eleven thirty, Ingrid was waiting on the riverbank at the rear of Earthshield's offices. It was a clear blue day with a light breeze carrying the sound of the traffic away from her. A jogger pounded past, hooked up to his Walkman, missing the wren weaving its way along the riverbank.

'Mrs Clarke?' Ingrid jumped. 'Sorry to startle you.' The young woman who had appeared from behind her held out a hand. 'I'm Sophie Cox.'

'Thanks for agreeing to meet me. You must have wondered what on earth is going on.'

'I meet a lot of worried people in this job. It's not a problem.'

'But not many implying your colleagues can't be trusted,' Ingrid said.

'True, but hopefully I can reassure you. Shall we sit?' She indicated a low wooden bench at the water's edge. 'You're worried about Alex?'

'Yes. If his father's firm is behind this then Steven Carmichael might... well, someone's trying to shut me up...' She gazed at a convoy of ducks heading across the river, a parent at either end and seven bobbing balls of fluff in between. 'It sounds ridiculous, saying it like that. I spent several days with him you see, up at Lynton. He was so...'

'Charming?'

'Yes.' Ingrid smiled.' How did you know?'

'Like father, like son. We know all about Steven Carmichael and Alex's possible conflict of interest. It's my job to make sure Alex stays focused and delivers what we need.'

'And I wouldn't want to imply that you're not totally capable of doing that, but I can't trust him.'

'Are you saying you don't want us involved?'

'Oh no. I need help - but not from Alex.'

'He's the only one who can get us documents it would take years to obtain any other way. Combined with your information it puts us in a very strong position.'

'What are you saying?'

'I guess I'm asking you to reconsider.'

'Don't take this the wrong way, Miss Cox...'

'Sophie, please.'

'Sophie, but my life has been turned upside down...' her voice wavered, 'since I got involved with this. Things have happened I can't believe... it's a nightmare and I want it to end. But I need help from people I can trust, that I know are working with me, not against me.'

'We need to keep Alex on board and your co-operation would help us do that, but I completely understand, Mrs Clarke. We won't pressurise you.' She paused. 'Would it help to know that Alex told me you were coming? That he asked me to sit in.'

'I suppose that's something,' Ingrid said. 'But I need to find out for myself.'

'That's absolutely your decision.' Sophie checked her watch. 'We should go in.'

Sophie ushered Ingrid into a small office and settled herself on the window-ledge, looking out across the river.

'Hello, Mrs Clarke; Ingrid.' Alex pulled out a chair for her. 'How are things?'

'You tell me.'

'Sorry?'

'I'd like to know why you haven't been straight with me. Last time we met, every possibility I raised you had an objection for. And how did you leave it? Don't do anything; give me time to come up with something. And what exactly have you come up with since then, Alex?'

'I've been doing some background research. I can play you a tape on stuff that's going on in the Antarctic right now.'

'Avoiding the subject of Lynmouth. Why's that, Alex?'

'I wasn't...'

'What's your real agenda? Why are you lying? To protect your father?'

'Why should I do that?'

Ingrid leant forward. 'It's my guess that your father's company was cloud seeding in August 1952. Making run after run, increasing the rainfall until the Exmoor Chains were so saturated one more cloudburst was all it took to turn moorland streams into raging torrents, devastating a village, killing thirty-four innocent people...'

'No, that's not how it was,' Alex interrupted.

'Are you denying SkySearch was cloud-seeding?'

'No, he's not,' Sophie interrupted. 'In fact he's brought something to show you. Haven't you, Alex?' She held his gaze.

Ingrid was impressed. Sophie was no more than a couple of years older than Alex but she knew what she was doing.

Alex pushed a file across the desk.

'What's this?' Ingrid asked.

'Copies of SkySearch documentation on their cloud seeding projects in the early fifties,' he said.

Ingrid spread the sheets over the desk. Was this it? Was she actually looking at proof that SkySearch had been cloud seeding before the Lynmouth floods?

'It confirms they were seeding in August '52,' Alex continued, 'but there's no evidence it reached Lynmouth.'

'Unfortunately I can confirm that,' Sophie said. 'There's nothing tangible, no actual proof SkySearch were responsible.'

'It was a government contract anyway,' Alex said. 'They were liable if anyone was. Not my dad. Or they would have been if it hadn't been for Richard Powell.'

'Powell? His partner?' Ingrid said.

'He negotiated a lousy contract - making SkySearch carry the can for any compensation.'

'Compensation! You're talking about money! Thirty-four people died. And for all I know your father was responsible for Guy's death.'

'No! He didn't know anything about that.'

'How do you know?'

'He told me.'

'And that's all you've got? Your father's word? What good is that? He lied to me, over and over. Pretending to care, to support me when all the time he was... what? Watching me? Working out how to shut me up?' Ingrid shouted.

'Of course dad doesn't want you to destroy his company, but he wouldn't harm you.'

'Bullshit. The truth's staring you in the face; you just won't accept it.' She paused. 'Why should you, he's your father.'

'So my father should have done something, but Powell was meant to buy your friend off, not let him die. Powell is out of control.'

'Powell? Or your father?' His resistance was understandable; Steven Carmichael was charismatic, it was impossible not to warm to him. But the evidence was there.

'Maybe the real issue is what Alex is prepared to do now.' Sophie's calm voice invited a compromise.

'The only way to stop it,' Alex finally said, 'is to expose SkySearch.'

'I guess we can all agree on that,' Ingrid said.

'The only question,' Sophie said, 'is how?'

'How long does silver iodide stay in the environment?' Ingrid asked, reaching into her bag.

'I don't know,' Sophie answered. 'Why?'

Ingrid placed her diary on the desk. 'Can you get the mud on this analysed?'

'Where does it come from?' Alex asked.

'The East Lyn River on the night of August 15th 1952.'

'No way!'

'If it shows silver iodide it's the nearest we've come to proof yet,' Sophie said. 'I'll get my mother's opinion.' She carefully picked the diary up between two sheets of paper. 'Won't be long. Get Ingrid a drink, Alex.'

'I could do with a coffee,' Ingrid said. She waited until the door closed then picked up the Lynmouth file. She'd seen a flight plan. The research team looked roughly the same each time. Murgatroyd, Goldsmith, Day, Grant...

Alex and Sophie returned together. Very together Ingrid thought. She wondered how far Sophie would go to get what she wanted. She turned back to the flight plan, to the last person in the crew.

'Oh my God,' Ingrid said.

Sophie was at her shoulder. 'What is it? What have you found?'

211

Suddenly it all made sense; his depression, the suicide, everything. 'All the proof I need,' Ingrid replied.

The carpet pile beneath the front window was pressed flat by the time Nick drew up outside the bungalow. Ingrid opened the door to him.

'Nick, I need you to drive me to Lynmouth.'

'You have to be joking!'

'I don't have time to explain. Please, I'll do anything you want but, please, please do this for me.'

'Why does it have to be now?'

'It just does.'

'We'll never find anywhere to stay, it's peak season.'

'We can take the caravan. I've got it ready. And I've packed a bag for you.'

'I'm not driving half way across the country tonight. It's been a long day. I want a good meal, a relaxing evening and bed. So I'm going to get out of these clothes, have a shower and settle in for the night.'

'I'm going tonight - one way or another,' she said to his disappearing back.

'Good, you do that. At least I'll get a peaceful weekend.'

'And I might not come back.'

He turned to face her. 'What the hell do you mean?'

'If you won't help me when I really need you, then we don't have a future.' She held her breath.

'Well, you've more spirit than I gave you credit for. I don't approve, I think you're crazy, I'm tired, and the last thing I want to do is drive you to Lynmouth but...'

She threw her arms around him. 'Thank you, Nick. You won't regret it, I promise you.'

It was an abysmal night. Horizontal rain, driven on by high winds, lashed the car as they climbed up onto the moor. The atmosphere inside was hardly less inviting. Glancing across at

Nick, Ingrid was reminded of the day she'd first mentioned Private Dean; of the way he'd stabbed at a few splashes of rainwater on his coat as though he'd been sprayed with deadly acid.

She gripped the edge of her seat. 'Take it easy on the bends, Nick, the river's down there.'

'Relax. I have towed before. I know what I'm doing.'

'And I know these roads. They're dangerous, especially in this weather.'

The car swung round another bend, giving her a clear view of the vertical drop into the gorge carved out by the East Lyn River. 'Please, slow down.'

'For Christ's sake woman.'

Ingrid froze.

'Do you want to drive?'

'No, of course not.'

'You're as bad as the prat on my tail. Sometimes you just don't know when to back off.'

She looked in the wing mirror. A black Mercedes seemed very close.

'I'll show you,' he said. The seat belt cut across Ingrid's chest as Nick slammed on the brakes.

'What are you...?' Her words were lost as the car jerked forward.

'So you want to play that game do you?' Nick accelerated then braked sharply again. The caravan rocked and pulled them to one side.

'Nick stop, this is madness.'

'Tell that to our friend behind. It's probably you he's interested in anyway.'

Ingrid released her grip on the door to twist her head round. But it was impossible to see anything in the darkness.

'Aaahhhh...' Ingrid braced herself against the dashboard as the Mercedes rammed the caravan again, over-riding their brakes, forcing them down the hill. A sharp bend appeared out of the darkness. 'Look out,' Ingrid screamed. The car's headlights caught a section of rough stone wall ahead of them.

It was strangely white, pristine. Why was that? 'There's no lichen on it,' she murmured. It had been recently re-pointed and the green mosses that covered the wall on either side hadn't had time to colonise the new crevices...

'You're becoming a regular,' the doctor was packing his bag. 'I'd prefer it if you chose better weather next time. How's your neck when I move it like this? And this?'

'A bit stiff,' Ingrid said.

'You've got whiplash but I don't think it's serious. How about the shoulder?'

'Tender.'

'Probably from the seat belt; should settle down in a day or two. Let's get you up.' He helped her to sit. 'Any other problems?'

'I don't know. What happened?'

'You didn't make it round the corner.' He nodded towards the remains of the stone wall.

'Where's Nick? Is he okay?'

'He's a lucky man; got away with bruising, lacerations to his head, whiplash - could have been a lot worse judging by the state of the car. Your caravan's a bit battered but still in one piece. They're towing it down to the site.'

Ingrid followed his finger, trying to make out the campsite below. But all she could see through the rain were soft night-lights dancing around the valley. It looked strangely wonderful, a flash of beauty in the middle of a nightmare.

'Why can't you follow it up now? He could be anywhere by the morning.' Nick's voice carried halfway to Lynmouth. Ingrid missed the constable's reply but Nick obviously wasn't happy with it. 'No, I don't want an appointment with him at ten, I want him here now.'

Ingrid smiled at the doctor. 'As you say, he's fine.'

'Maybe, but I'm taking you both in for observation overnight.'

Twelve hours later they were standing beside the caravan. 'We won't be towing that anywhere,' Nick said.

'Oh I don't know. Some panel beating, a re-spray and it'll be fine.' Ingrid stepped inside, clearing a path through the broken crockery littering the floor. 'Put your bag in the bedroom. I'll make a start on this.'

'You're not staying?'

'I can't go back, not yet.'

'Bollocks. I've called a taxi. We're getting out of here right now.'

'No. Please, Nick, I need your support.'

'Go to the police. Right now. Tell them everything. Even better, I'll put it out to a national. With their resources they'll have it cracked in a fraction of the time and without risking their necks either.' He put his arms around her. 'It's never worth it, Ingrid. It's not down to you to see this thing through. I'm putting the bags out for the taxi; we're going home.'

'I'm not leaving.'

'Don't be so bloody stubborn.'

'Will you listen for once?'

'You'll be grateful when we get home. We can make some changes to the house, make it ours, then get away, do some travelling. Get someone in to look after the...'

He was like a runaway train. Well he was about to hit the bumpers. 'There is no house.'

'Don't be daft. We've got your place.'

'No, we haven't.'

'Oh, I get it. I do mean to make an honest woman of you, Ingrid if that's what you're worried about.'

'I'm not.'

'What is it then? Your place is a damn site more comfortable than my postage stamp of a flat.'

'Jack left it to charity. I'm only allowed to stay until it's sold.'

'Yeah, right. As if he'd do that. He idolised you.'

Ingrid looked at the man standing in front of her. Who was he? Part of another life, another time? *The truth Ingrid. Always the truth.* Jack was right. 'Why? I'll tell you why. Because he found out that I was a bigamist and a liar; that I'd stolen someone's identity; that I'd run away when life got... complicated. Is that enough or would you like some more? There's plenty more.'

'What the...'

'I don't believe we've been formally introduced. I'm Moira, Moira Williams. Pleased to meet you.' She extended a hand. It was shaking.

'Cut the crap, Ingrid. This is ridiculous.'

'Ridiculous? Ridiculous that meek little Ingrid, or even Moira, yes especially Moira, should have such an evil past? Or ridiculous that you've got involved with someone who isn't who she says she is? Which is it, Nick?' *Surely you don't need to be quite so harsh*, a voice whispered. But it felt like the only way.

'You've had a shock, you're not yourself.'

'I assure you I am, more than I've ever been.'

'What the hell do you mean?'

Ingrid smiled. 'I've been picking up bits of me lately, a lot from round here; not very pleasant bits but then you can't go leaving your garbage for someone else to clear up can you?'

Nick stared at her. 'You need help, Ingrid.'

'Are you offering?'

'I don't mean that kind of help, I mean...'

I know exactly what you mean, but you're wrong. I'm not mad, even though I've done things I can't begin to forgive myself for, things you need to know about if we're going to be together. Would you like me to tell you about my husband, the real one that is, not Jack, and about the children who died? How much reality can you take, Nick?'

'I don't know what you're playing at but...'

'Oh I'm not playing, not any more. I did enjoy working with you, Nick. We should have left things as they were.' She opened the caravan door. 'Your taxi's waiting. Goodbye, Nick.'

It was his choice. But there was never any doubt, not really.

He picked up his bag. 'Be careful, Ingrid... Moira... whoever you are.'

'Thank you, Nick, you too.' Ingrid closed the door behind him, locked it, checked the windows, closed the curtains, rechecked the door, and sat down.

She was sitting in a battered caravan, quite alone and someone was trying to kill her. Could it get much worse? 'Oh Jack. What would you do?' Ingrid curled up on the seat. She wanted his certainty now more than ever. But Nick was right about one thing; she had to go public. All she needed was the last part of the jigsaw.

Chapter Twenty-one

'Mr Carmichael? Mr Steven Carmichael?' Steven had never knowingly met anyone from MI5, but he recognised the two men standing on his doorstep immediately. 'May we come in?'

'Do I have a choice?'

'This is an informal visit, Mr Carmichael. We'd like to keep it that way.'

'I bet you would.' He stood back.

'I am Mr Harrison, and this is my colleague, Mr Wilson.' The short arrogant looking one was obviously going to do the talking. 'Are you alone?'

'Yes. Until my son gets back.'

'I believe you're acquainted with Mrs Ingrid Clarke, otherwise known as Mrs Moira Williams.'

They obviously didn't intend to waste any time. 'Yes.'

'You recently spent some time with her. Why?'

'She's an attractive woman. We get on.'

'Mr Carmichael, we know why you went to Lynmouth.'

'So why ask?'

'May I?' Harrison sat. Wilson positioned himself between Steven and the door. 'We're on the same side here Mr Carmichael.'

'Meaning?'

'We both want Mrs Clarke and her colleagues to forget they ever knew anything about cloud seeding. We made a suggestion; she decided to ignore it. Your partner paid Hoskins to devise a rather more permanent solution to the problem.'

'That was none of my doing. I can prove it.'

'We know. Hoskins has been debriefed and Mr Powell is currently helping us with our enquiries.'

'You've arrested him?'

'Let's just say he's been detained. But there's still one problem. Or maybe you found a solution on your visit to Lee Abbey, Mr Carmichael?'

'If you know I was there you'll know that I had to return to Salisbury for a few days. She'd left by the time I got back. I haven't seen her since.'

'Have you heard of an organisation called Earthshield, Mr Carmichael?'

'Earthshield? I don't think so.'

'That's odd.'

'Why?'

'Because your son works for them.'

'What? Well... I know it's an environmental organisation of some kind.'

'So you do know.'

'I didn't know the name.'

'But you know what they're involved in?'

'Not exactly.'

'Maybe you know what your son is researching then?'

Steven paused. 'No, he hasn't said.'

'Hasn't said? That's a bit strange isn't it? With him living here.'

Steven wanted to argue but Harrison was right. It was strange. 'I've been preoccupied. I never asked.'

'Not even when your son asked for a job at SkySearch?'

'He said he was short of cash...'

'He *said* he was short of cash.'

'I had no reason to doubt him.'

'Had? So maybe you doubt him now?'

'No... I don't know. What are you saying?'

'Earthshield are using your son to get at classified information held by your company. They intend to sabotage the work you're doing on weather modification.'

'No. No. Alex wouldn't do that. He knows how much SkySearch means to me. He's my son.'

'A son who hasn't shared any information with you about his work; a son who has access to all your top secret files; a son who has ingratiated himself with the man behind LYRE.' Harrison paused before delivering the final blow. 'A son who is working with Ingrid Clarke and Earthshield to destroy your company.'

'No! He wouldn't do that.' But Ingrid had come to see Alex. Why else if not about Lynmouth?

'Believe me, your son *is* working against you. And Ingrid Clarke was seen leaving Earthshield's offices earlier today. You need all the help you can get, Mr Carmichael, and right now we're it.'

Ingrid peered through the slit in the curtain. The family on the next site had packed up, giving her an open view of the campsite. Who was in the black Mercedes? Maybe no-one. After all, Nick had braked first. Did she believe that? Maybe. Maybe not.

She slumped back and closed her eyes. The smell of the upholstery sparked a domino-run of sensations from a deep-seated familiarity to... to what? Unease? No, stronger than that. Fear. What was Steven Carmichael capable of? Could he really be behind all this? Her chest began to tighten. 'Oh God... no... not now.' She reached for her bag, scattering the contents across the floor, grasping her inhaler. This was not the time. She had to stay alert. She nudged the curtain aside and scanned the campsite. There was no way of knowing if anyone was out there: if Steven was out there - watching, waiting.

As dusk began to fall, automatic sensors switched on the overhead lights one by one. For a few seconds they cast the caravan into shadow. This was the time. She slipped through the door and dropped down alongside the riverbed. She constantly lost her footing amongst the boulders but managed to pick her way as far as the bridge by the Cottage Inn. Seconds later she was hurrying along Lynway, a quiet path that wound its way past a few isolated cottages before reaching the back lanes of Lynton.

The clock was striking ten when she crept beneath the towering walls of the Valley of Rocks Hotel and into the churchyard. She dropped onto the porch bench, made a pillow of her rucksack, pulled her grey coat tight around her and sank into the protective camouflage of the worn grey stone.

Mark leant his bike against the imposing porch at the front of the Manor and pulled off his trouser clips. Satisfied he was presentable, he turned to ring the bell - only she'd beaten him to it.

'Saw you coming up the drive,' Julie said. 'Come in.'

'I've brought this morning's reading up. Are you still game?'

'Are you kidding? Being able to say that Mrs Bryce Jones has let you down is worth its weight in gold.' She saw Mark was about to object. 'Not that I'll rub her nose in it. Trust me. I know how to make a point tastefully.'

'I wish I did.'

'Ah.' Julie offered him a seat. 'I gather this afternoon's meeting is likely to be a full house - sorry, that wasn't exactly what you wanted to hear was it?'

Mark smiled. 'It's okay, I already knew. One day I'll learn to think before I speak.'

'Oh, Mark, don't give yourself such a hard time. It was just a word. We all knew you weren't suggesting we celebrate the floods.'

'I meant commemorate.'

'I know. You're a convenient focus for the few who think the whole idea of an anniversary of any kind is wrong.'

'And how about you? Do you think we should be remembering the floods?'

'I don't know. Sorry, not very helpful is it?'

'Oh, well, I'll leave it to the meeting. Fingers crossed it will go clearly one way or the other so I'm not left with the casting vote. But if we're going to do something I need to get on and organise it. If you'd rather not be involved that's fine.'

'No. If the town decides to go for it, I'll help.' She paused. 'Can I change the subject?'

'Sure.'

'Are you any good at picking locks?'

He looked at her. 'Not something I get asked every day.'

'It's all legit. trust me, only I can't afford to lose any more of these.' She held out the butchered remains of her fingernails.

'You're either in need of some strong tranquillisers or a set of lock picking tools. And I can't help with either. What are you trying to break into?'

Julie disappeared for a few seconds and returned with Hugh's case. 'This. I found it down the cellar - only it's locked and I can't find the key.'

'Surprising to have a lock like this on a briefcase.'

'I know.'

'Which is why you have to get into it, right?'

'Right.'

Mark checked his watch. 'We need to get to the church. I could take it with me; have a go after the service.'

'Yes please; but wait for me, I want to be there.'

The key turning in the lock echoed through the empty church. Mark walked up to the altar and knelt. Outside the occasional car drove past, someone called out, a child laughed; but inside these walls all was silent. Apart from the footsteps.

'Say one for me will you, Mark.'

He half turned. 'Why don't you come and say one for yourself Ingrid?' He waited, sensing her moving closer until she was kneeling beside him. She looked strained and very much in need of his support.

'Does the notion of sanctuary still apply?' she asked.

'Are you in need of it?'

'I think so.'

'Then it applies.' He guided her to a seat. 'I heard about your husband. I'm so sorry.'

'Talk about lousy timing. It was over. No more digging around in the past, no more heroics,' she wiped the tears away with her hand, 'definitely no more heroics.' She glanced at Mark, then back to the altar. 'Only it doesn't work like that does it?' She pointed towards the crucifix. 'He's got other plans for me. Let her carry her peace away with her? You must be joking! Give her enough time to beg her husband's forgiveness? No way. Let her leave a job half done? Definitely not.'

Mark put his arm around her. 'People will be arriving soon. Come through to the vestry.'

He placed Hugh's briefcase on the desk and helped Ingrid to an armchair, recently retired from the vicarage. 'There are biscuits in the cupboard. Help yourself. Nothing more exciting than water to drink, other than the communion wine, which I can't in all conscience offer you. But if you happen to forget what it's there for I'm sure God will understand. Have a rest and we'll talk as soon as the service is over.'

There was something comforting about the subdued light of the vestry and the sound of 'Immortal, invisible...' drifting in from the church. She began to sing. 'Unresting, unhasting and silent as light. Not wanting, nor wasting, thou rulest in might; Thy justice like mountains high soaring above, Thy clouds which are fountains of goodness and love...'

'Goodness and love! You'll be telling me every cloud has a silver lining next.' Ingrid began to shake. 'Silver linings...' It was the ultimate joke. A silver lining meant only one thing - clouds that had been seeded with silver iodide, clouds that deluged Exmoor with nine inches of rain, clouds that killed.

Silver lining. Had they found silver iodide on her diary? It was all the proof she needed to face them, the government... and Steven Carmichael? 'No, not Steven.' She dropped her head into her hands. 'Such a fool.... Will I ever learn? What do you think God?' she said to the simple wooden cross hanging over the mantelpiece. He was silent, no more communicative now than when she turned to him for help in Salisbury cathedral.

But what if the government decided she was a loose cannon? With Jack gone, blackmail was useless. What else would they try? 'Did they force us off the road?' The Mercedes would never be traced; any investigation would be quashed one way or another. So much power. 'No!' It didn't happen here, not in Britain. No, it had to be Powell. But she only had Alex's word that Powell was behind everything. And that relied on the so-called 'facts' Steven had planted in his mind. Steven Carmichael was implicated in blackmail, bribery and deception; would he stop short of murder?

Mark's voice filtered through from the church. 'And may the peace that passes all understanding remain with you now and always. Amen.'

'Amen,' the congregation responded.

Thank God for one person she could trust.

'Are you fit for some lock busting then?' Julie asked, balancing the last of the hymn books in a neat stack by the door.

'Sit down, Julie. There's something I need to say first.'

'That sounds ominous.'

'It needn't be, but that depends on you.' He took a breath. 'Moira's here.'

'Where?'

'In the vestry.' Julie turned away. 'Please, Julie, hear me out.' She paused. 'Did you think about what I said last time, about needing resolution for all of you?'

'Yes.'

'And...?'

'You're right. But it's hard, realising everything I've thought, or said... that it's all been about protecting me.'

Mark waited.

'I... I hated Moira because... I needed someone to blame. She was supposed to be dead wasn't she?'

'Only now you know she isn't dead, what's happened to all that hatred?'

Julie pressed her hand to her chest.

'It will eat away at you, Julie.'

'I know.'

'It's time to let it go.'

'But I loved them so much,' she sobbed. 'Why did he take them from me?'

'So you want to hate God now? If you do he'll understand and it won't change his love for you in the slightest; but is that what you really want?'

'What can I do?'

'It's the most natural thing in the world to want to keep your children alive; to hold them in your heart and never let them go. But is that what's best for any of you? Maybe it's time to set them free.'

'That sounds so beautiful, for them, but I don't know how.'

'Are you willing to try?'

She hesitated. 'Yes.'

'Then you'll find a way; we'll find a way. If you look into your heart right now what is it telling you to do?'

Julie looked across at the Vestry door. 'I don't know if I can.'

Ingrid was sitting in the armchair, the blanket pulled up under her chin, her head slumped to one side.

'Hello, Moira.'

She opened her eyes. 'Julie?'

'I need to say something... the last time... when you came to the Manor... I...'

'I deserved every word of it.'

'Please Moira, let me say this, only it's not easy.' She took a breath. 'I blamed you for Michael and Alistair's death. What I said to you was unforgivable but... if you'll forgive me, for that day, for every day of the last thirty years that I've... I've...'

Ingrid stood and held her arms out. 'Of course you blamed me; there's not been a day when I haven't blamed myself. Can you ever forgive me, Julie? For not saving your boys...' The words caught in her throat.

Mark disappeared into the church. Fifteen minutes later he was back at the door. 'Would you both like to come back to the vicarage for some lunch?'

'Lunch!' Ingrid laughed.

Mark and Julie exchanged glances. 'Or we could go to the Manor,' Julie said.

'I'm sorry,' Ingrid said. 'It's just... do you remember I tried to tell you about how the government were experimenting with artificial rainmaking? How they're responsible for the floods.'

'I wasn't in any state to listen; sorry.'

'Because of what I know I've been blackmailed, forced out of my job, witnessed a murder... and you're talking about lunch. It's all so bizarrely normal.'

Julie put her arm around Ingrid. 'What will you do now?'

'Nick was right about one thing...'

'Nick?' Julie interrupted.

'My boss. Correction ex-boss. He was helping me with this for a while. Anyway, he said I should go public.'

'There's an obvious time and place for you to do it,' Mark said.

'The meeting!' Julie exclaimed.

'Precisely. At four o'clock this afternoon the town hall will be packed with people, every single one of them interested in the floods. We've got a journalist coming down from London to cover it...'

'You didn't say,' Julie interrupted.

'The MP organised it. Bound to have more to do with him being up for re-election than us, but you'll get national coverage, Ingrid.'

'It's perfect,' Julie said.

'Are you sure you won't go to the police first?' Mark said.

'I might as well put a signpost outside the door telling MI5 I'm here.'

Julie said. 'Do they know what happened between us, when you came to the Manor?'

'Probably.'

'In that case, it's the last place they'll be looking for you. I'll get my car. Mark, I'll leave it to you to get her out without being seen. And bring the briefcase.'

'Wait here, Ingrid,' Mark said.

She leant against the vestry door, grateful to be alone.

The walking party was a godsend, literally according to Mark. They were delighted to find the vicar present and happy to offer a free guided tour. Fifteen minutes later Mark completed his potted history of St Mary's, coincidentally right in front of the donations box, and escorted the group through the churchyard. Concealed in the group, Ingrid slipped out of the church and into Julie's car.

A few minutes later, Dave Harrison left the walkers and doubled back to the phone box.

'Mr Carmichael? We've found her. There's going to be a meeting this afternoon... yes, she intends to go public... Just a minute. This could be exactly what we need... You said you have evidence to prove that seeding couldn't have caused the floods... Right. Well this is the time to use it... Yes... Yes... If you're absolutely certain he'll corroborate your findings then bring him. And any documentation you've got. We discredit her now, publicly, and it's over.'

Alex waited for his father to hang up then put the extension down. He picked it up again almost immediately... and paused. He had to call; the information he'd just overheard was crucial but... there was always a but.

Moments later Alex made his decision. He lifted the handset and punched in the now familiar number. 'Sophie?'

Elliott Grigg was beginning to enjoy retirement. He'd been accepted as a weather recorder by the Met Office, which more or less filled his mornings; the afternoon was devoted to developing some ideas in the workshop he'd installed in the garage, and in the evenings he sorted and stored a lifetime's work on weather modification. But being at home had its downside. For years now, he and Elizabeth had lived in the Lodge to Woolmer House, a stately home six miles north of Salisbury. He had a nodding acquaintance with the chief warden but within a week of retiring he'd been cornered into accepting a summons to coffee.

'We're looking to expand local support for the House,' Commander Hunt had stated when Elliott was barely through the door. 'Lord Woolmer suggested using the hall for talks, exhibitions, conferences, that sort of thing. Looking for some speakers to kick the thing off. Elizabeth tells me you're something to do with the weather. Always a topic that goes down well and you're just the type we need to present it. Can I book you in?'

It was Elliott's worst nightmare. 'I'm not sure that I'm...'

'Elizabeth said you'd be too modest to offer yourself so I've put you in for September, the 24th I think it is. We'll do all the publicity, get a good crowd, no need for you to worry about that. Might even get a national down.'

'But what...'

'Yes, the topic. Leave that to you. Make it something memorable to kick the autumn season off. Just keep away from politics - should be safe enough with the weather eh?'

He was in the sanctuary of his workshop when Elizabeth called him to the phone. 'Yes?'

'Elliott? It's Steven. I need you to come to Lynton with me, this afternoon. I'll pick you up in fifteen minutes.'

Elliott would have expected it of Powell but it wasn't like Steven to miss the finer points of retirement.

'Fifteen minutes will be fine.' Elliott was also having trouble adjusting.

'So what now?' Julie asked as they moved to the conservatory.

'Can we try the sitting room?' Ingrid said, hanging back in the doorway.

'Of course, I didn't think.'

Ingrid selected a chair away from the windows.

'Listen, there's something we have to sort out,' Julie said. 'What do I call you? Moira or Ingrid?'

'I think you were right; Moira's dead.'

'So it's Ingrid then. How does that feel?'

'Good... it feels good.'

'We need to get you to this meeting, Ingrid,' Mark said.

'But I don't know what to say, I haven't had time to put anything together, I need to get it clear in my head...'

'Just say it as it comes, like you did over lunch. I got it, so will they,' Julie said.

'I'd better get back.' Mark stood.

'Just a minute, the briefcase.' She fetched it from the hall.

'Ingrid, I want you as my witness that Mrs Davenport actually asked me to break into this briefcase,' Mark said.

'Break into it?'

'It was Hugh's, only I don't know where the key is,' Julie replied.

Ingrid stared at the case. 'I do.'

'What?'

'I think I know where the key is.'

'How? It's been buried in the cellar for God knows how long. How can you possibly know?' Julie demanded.

'Did you keep Hugh's desk?'

'Yes.'

Ingrid was on her feet and running up the stairs. She burst through the door as she had done all those years before. She could still see him standing there, his briefcase lying on the open desk, the small drawer pulled right out, his hand reaching into the space it had left. She pulled out the drawer and felt behind it. Moments later she handed Julie the key.

'I don't understand,' Julie said, gazing at the flight plans, SkySearch bulletins and technical cloud seeding data she'd pulled from the case.

'It's why I came back.' Ingrid hesitated. 'I discovered Hugh was working for SkySearch, for Richard Powell and Steven Carmichael. He was their pilot, taking their research team up.'

'But if he was only doing a few experiments for a private company why all the secrecy?' Julie asked. Mark guided her to a chair.

'SkySearch had a contract with the government to conduct cloud seeding experiments. It was all covered under the Official Secrets Act.'

'But trying to make it rain is hardly earth shattering stuff.'

'It is if your client is the Ministry of Defence and they're looking at weather modification as a weapon of war.'

Julie flicked through the flight plans. They began in the early 1950's; just a series of dates and flight times, crew members, purpose of flight. Page after page of details. Ingrid scanned the sheets over Julie's shoulder. Most of the flights concentrated on cloud physics research - actual seeding was relatively rare. Then Julie's hand froze on the sheet for August 15th 1952.

The silence was finally broken as her words began to fall. 'He'd promised to be at the children's play. They'd rehearsed so hard. I remember now, he talked about conditions. The conditions changed and he was gone. Alistair and Michael were so disappointed he wasn't there. Alistair barely remembered his lines. And Hugh was going to help us with the dance.' She turned to Ingrid. 'You remember, all that heavy equipment we had to move. He promised he would be there. I thought he'd broken his promise.' Julie looked towards the desk. She spoke as though Hugh were standing there. 'But you hadn't had you? Of course you hadn't. You always kept your word didn't you darling?' Her face was strangely immobile.

She stood up and went over to the desk. Ingrid made to go after her but Mark held her arm. 'Not yet,' he mouthed.

'But you were there,' Julie said, her voice harsher now. 'Not in the school hall, not at the dance beneath all those damned corrugated sheets, but up there,' she jabbed her finger skywards, 'above the clouds. You knew we were there, dancing by the river, but you carried on with your little experiment; still sent the rain to wash our happiness away.'

Ingrid wrenched her arm away from Mark; she had to stop this. But before she could move the words exploded from Julie.

'YOU MURDERED OUR CHILDREN.'

Mark went over to Julie, held her in his arms and rocked her as you would a child.

'His depression... blaming himself... all true,' she gasped.

'I'm so sorry you had to find out, Julie,' Ingrid said.

She looked up. 'You knew?'

'Only for a couple of days.'

'You knew! When you hugged me in the church you knew! When you came home with me you knew!'

Mark pulled Ingrid out of the room. 'Get the housekeeper to ring the GP, then wait downstairs.'

It was a while before Mark appeared. 'Are you okay?' he said.

'Bit shaken but nothing compared to what Julie's going through,' Ingrid replied. 'Will she be all right?'

'If what I saw and heard in the church earlier today is anything to go by, then yes.'

'Will she see me?'

'Maybe, later. But first we have to get to this meeting.'

'What, now?'

'Especially now. Are you going to let her go through all that for nothing?'

Chapter Twenty-two

Ingrid paced the worn floorboards of the anteroom inside Lynton Town Hall. There was a constant stream of footsteps on the stairs outside the door. Everyone in Lynton and Lynmouth wanted to have their say. 'Oh God,' Ingrid whispered. She wrapped her arms across her stomach.

'How are you doing?' Mark slipped through the heavily panelled door that led straight into the main hall.

'Pass.'

'There are some faces I don't recognise. Do you feel up to taking a look?'

'Do I have to?'

'No. But better now than when you're standing in front of them.' He held the door open.

Ingrid walked across to the curtain at the edge of the platform. 'Where?' she whispered. He pointed towards two men sitting half way along the hall. 'Oh God, they're the ones who tried to blackmail me.'

'So we can safely assume Her Majesty's Government are with us. Anyone else you recognise?'

'No. I can't see Steven - but Powell could be there. I don't know what he looks like.'

Mark led her back to the anteroom. 'Back in a minute.'

'Do you have to go?'

'I'm only on the other side of the door.'

'I know... I'm sorry. It's just that...'

He took her hand. 'It will all be over in a few minutes. Just hold on.'

Ingrid nodded.

'Stay in the wings until I give you the cue. Good luck.'

Elliott stepped out of the car at the door to the Town Hall. The bodies funnelling up the steps ahead of him intensified the feeling in the pit of his stomach. He should have let Elizabeth save him from the terrifying prospect of speaking in front of all these strangers.

'I'll find somewhere to park,' Steven said. 'But you know what to say if they need the facts before I get back.'

Elliott knew all right; Steven had made it quite clear. The future of the company was at stake. No company - no pension. Where was the choice? A few cloud seeding flights couldn't have caused major flooding anyway, not with the prevailing westerlies here. No, he would stake his professional reputation on it.

Twenty minutes later, several outspoken residents were still drawing up their battle lines over whether or not to commemorate the thirtieth anniversary of the floods. Ingrid listened from the anteroom as Frank Williams imposed himself on the meeting.

'This town has had tragedy written over it for too long. We're trying to get the grockles back but we're hardly going to do that by reminding them they might get drowned if they stay too close to the river!'

'I know this is a concept you'll struggle with, Mr Williams, but this isn't about money,' Mrs Bryce-Jones bristled. 'We are a community here, a community that suffered a grave tragedy, one that deserves commemoration.'

Cries of, 'hear, hear,' sounded round the hall. Mark seized the moment. 'I propose we take a vote.'

'On what?' Frank Williams shouted.

Ingrid could have strangled him. There was no time for small-minded bickering. Didn't they realise what was at stake?

Mark glanced her way. 'I propose that a commemoration, the exact nature of which to be decided after extensive consultation, be held to mark the thirtieth anniversary of the Lynmouth floods. All those in favour?' The clear vote was a relief. He turned to the clerk to ensure it was recorded.

'Well, on your bloody heads be it.' Frank Williams was on his feet and pushing along the row. Others took their cue and the hall filled with the sound of chairs scraping back on the wooden floor.

'Wait.' Mark called. 'There's something else.'

The town clerk raised his hand. 'This meeting was called for a specific reason. I don't know that any other business is in order. I could check the...'

'In order or not, this is something you'll want to know. It's about the floods,' Mark continued.

'What about them?' Frank Williams grunted.

'We haven't got all day vicar,' another voice called from the doorway.

'There was a lot of talk at the time about what caused the floods. Bill,' Mark turned to his committee member, 'You spoke to a reporter about a strange sulphurous smell in the air.' He pointed to a man sitting in the third row. 'Mr Keane, you talked about a peculiar pink shade in an ugly threatening sky. Many of you thought that artificial rainmaking had something to do with what happened that night...'

Mrs Bryce-Jones leapt to her feet. 'Vicar, I would have thought you'd be the last person to perpetuate idle rumour and gossip. I think I speak for everyone here when I say it serves no purpose to give these accusations any credence. We all wanted, needed someone to blame. Our loved ones had been torn from us, we were angry. But it was an act of God. We have come to terms with it. Don't open those wounds again.'

'Thank you Mrs Bryce-Jones. You may be right. But a few months ago someone began to investigate whether or not the government, despite denials, had been cloud seeding in the early

234

fifties. She has uncovered facts - not rumours, not gossip - but facts that show conclusively that cloud seeding was happening. Someone has gone to extreme lengths to suppress this information; but she believes you have a right to know.'

'What facts?' a voice called.

'I'd like to bring her over to answer that.' Mark beckoned Ingrid onto the stage.

'Is this a joke?' Frank Williams blurted. 'This woman's a liar, a bigamist and God knows what else. What's in it for her? That's what you should be asking. You can't believe a word she says.' He was addressing the audience, not Mark.

'It's not a matter of belief,' Mark retaliated, 'but facts.' Whatever you think of Moira's actions you can't...'

'Don't tell me what I can't do. If you want facts I've a few...'

'Shut up, shut up, shut up!' The woman at Frank Williams' side was on her feet. 'We've all heard quite enough of you. For goodness sake sit down and let the vicar speak.'

Applause rippled through the hall. Then the audience fell silent, curious to hear whether the first Mrs Williams deserved their support.

Ingrid swallowed, anxiously scanning the faces before her.

'When you're ready, Ingrid.' Mark sat.

'Excuse me,' Steven approached the woman pacing back and forth across the foyer. Where is the meeting being held?'

Julie nodded in the direction of the stairs. 'Up there. It's straight ahead of you at the top.'

'Thanks. Are you going up?'

She clutched the briefcase closer to her chest. 'I'm not sure.'

Steven paused. 'Likely to be long-winded is it?'

As if on cue, Frank Williams raised yet another objection. Julie smiled, 'Yes, but not for the usual reasons.' She looked at Steven. 'You're not local are you?'

'No.'

'Press? Mark is expecting someone from a national to cover the story.'

'No, I'm not press. What story is that?'

'About whether the town should commemorate the floods.'

'Of course.' He paused. 'What do you think?'

'I haven't decided.'

'It was so long ago, isn't it time the victims were allowed some peace?'

Julie shrugged. 'I suppose it depends on whether their survivors can do that.'

'How do you mean?'

'A lot of us are still asking why.'

'It's understandable with any natural disaster to want someone or something to blame.'

'But was it? Was it a natural disaster?'

'Yes it was.'

Julie looked at him. 'You seem very sure.'

'I study the weather. This was like the floods along the East coast the year after. Massive weather systems produce freak conditions all the time. The tragedy is that sometimes we get in the way and lives are lost.'

'But what if someone can't resist trying to manipulate all that power...?'

'We can try, but anything we do is nothing more than a drop in the ocean compared to the natural forces at work on this planet.'

'Are we really that insignificant?'

'I may be shooting myself in the foot for saying this but yes, I believe we are. Anyway, I'd better be getting upstairs. Are you...?'

'No... no, I don't think so.'

'Cloud seeding has never been a priority in this country.' Elliott had finally summoned up the courage to speak.

'But you're not denying it was happening?' Ingrid retorted.

'No. It was simply done on an ad hoc basis.'

'And did ad hoc include August 14th 1952?'

'Yes, but...'

'And August 15th?'

'Yes, but just a few cloud physics experiments.'

'I've read reports stating that an increase in rainfall of up to fifty percent is possible.'

'Those reports relate to one experiment conducted at high altitude in the mountains of western USA. Most reliable research quotes ten percent, fifteen as an absolute maximum.'

'But can the effect be cumulative?'

'If one area is repeatedly targeted that's possible but the experiments you are talking about were conducted up country.'

'Do you deny seeding can have an impact on weather up to three hundred miles away?'

'No, but circumstances have to be right. Cloud conditions are rarely right for seeding to make any significant impact and for this area to be affected it would have to take place in Cornwall or Wales because of the prevailing westerlies. The experiments you quote are irrelevant.'

'You see,' Frank Williams interrupted, 'she comes back here causing trouble and hasn't even got her facts straight.'

'But the wind could have come from a different direction at the time couldn't it?' Ingrid persisted.

'It could have. But it didn't. Met Office reports clearly state the wind was travelling from west to east.'

Ingrid grimaced. Why hadn't she checked? Nick had said ages ago that it would all depend on wind speed and direction. Why hadn't she taken more notice?

People were starting to move. Steven grasped the opportunity to find an empty seat. Ingrid followed him as he worked his way along the row.

'Who do you work for Mr Grigg?' Heads turned to identify the new voice.

Elliott swivelled to face the young woman leaning against the window. 'I'm retired.'

Sophie continued. 'But you used to work for a company called SkySearch. Isn't that right?'

'Yes.'

'And SkySearch provide cloud seeding services.'

'Yes.'

'Who for?'

'I'm not at liberty to reveal that information.'

'Isn't it true that you worked for the Ministry of Defence?'

'As I said, I'm not at liberty to reveal that information.'

'So, speaking hypothetically, it might well be in your interests to prove that cloud seeding was not responsible for the tragedy that occurred here.'

The hall was silent. A hint of conspiracy made all the difference.

'I am a scientist. My only concern is for the facts. On August 15th 1952, the wind was westerly.'

'I can confirm that.' Steven stood.

'And you are...?' asked Mark.

'Steven Carmichael, co-director of SkySearch UK. I have the relevant file here,' he waved a red folder in the air, 'which details all, or I should say, the little work that SkySearch were doing in cloud seeding at the time.'

'Can I see that?' Mark asked, walking towards Steven.

'Of course.' Steven passed the file to him.

'Mr Chairman, I think you should compare the contents of the file Mr Carmichael has given you with these notes, copied from that file less than a week ago.' Sophie raised a folder above her head.

'How the hell did you get hold of that?' Steven said.

'Fortunately your son had the vision to see where this was headed and the courage to do something about it Mr Carmichael,' Sophie said.

Steven scanned the crowd until he found Alex. 'Is this true?'

'And he has evidence,' Sophie continued, 'of your attempts to suppress this investigation, attempts that led to the death of an innocent person. Why is it Mr Carmichael that both the authorities and yourself were so keen to shut these people up?'

'That's not how it is.'

'Are you denying that one of the team of three who began this investigation with Mrs Clarke is now dead?'

'No, but...'

'How did he die Mr Carmichael?'

'He drowned, in the West Lyn.'

'By accident or design?'

'I... I don't know.'

'Really?'

'Stop. This has nothing to do with my father. It was all Powell.' Alex was on his feet.

'Richard Powell, the co-director of SkySearch,' Sophie stated.

'Yes. My father's got proof that it was all down to Powell,' Alex said.

'Proof that Richard Powell was behind this man's death?'

'Yes.'

'Let's be clear on this. You're saying that the co-director of a firm under contract to the government was responsible for the death of a man who was about to prove that cloud seeding caused the Lynmouth floods.' She had reeled him in to perfection. 'Why would they do that, Alex? Why would SkySearch take such extreme steps?'

Alex was visibly shaking. 'Because...' he stuttered, 'because...'

'Because *if* SkySearch were responsible,' Steven interjected, 'Richard Powell and I were personally liable for any compensation.'

'*If*, Mr Carmichael?'

'You've had your say. Playing to people's fears here, stringing together a load of supposition to fit the conclusion you've already decided on. Elliott Grigg and I are scientists. And it's science this meeting should be concentrating on - not scaremongering. Whatever Powell did or didn't do - however despicable - doesn't change that science.

'Firstly, heavy rain fell across the whole of the West Country and Wales that night, caused by a depression that had stagnated in the Southwest approaches for two days.' Steven pointed at Elliott. 'And secondly, you've heard it from the expert. The wind was blowing from the wrong direction. The conditions were wrong for anything we did to have any effect on Lynmouth. That's the truth. Not some mock science dished up by a group of amateurs hell bent on holding back progress at any cost.'

'As far as I can see the information in this file supports that conclusion.' Mark held up the red file.

'Of course it does,' Steven continued. 'The Lynmouth floods were a dreadful tragedy. My heart goes out to all whose lives were devastated by what happened. It's natural for you to want someone to blame. Yes, I've made mistakes. I should have acted sooner to stop Richard Powell, I bitterly regret that I didn't, but we all do the best we can, when we can. Which is why I'm here now. You have a right to the truth.'

'The truth?' Ingrid moved to the front of the stage. 'You dare talk about the truth. Do you deny you lied to me?'

'No, but...'

'And that you - *you*, not Powell, not anyone else - tracked me down for one reason and one reason only, to stop me talking.' Ingrid fought to keep her composure. He wasn't going to have the satisfaction of putting it all down to an emotional outburst of some middle aged woman who had got the wrong end of the stick.

'It wasn't like that...'

'No?' She had to keep her voice steady. 'Well it doesn't matter now. You want proof, scientific proof, then you'll have it.' Ingrid looked at Sophie. 'The seeding agent most commonly used in these experiments was silver iodide.' Sophie scowled but Ingrid forged on. 'On the night of August 15th, 1952, I was caught up in the floods. My clothes, my hair, everything on me that night was covered in a layer of mud - including the diary that I gave to Miss Cox a couple of days ago to test for the presence of silver iodide. Sophie?'

A motion like a breaking wave spread across the hall as row after row of heads turned to face Sophie Cox.

'We sent samples of mud from Mrs Clarke's diary for testing for traces of silver iodide. If found these will prove beyond any doubt that seeding did affect the amount of rainfall that fell on Lynmouth on August 15th.'

Ingrid looked puzzled, 'But you said...'

'That we will have to wait for the results. That's right.'

'Is that right, Ingrid? Is that what Miss Cox said to you?' Steven asked. 'Only you seem surprised by her response.'

'I... I don't know.'

'You were talking about the truth earlier. This is very important Ingrid. Exactly what did Miss Cox say to you about the tests?'

Ingrid looked from Sophie to Steven. She had torn into him for straying from the truth and now here she was... 'When I called her this morning she said the results were back but she hadn't had a chance to look at them yet.'

'Miss Cox?'

'Investing too much in these results will cloud the issue,' Sophie said. 'All the evidence indicates seeding was happening at exactly the right time to have had an impact on Lynmouth.'

'Not all the evidence, surely. We've already established the wind was blowing in the wrong direction. So tell us please, Miss Cox, what did the results show?'

'The results were negative.'

'In other words, there were no traces of silver iodide,' Steven persisted.

'Not as yet. But this was just one line of enquiry.'

'The truth is, Miss Cox, that there is no evidence to find. The Lynmouth floods were a tragic natural disaster and had nothing whatever to do with cloud seeding.' He sat down.

'I told you.' Frank Williams was on his feet. 'Personal vendetta, all of it. The only reason you've have to sit through this load of bullshit is because of this woman's personal agenda.' He pointed at Ingrid. 'The truth is that two kids died because of her and she faked her own death to cover it up. This woman will do anything to get herself off the hook.'

'That's not true,' Ingrid shouted. '*They're* the ones with the agenda,' she pointed at Harrison and Wilson, already making their way out, 'and Richard Powell and...' she hesitated, 'and Steven Carmichael. I *will* prove it.'

Mark stood. 'I suggest we take some time to consider what has been said here today. Thank you all for coming...'

'No,' Ingrid interrupted. 'You've got to listen, please...' but the hall was already emptying; people were shuffling along the rows, refusing to meet her eyes. 'I know they're to blame. You can't let them get away with it like this. Please, they've twisted it all around. You've got to believe me.'

Mark put his arm around Ingrid and guided her to a chair. 'This isn't helping Ingrid. Let them go.'

'Is that it?' Ingrid said, her legs giving way beneath her. 'It's all been for nothing?'

'It's a setback; that's all. We need to think about what happens next.'

'Ever since I found Private Dean's photograph I've lurched from one crisis to the next, all leading up to today - the day everyone saw exactly what was going on and rose as one to do something about it. Great fantasy eh?' She rested her head against the wall and closed her eyes.

'What happens now? I haven't a clue.'

Chapter Twenty-three

Julie stepped back as the doors burst open and the first wave spilled out of the main hall and down the stairs.

'Woman's deranged. Inventing all that conspiracy stuff to save her own skin. How she ever thought she could come back here I don't know.' A group clustered around the outspoken woman. 'And to think she let those two little boys die then had the nerve to pretend to be someone else all those years. She should be locked up.'

'It's the vicar I don't understand. Supporting her like that!' another said.

'Well I'm not going back to church, that's for sure.'

'Nor me. Never did like him. Too much of the city about him.'

'It'll be on the agenda of the next parish council meeting, you can be sure of that. It's the least we can do for poor Mrs Davenport.'

'Poor Mrs Davenport,' Julie whispered under her breath. Was that what she was to become? And Ingrid cast as the local pariah; Mark moved on to another parish. They would do it. She had no doubt of that. But to force her way into that room, to raise her voice and bring all that hate and vitriol down on Hugh's memory... Julie shuddered.

'Excuse me,' Elliott edged across the landing, 'but is the gents anywhere around here?' Julie pointed to a door behind her. 'Thank you.'

Ingrid's pleas fell on deaf ears as the exodus continued. Julie stepped forward. She had to do it - but the SkySearch man was adamant that seeding had nothing to do with the floods.

'That's better.' Elliott was standing beside her, waiting for the flow of people to ease up.

'It's Mr Grigg isn't it?' she asked.

'Yes.'

'I heard what you were saying, about the wind direction. If there was something else, something new, would it make any difference?'

'That would depend on what it was. Why do you ask?'

'I...' There were still so many people milling about in the hall, standing in clusters, gossiping. But she had to be sure. 'There's something I'd like your opinion on, as a scientist.'

'I imagine we'll be leaving very soon.'

'Please, it's important.'

'Very well. Shall we?' he said, indicating the door to the anteroom.

At the far end of the hall Alex leant against a window, his eyes fixed on the woman pushing her way through the crowds to her car.

'Let her go, Alex,' Steven said, resting a hand on his shoulder. 'Sophie Cox is a professional. You're not the first she's sucked in and you certainly won't be the last.'

Alex shrugged his hand away. 'You don't understand, it's not like that.'

'No? So tell me, what *is* it like - being used as a pawn to get at your father?'

'It wasn't personal. If you hadn't gone ahead with LYRE none of this would have happened. They couldn't let you sign that contract.'

'They?'

'Sophie and Madeline. They don't let sentiment or vested interest get in the way. They live their beliefs - just like mum.'

'Oh. And I don't?' They stood in silence. 'Who were you doing this for Alex?'

'What do you mean?'

'For yourself, for them... or your mother?'

Alex shrugged. 'I don't know. Mum maybe.'

'Martha is dead Alex; it's time to start making your own decisions.'

'You have to meet Madeline dad.'

'I don't think so. Anyone who could use you as they did will never have a place in my life.'

'They didn't use me. They're just passionate about protecting the earth; and prepared to fight for it.'

'That's the point. They're fighters - and not too concerned about who gets caught in the crossfire. Your mum was passionate about what she did; I'm passionate about my work. Before you make any decisions, be sure what you're passionate about.'

Alex looked at him. 'I don't get it. You should be giving me a bollocking.'

'Maybe.' He paused. 'But I've done more than enough to drive away the people I care about for one day.'

Alex followed his father's eyes to where Ingrid sat, her head propped against the wood panelling, eyes closed.

Words were falling like a warm, soft blanket wrapping themselves around her, supporting and protecting her. But as she relaxed into its comfortable embrace, the blanket fell over her face. She tried to push it away but it was suffocating her.

'Be sure to keep the house in sight. And be back well before dark.'

'Yes dad.'

'Put your winter coat on or you'll catch your death.'

'But they're going.'

'Be careful.'

Her legs carried her along the track. She wouldn't look back: she looked back... at her father, watching her, fearful of unseen dangers. It trapped her breath. Was that when she'd first fought for breath - all those years ago? No wonder she'd run, she had to be free of him. Free to marry, free to cower, free to cover her bruises with make up; free to watch as Michael and

245

Alistair drowned. Of course she kept running. No-one could live like that. With the fear - with the guilt. Always the guilt...

Ingrid's harsh breaths echoed through the empty hall.

'Ingrid... Ingrid, what can I do?' Mark said.

Ingrid forced her eyes open. 'Inh...aler.'

'Where is it?'

'Bag...'

Mark looked around. Steven had almost reached them. 'Stay with her,' Mark said, disappearing into the anteroom.

Steven knelt by Ingrid. 'Take my hands. That's good. Now close your eyes and breathe out for me, very gently.'

'Can't.'

'Give me your widest possible grin. I'm doing it and I don't appreciate looking like an idiot alone so please, grin and breathe out.'

The grin was lopsided but it was there and just for a second the awful sound eased.

'That's great. Now focus on your scalp. Really concentrate on releasing it. Release and relax. Start a wave that's going to cascade all down your body relaxing everything it touches. Let it flow down your face, past your cheeks, your chin, your neck. Let it flow down your chest, a wonderful warm wave of relaxation releasing everything in its path.'

'Where's... Mark?'

'He'll be right back. Now say to yourself, I breathe for myself, I take charge of my life.'

'What... on... earth...'

'Please. Let the words flow through your mind. I breathe for myself, I take charge of my life.'

Very slowly, Ingrid's breathing began to ease. '...myself, I take... charge of my life. I... breathe for myself... I take charge... of my life. I... breathe...'

'That's great, and when you're ready, open your eyes and, very gently, breathe out again.'

Ingrid's grip on his hands gradually relaxed as her breathing slowly returned to normal. 'How did you do that?'

'Martha had asthma. It's something she taught me.'

'Thank you.' Ingrid was suddenly conscious of his hands gently holding hers. It wasn't the kind of touch that wanted to steer and control; no, this felt more like the touch of a sensitive guide.

What rubbish! This man had lied, deceived, conspired to murder and God knows what else. Hadn't he? She pulled her hands away.

Mark reappeared with her inhaler. 'Thanks, Mark, but I think I'm okay.'

'If you're sure...' Mark began.

'Absolutely, thanks.'

'In that case I think you should come next door. You too, Mr Carmichael. Julie has something to say.'

Across the room, Alex checked his tape recorder and caught up with his father at the anteroom door.

'Julie!' Ingrid exclaimed. 'Were you here? I didn't see you.'

'Yes and no. I'm sorry, Ingrid, I couldn't do it to Hugh, not in front of all those people. I couldn't bear the thought of them gossiping about him, pulling his memory through the mud. It's one thing for me to know but...'

'It's okay,' Ingrid said. 'It wouldn't have made any difference. Apparently there's no way anything SkySearch did could have had an impact on Lynmouth. It was a natural disaster. Case closed.'

'Mr Carmichael,' Julie's voice was surprisingly confident. 'You said there's no evidence your seeding affected Lynmouth.'

'Yes, the wind...'

'And you're sure of that?'

'Elliott has all the records, there's no mistake.' Steven glanced at Elliott.

'Well you're wrong.' Julie picked up the top sheet from a sheaf of papers lying on the table next to Hugh's briefcase. 'This is a letter from a Mr Sutton to the West Somerset Free Press on November 23rd. 1952. He says, *the flood must have been the result of a freak storm or cloudburst.* And further on, *on the morning of August 15th the wind was fresh to strong from almost due East...'*

'But our flight went up later in the day didn't it Elliott?'

'When exactly?' Ingrid said.

'If you have Mr Davenport's log book there it should say,' Elliott said.

Ingrid sorted through the pile of papers until she came across a large leather bound record book. She flicked through the pages. 'It says, *on August 14th three flights went up at 11.30, 14.30 and 15.25.'*

'There's nothing here to say they were cloud seeding flights,' Steven interrupted.

Ingrid looked up. 'But if they were it must have had an impact on Exmoor. There's an iron pan under the peat on the Chains. Once it gets waterlogged there's nowhere for the water to go other than into the rivers.' She read on. 'On the 15th there was a flight at 14.35 lasting one hour forty minutes. So allowing time for the run out and back they could have been seeding for an hour between... 14.55 and 15.55.'

Mark said, 'There's another record here, an Air Ministry Met office table showing hourly rainfall over Exmoor on August 15th 1952.' They waited. 'The heaviest rainfall over the Chains began at 16.00 - four o'clock.' He looked up, 'immediately after that flight.'

'But it's all irrelevant. Even if they were seeding, it was up country and the wind was westerly by that time,' Steven finally said.

Mark looked back at the sheet in his hand. 'Mr Sutton seems to confirm that. *At 12 noon... it was noted that a very dense layer of cloud of the nimbus variety was moving slowly from WEST to EAST...'* he paused, looked at Ingrid, then continued... 'but, *underneath that was curling wisps of cloud, like broken cumulus, travelling at tremendous speed from EAST to WEST.'* Mark looked at Steven. 'He says that the east/west cloud was moving at anything between 60 to 70 m.p.h. Could it have carried the seeding over Exmoor?'

Steven thought for a moment. 'It's possible. But for it to have had a serious impact it would need to get drawn up into clouds at an altitude of at least 45,000ft and that's rare over England.'

'I think you'd better listen to this,' Ingrid held up the final piece of paper. 'On August 15th Captain Singleton, a pilot with the U.S.A.F. reported a line of cumulonimbus extending northwestwards over Southern England. *Captain Singleton estimated that the tops away to the west were rising to 45000-50000 ft. It was on this day that severe flooding took place in southwest England.*'

Chapter Twenty-four

It was a victory - wasn't it? Ingrid waited for some sensation to filter through her exhausted body and mind. How should she react? Not with whoops of delight certainly, but surely there should be something? She'd been quick enough to feel anger and despair when Steven turned the meeting against her. Shouldn't this be sweet revenge? She watched as he read and re-read the yellowing sheets from Hugh's briefcase, his face ashen.

Alex sat beside him. 'Are you okay?'

'I was so certain. So bloody certain that you, Ingrid, all the others had got it wrong...'

'You can't blame yourself.'

'I honestly believed there was no way...'

'I know.'

'But according to this, if those flights were seeding, then...' He paused. 'If... if I was in any way to blame for all those deaths... if I'm responsible...'

The silence lengthened. Ingrid wanted him to suffer, as she had, as so many had, but... 'Not you alone,' she said finally. 'You were the government's agent. They wanted this work done; it was their intention to use it as a weapon of war causing God knows how much more suffering without blame or accountability. They're the ones we have to stop.'

'What will you do?' Mark said.

'I don't know,' Steven said. 'I suppose... the first thing is to make this new evidence public.'

'I'm afraid not.' Harrison appeared from the hallway and

snatched the sheets from Steven's hand. 'This matter will go no further than this room. Mr Carmichael, Mr Grigg, you are both subject to the Official Secrets Act. The younger Mr Carmichael too I believe.' He looked at Ingrid. 'And you will be signing it in just a few moments Mrs Clarke, and you too Mrs Davenport.'

'I will not. I haven't come through all this to be silenced now,' Ingrid said.

'Mrs Clarke, please don't deceive yourself that you can take us on and win. There are many ways I can make your life extremely uncomfortable. I strongly advise you not to put yourself in that position.'

'It's okay, Ingrid, you don't have to,' Alex said. He looked straight at Harrison. 'Everything we know will be public knowledge in a few hours.'

'You're in serious trouble if that's the case,' Harrison said.

'Nothing to do with me. A national had a journalist at the meeting. He picked up on everything - rainmaking, witness testimony from Mrs Davenport...'

'And how exactly could he have obtained that when you only heard about it moments ago and no-one has left this room since?'

'He clocked Mrs Davenport listening at the door and got curious. It's exactly what I'd have done.'

Ingrid sensed rather than heard Julie's intake of breath. She touched her arm.

'I bet he's faxing the copy as we speak. The paper won't believe their luck: a government conspiracy, dear little middle aged lady - no offence, Ingrid - threatened, attempts made on her life, when all she's trying to do is bring justice to the memory of all those innocent lives lost. It's an editor's dream.'

Harrison strode up to Alex. 'I suppose you think you're safe. Well think again.'

Alex held his gaze. 'Just try to...'

Steven gripped his son's shoulder. Alex remained silent for the few moments it took for the agents to leave.

'Arrogant bastards!' Alex exploded. 'Who do they think they are?'

'People with more power than you know. Tread carefully, Alex.'

Alex began to laugh. 'Mum always used to say that was your motto. She got so frustrated with you always taking the safe option.'

'She had more guts than anyone else I knew - but that's not true anymore is it? She'd have been so proud.'

Ingrid sank into a reclining chair on the terrace outside the Manor. It was over; for her at least. She shaded her eyes to look for Steven. He'd taken himself off and was standing by the stream, a lonely figure facing God knows what in the days and weeks ahead.

'What will you do now?' Julie said, pulling a chair over.

'I don't know.'

'Do you remember, years ago, I said you could stay at the Lodge if you ever needed somewhere?'

'I should have taken you up on it.'

'Well, the offer's still there.'

'Thanks, Julie,' Ingrid said.

'Say you'll take it, please.'

'I don't know...'

'Please.' Tears were filling her eyes. 'I'd understand if you didn't want to be near me... after the way I've treated you...'

'It's not that. And if anyone's sorry, it's me. For what happened before and the way you found out, about Hugh.'

'Don't be. I hated him all those years, for not being there for me. But now I understand, in a weird way it helps.'

'Helps? How?'

'I thought he was being selfish. Claiming all the grief for himself, not allowing me to be the one needing support. But he wasn't was he? His guilt was real. I couldn't have lived with that burden. Maybe understanding means I can stop hating him.'

'I don't know if I could do that.'

Julie nodded towards Steven. 'Now's your chance to find out.'

Ingrid walked across the parkland. Steven Carmichael was sitting by the river, his arms gripping his legs, the muscles of his face and chin visibly taut.

'Mind if I join you?'

He shook his head.

'I wanted to say... to, well, apologise I suppose.'

'What for?'

'There's a lot I'm not exactly proud of. My past, the cloud seeding, everything... You remember that woman at the meeting, Mrs Bryce Jones, talked about the people here needing someone to blame?'

'Vaguely.'

'Well she was right. I needed someone to blame. That's why I couldn't let it go. From the moment I saw Private Dean's photo something took over.' She glanced at him. 'I suppose psychologists would call it an obsession. But there it was, my chance to be free of guilt. I could hand it to someone else - it wouldn't be mine any more but theirs. Does that make sense?'

'In a way.'

Ingrid waited. His silence threw her. Where was his take on her situation? Why wasn't he telling her what came next? 'I'm sorry, you've more than enough to think about.'

'Yes I have.' He released his grip on his legs and turned towards her. 'But go on.'

Ingrid hesitated. 'Giving my guilt to Powell or Hoskins, Harrison, whatever his name was, that would have been okay; but not you. I never meant...' Ingrid paused. 'I never wanted it to get personal. Not with you. And if it did, then I'm sorry.'

'Thank you. That means a lot.' His face relaxed.

'Please, don't let guilt destroy your life, like it has mine.'

'Has it? Destroyed your life?'

'Two lives more like. Moira's and Ingrid's.'

'Does that have to be a bad thing?'

Ingrid paused. 'When I was with Jack, some days I felt as though the pieces of my life had been thrown up into the air and fallen back in the wrong place; and that one day I'd have to put them together all over again. I guess one day is now.'

He put his finger to his lips as a heron appeared on the opposite bank. It stood motionless searching the water; then in one effortless move, speared and swallowed a fish. Satisfied for the moment, it shook its wings and hopped from boulder to boulder down river. 'Let's walk,' Steven said, holding out his hand.

'When I first came here I couldn't believe my luck,' Ingrid said, picking her way beside the stream. 'The rivers were my sanctuary, the place where I belonged.'

'Where do you belong now?'

'I don't know. There's nothing left for me in Salisbury. It's time to move on. But as to where...'

'Your friend said something about the Lodge didn't she? Is that it?' They were alongside two enormous copper beeches at the end of the drive. On their left was a stone and timber-framed building surrounded by a picture postcard cottage garden. 'You can't turn this down, Ingrid, it's perfect.'

'But it's probably suffering from rising damp, dry rot, death-watch beetle and goodness knows what else. It hasn't been lived in for years.'

'So?'

'Lynton has too many memories.'

'But you said it yourself, this is where you belong. Someone up there has granted your wish. What's the problem?'

'I don't deserve it.'

'How do you work that out?'

'You know how!' Ingrid pulled her hand away.

He walked up the front path and tried the door. 'Would Julie mind?'

Ingrid shrugged. 'She always kept a key under the watering can in the outhouse.'

He disappeared round the back of the cottage. Moments later he opened the door. 'Welcome to the Lodge.'

She stepped inside. It was damp and uninviting, an air of neglect reinforced by a mound of advertising flyers choking the hall floor.

'Well,' Steven lifted the carpet, 'it has possibilities. These tiles would look great cleaned up. And it's a bit difficult to tell with all the perished underlay stuck to it, but I think the living room floors are solid oak. You could do a lot worse Ingrid.'

'But...'

'If this was mine I'd open up the two rooms, enlarge this window - you could definitely do that without compromising the integrity of the building - and let more light through to the back.

'You've missed your vocation.'

'Maybe, but a seven year slog and hours spent with only a slide rule and a sharp pencil for company didn't appeal.' He sat on the stairs. 'How about you? They may have booted you off the paper but it's much too soon to retire.'

'I don't know. Everything's up for grabs. Where I live, what I do...'

'Come here.' He led her into the sitting room. 'How do you feel when you look at that view?'

'Peaceful. At home.'

'So what's stopping you making the decision?'

'I don't know.'

'Imagine the sofa along there,' Steven pointed to a space beside the fire, 'and,' he walked over to the window, 'the dining table right here. Great setting for dinner.'

'Maybe you'd better come and try it out.'

'Is that an invitation?'

'Possibly.'

'In that case I accept.' His mood suddenly changed. 'Depending on how things go I may need sanctuary myself.' He looked at his watch. 'Can't put it off any longer. Better get Alex and Elliott back home.'

Ingrid walked through the hall, pausing to pick up a stray flyer. It was an advert for a local guesthouse.

'Steven, could you drop me in the village on your way?'

'Sure, but will you have a word with Julie, about taking the cottage?'

'Later, I promise. There's something I need to do first.'

The bell echoed down the hallway of the terraced guesthouse, one of several fronting onto the river.

'Yes?' The elderly lady who answered the door had such a wonderfully open countenance. Ingrid immediately felt at ease.

'You had a Mr Fairweather staying with you a few weeks back. I wondered if you had an address for him?'

'Come in my dear. Make yourself comfortable through there; I'll be back in a minute.' She placed a hand on Ingrid's back and guided her into the front room.

It was so homely; that was the only word for it. The furniture, curtains, pictures were a hotchpotch of styles, none of the soft furnishings matched and the colours were... original, but she felt like taking out a pair of slippers and curling up on the sofa. If she'd been alone she probably would have done, but a man's head was just visible over the back of an armchair. She wandered over to the window.

'Hello, Moira,' he said.

The voice was weaker, but this time there was no hesitation. 'Dad... you're here.'

'Where else would I be?' he said.

Appendix
References

BBC archive

30/8/2001   BBC Radio 4 Broadcast, 'The Day They Made it Rain'. Seeding from glider by Alan Yates. Interview with Flt Lt Otley and others. Review of source material and summary of evidence.

Public Record Office
AIR 2/13343

15/8/52   Cloud to SW at 45000-50000ft.

15/8/52   Morning - Wind fresh to strong due east.
              12 noon - Some cloud travelling east to west.

15/8/52   Heaviest rain 1600-1800 & 2000-2200.

7/9/52   Report of conditions at Pinkworthy Pond.

5/3/53   Opinions of Mr Bleasedale (Met Office) sub soil drainage loosening valley floor to form peat rafts. Sub soil drainage formed tunnels. '...volume of water carried just beneath the soil... was very much greater than in any normal rainfall.

27/3/53   Reply from Geological survey, West Ken. (Green). Considered opinion that '...the storm centre must have been nearer the Farley Water headwaters than the Shallowford headwaters... the rate of increase in the flood cross sections of the Farley and Hoar Oak Waters suggested a storm centre north of the main watershed and a little north of their sources.'

22/9/52   Met office investigation of Lynmouth flood

area. Call for eye-witness accounts.

Re 15/8/52   Eye witness report at 8am... curious pink shade in an ugly threatening sky... rain commenced as gentle fall at noon... an hour later... really heavy... 8pm bright sheet lightning (pink).

AVIA 1 27
14/8/52   Met Research flights undertaken.

15/8/52   Met Research Flight at 14.35 lasting 1hr 40 min.

B1 21T/1892
8/1/48   Times article re cloud snatching and spectre of interstate disputes about who owns which clouds.

AIR 2/10467
13/9/49   Flying Training Command, Reading, to Under Secretary of State re rainmaking. 'I have the honour to refer to recent experiments at Middleton St George...'

3/8/49   Dry ice seeding experiment. Flt Lt Otley - Captain. Seeded cumulus at 10,000ft, temp. -4C. Slight shower resulted.

8/8/49   Seeded cumulus at 10,500ft, -4C with dry ice. Cloud top rose, produced a good shower.

11/8/49   Cumulus 8000ft at -1C. Little upward growth, no rain. Cloud development hardly penetrated beyond freezing level.

          Appendix B -Report on technical aspect of rainmaking trials.

15/3/51   Unidentified seeding noticed from East Hill.

24/9/51	Met Research Flight. Clearance of layer cloud by seeding.
12/11/53	Sutton (DMO) minute to A.C.A.S. (Ops) Re Tactical use of Rainmaking. 'The greatest caution should be exercised in dealing with this group of people (Krick & co) and no contract should be placed or public money allowed to pass to them, without consultation with the Meteorological Office.'
17/11/53	Air Vice Marshall Sinclair. 'I had heard about the tactical use of rain-making while I was Commandant at OLD SARUM...'
18/11/53	Tactical use of rain-making. 'This subject is rapidly flying off the rails.'
Loose minute.	Paper from Krick brought up at October 16th meeting of the land/air warfare offensive support sub-committee to obtain views of war office re the tactical value of rain made by artificial means. (Air Vice Marshall Sir Harry Broadhurst persuaded to do this by Grp. Cpt. Searl, Krick's UK agent.)
November 3rd	Krick spoke at War Office on the subject.
Loose minute.	Response to Krick's paper, 'Suggestions for the Tactical Application of Weather Modification Techniques.' Discussion of possible application where soils are right to bog down tanks - Lowes, common in NW Germany. Mention of Krick stating that maximum increase to be expected is about 50% above normal.
16/12/53	Letter from Searl to Air Vice Marshall Sinclair. Ref. US investigation of linking rainfall increase

to the strategic use of the atom bomb. Reference to Congress appointing a Weather Evaluation Board on which the Dept. of Defense is represented.

Loose Minute. Sinclair to DMO. Added note - 'We ought to keep our ears very close to the ground on this subject. Quite obviously one side or the other is leg pulling but if the U.S. Types are right there is a whole of a lot to it operationally.'

DSIR23/22274

4-15/8/52 Project Cumulus. Cloud investigations made by Met Research Flight to investigate structure & environment of cumuliform clouds. Flights coincided with 'other' investigations made by Dept of Meteorology, Imperial College, Surrey Gliding Club, RAF Farnborough and a network of ground observing stations.

BJJ/94 Air Ministry, Met Research committee minutes of 50th meeting, pg 660, Production of rain. Discussion of Langmuir's work.

BT 217/1892

27/11/47 Min. of Civil Aviation notes re request for permission from Airworks Ltd to conduct cloud seeding experiments.
1. Need to know all details to ensure no danger to third parties.
2. Establish L.A. over which seeding is to take place has no objection.
3. Need to establish what results are to be expected.
4. Important 'in relation to the public' that the desirability of permitting such a practice will arise.

13/1/48	Letter from Ministry of Civil Aviation (Atride) to Airwork Ltd. (Jaques) re rainmaking experiments already conducted & planned. Request for 'lengthy notice of intended resumption of experiments.' To allow for further consideration of implications.
30/1/48	Reply. No further work contemplated in UK but practical trial may take place later this year in East Africa.

CO927/134

Jan-April/51	Report on experiments at Kongwa on artificial stimulation of rain. Description of method and conclusions. Statement of Irving P Krick, Director of the American Institute of Aerological Research and President of the Water Resources Development Corp., Denver Colorado. Krick's C.V. And details on work on artificial nucleation - beginning in the winter of 1946-47. Detail of '...the proper conduct of a cloud-seeding program.'
15/3/51	Statement before the Joint Weather Control Hearings of the US Senate by Robert McKinney, Chairman, New Mexico Economic Development Commission. Re - urgent need for legislation proposed in Senate Bill 222 Weather Control Act of 1951. 'Three of the storms which occurred in New Mexico at times when our School of Mines scientists were engaged in rainmaking activities were accompanied by floods and property damage.' 'There exist in New Mexico today, or are being negotiated at this time, contracts with commercial rainmaking firms virtually blanketing the state.'

'Evidence is accumulating daily which indicates a concerted plan on the part of special interests to avoid legal responsibility for their action in this field.'
No controls to keep fakers from operating in this field. Cleverly drawn contracts, the rainmaker takes no risk.

5/3/51   Met Office (Johnson) to Colonial Office (Eastwood) General advice on rainmaking Ref Kongwa. Difficulty of distinguishing success of seeding from natural precipitation. Various possibilities then... 'it has been suggested, though apparently not yet tried, that correct quantitative artificial seeding might result in a reduction of rainfall in such areas (e.g. Along coastal high ground with off sea air flow.)...'

4/3/51   Met Office (Goldie) to Colonial Office (Eastwood) Ref possibility of seeding in Aden & refuting suggestion that American 'experts' should be employed.

28/7/51   Note from Advisory Council on Scientific Policy. Ref request by PM for 'report on the work which is being done in this country in the field of weather control and the extent to which we are in touch with the research and practice on this subject abroad, especially in the United States.' Attached are a reports by Sir David Brunt - on the artificial production of rain; Dr EG Bowen - Australian work on weather control; BCSO Washington - current legislation in the United States dealing with artificial rainmaking.

1/8/51   Extract from meeting of the Advisory Council on Scientific Policy. Paper by Sir David Brunt discussed. 'Sir David Brunt... described experiments which had been undertaken in this country and abroad into methods of producing rain artificially. Necessary conditions for a successful experiment include:

- availability of cumulus cloud of considerable height.
- temperature at the top of -7degrees C for dry ice, -10 degrees C for silver iodide.

Australian results - 100% success using dry ice if cloud -6 C. or below.

Increase in annual rainfall that could be achieved: 5%-10%.

14/9/51   From Secretary of State for the Colonies summarising stand on artificial rainmaking:

- Artificial methods of inducing rain could not be expected to increase average rainfall over a wide area by more than a small amount.
- Exceptional conditions which would justify this method of producing rain seldom present in this country...
- Exaggerated claims made by commercial interests in the US could be wholly disregarded.
- No present need to introduce legislation for controlling experiments in this country.

29/10/51   Suggestions for experiments in 'seeding' of cloud at Aden.

29/11/51   NATURE article on 'Natural and Artificial Production of Atmospheric Precipitation.' Report of discussion held at British Association for the Advancement of Science meeting in Edinburgh. Contributions by BJ Mason

(Imperial College of Science & Technology), FH Ludlam (Imperial), RF Jones (Met Office), HP Palmer and Dr AW Brewer (Oxford), IC Browne (Cambridge)

CO927/135/1

14/9/51

From Secretary of State for Colonies re Artificial Rainmaking. 'The Advisory Council on Scientific Policy has recently had under review the work which has been done in the United Kingdom in the field of weather control.' Newspaper references giving a misleading picture. '...purpose of notes which follow to describe the problem and to indicate the degree of success achieved in solving it.' July 1950 summary of US work on cloud physics and artificial rain production (Project Cirrus) - sponsored by Dept of Defense... 'The question 'can you make it rain' has received an answer in the affirmative in many experimental instances where atmospheric conditions were suitable, but the question of how much precipitation can be artificially induced or if the amount would be of any economic significance is yet to be determined.'

19/9/51

Met office (Goldie) to Colonial office (Hibbert) re rainmaking in Cyprus. 'Orographic clouds may provide the only practicable source for artificially induced rain... The science of rainmaking is in its infancy and one cannot be sure that good results would be obtained but I think that there is a definite possibility that... rainfall could be increased by artificial means.' The Met office would certainly be interested in (rainmaking experiments) whether in Cyprus or elsewhere.

29/12/51	Met office (Goldie) to Colonial office (Hibbert) '...the two officers who have been directly concerned in this country with experiments of cloud seeding... cannot be spared at the moment from other urgent work...' Report to be prepared by an officer who has made a study of artificial production of rain. Report: Possibility of augmenting rainfall over Cyprus by artificial means. Comprehensive summary covering theory and practice of artificial rainmaking.

AIR 2/15153

7/2/54	Parliamentary question re work on 'improving weather', staffing, cost and priority.
19.2.54	Notice re de Frietas & Adjournment debate on rain-making. Most promising method coke furnaces not aircraft.
20/2/54	Met office brief for adjournment debate on weather modification. Background. 'Grave doubts about claims made by commercial rainmakers'. Subject of rainmaking in need of review. Recommended that any experimentation should not be done by commercial bodies.
23/2/54	Background info for U.S. of S. for adjournment debate on weather modification. Info re Krick, UK agents, rainmaking background, problem in UK that relatively small number of days when clouds thick enough. Doubtful whether could succeed in producing more than a few local showers and these would have no economic significance. References to seeding in Tanganyika, California, Arizona, Denver, New Mexico,

Australia, Canada, France, India, South Africa.
In Great Britain - few small-scale experiments
made by Met. Research Flight + unpublished
work done with silver iodide by one of the
universities.

23/2/54   Aide Memoire - Weather Modification
Adjournment debate. Probably for De Frietas -
pro rainmaking research.

23/2/54   Parliamentary question from de Freitas asking
for increased research into weather
Modification.

3/54   Anti-hail rockets first tested in Italy 1949.
Artificial rain - producers of patented rockets
with silver iodine - SIPE, Soc. Italrazzi

0/3/54   Meeting led by U.S. of S. De Freitas (MP)
requested high level committee to look into
weather modification. Grp. Cpt. Searl & Major
Anstruther (Krick's UK agent) representing
British Institute of Aerological Research.
Institute keen to launch UK scientific
experiment at no public expense. U.S. of S.
declined. Referred back to Met. Research
committee. 'Grp. Cpt. Searl said that the Air
Ministry would be expected to accept (legal)
liability. Major Anstruther then said that the
Institute would do so.'

16/4/54   Krick making $50,000 from one scheme alone,
covering 2 million acres in Saskatoon. 12
generators; a billion silver iodide crystals.

17/6/54   DMO to Krick, 'no reliable evidence that
rainfall had ever been artificially increased on
any economically useful scale...' Errors in data
from Spain.

| 3/8/54 | Krick to DMO 'astonished by your statement that there was "no reliable evidence" etc.' |
| 5/7/54 | French experiments over Massif region and project with 5/6 generators in Brittany planned. |

Misc. references
BJJ/94

July 1948	RAF Farnborough. Technical paper on cloud icing including Langmuir and Schaefer's work on artificial nucleation.
29/1/48	Minutes of 53rd meeting of Air Ministry Meteorological Research Committee. Functions of the committee.
12/10/48	Minutes of 55th meeting of the Met Research Comm. Temp. and wind in the Upper Air.